BLOOD ON THE TABLE

BLOOD ON
THE TABLE

GERRY SPENCE

A TOM DOHERTY ASSOCIATES BOOK

NEW YORK

BLOOD ON THE TABLE

Copyright © 2021 by G. L. Spence and Lanelle P. Spence Living Trust

A Forge Book
Published by Tom Doherty Associates
120 Broadway
New York, NY 10271

www.tor-forge.com

Forge® is a registered trademark of Macmillan Publishing Group, LLC.

The Library of Congress Cataloging-in-Publication Data is available upon request.

ISBN 978-1-250-77426-2 (hardcover)
ISBN 978-1-250-77429-3 (ebook)

Our books may be purchased in bulk for promotional, educational, or business use. Please contact your local bookseller or the Macmillan Corporate and Premium Sales Department at 1–800-221-7945, extension 5442, or by email at MacmillanSpecialMarkets@macmillan.com.

First Edition: March 2021

Printed in the United States of America

0 9 8 7 6 5 4 3 2 1

To one of the great trial lawyers in America who has spent a lifetime fighting for the rights and lives of the poor, the lost, the forgotten, and the damned, John P. Zelbst.

BLOOD ON THE TABLE

CHAPTER 1

Laramie, Wyoming, Winter, 1947

RINGO FELT SOMETHING hard poking him in the ribs. He couldn't remember where he was. When he pulled his head out from under his bedroll, he was attacked by a blinding light.

"Get out of there," a harsh voice demanded. "I said, get out of there!"

When the cop prodded him again, Ringo bolted straight up. He grabbed for his hat and stood up in the pickup bed, naked, all that belonged to him in plain view. He tried to cover it with his hat.

"Whatcha doin' here?"

"I was sleepin'," Ringo said.

"I could run you in for sleepin'," the cop hollered.

A scruffy tramp stumbled up in a dirty gray overcoat with a gray woolen cap pulled over his ears. "Ain't no law in Laramie, Wyoming, against sleepin'," the tramp said. The bottoms of his ragged pants were dragging on the sidewalk.

"Get your ass down the street, or I'll haul you in, too," the cop yelled at the tramp.

"Been tryin' to get one of you cops to haul me in for three days," the tramp said. His thick whiskers held his face together. "It's colder than a well digger's ass in January out here." He walked over to where the cop was standing. "And I'm hungry. I could eat the ass off a skunk." He stood huddled, his hands in his coat pockets.

"Get down out of there," the cop ordered Ringo. He reached for his pants, but the cop started at him with his stick again. "I said, get out of there." Ringo slid down from the back of the pickup onto the street in his bare feet. His toes recoiled from the cold, rough pavement, and he tried to balance himself on his heels.

"Turn around." The cop prodded him with his stick. Ringo jumped and spun around. "Stand up against that pickup door and don't move, or I'll shoot your ass off."

"Ain't much to shoot off," the tramp said. "Anyways, you'd probably miss."

The cop climbed into the pickup bed. He shook Ringo's bed-roll, and, satisfied it contained no illegal contraband, he began to untie the rope that held Ringo's old suitcase closed.

"Hand down this boy's clothes," the tramp ordered the cop. "It's cold out here, in case you didn't notice."

"He ain't gonna run no place without no clothes," the cop said.

"Well, you can deputize me. I'll watch him. Hand down his clothes."

"Get the fuck out of here," the cop said. He began rummaging through the suitcase and scattering its contents across the length of the pickup bed—two pairs of socks, a pair of old boots, a couple pairs of patched Levi's, and a faded western shirt, town pants and boots. The cop ripped open Ringo's old lunch bucket and dumped out a toothbrush, toothpaste, and a bar of soap, along with a small box of Ex-Lax his mother insisted he take "just in case." Finding nothing of interest, the cop jumped down from the pickup and walked over to Ringo, who, by this time, had begun to shiver in spasms.

The tramp stuck his whiskers in the cop's face. "I am hereby orderin' you in the name of the law to give this boy his clothes. If you don't, I'm makin' a citizen's arrest and turnin' you in for cruel and unusual punishment."

The cop beamed his flashlight into the tramp's eyes.

"You are a cruel motherfucker," the tramp said. "I should take that billy club from you and stick it up your fat ass."

The cop raised his nightstick, and the tramp backed off, telling the cop, "You lay a hand on me and I'll sue your fat ass plum off you. My brother's a lawyer in this town."

"Yeah? Who's your brother?" the cop asked.

"Christopher Hampton. Ever hear of him?"

The cop poked his nightstick into Ringo's belly. "Whatcha doin' in Laramie?"

"Goin' to school, the university."

"Don't give me no bullshit," the cop said. "You ain't no schoolkid. Where you from?"

"West of town at Bear Creek."

"More bullshit. Just a bunch of rich ranchers live out there." The cop stuck his nightstick under Ringo's testicles and gave it a small, quick, but hard upward lift. Ringo jumped, and when he did, he grabbed the cop's nightstick and pulled it loose from his hand.

Ringo hollered at the tramp. "Get my clothes." He stood waving the stick in front of the cop. "Don't be goin' for your gun. Throw it down there on the pavement, or I'll break your head wide open."

"Go ahead and smack him," the tramp said. "He's got it comin'. And there ain't nothin' inside his head but donkey shit. That's why we call him 'Shithead Henry.'" The tramp picked up the cop's service revolver and handed Ringo his pants and shirt.

"You hold his gun on him while I get dressed," Ringo said.

"If you do, I'm charging you with aidin' and abettin' a crime," the cop said to the tramp.

"Finally!" The tramp pointed the gun at the cop's nose. "I admit it. Take me in." The tramp started to shiver. "I'm gonna make you a deal. Number one: You let this kid go. He's goin' to school. See here?" The tramp picked up a copy of Ringo's registration from the hodgepodge the cop had spilled over the truck's bed.

"Number two: You gotta haul me in for vagrancy. It's too fuckin' cold out here. Okay?"

The cop thought about it for a minute. "Okay, but don't tell nobody about this."

"Right."

"You a man of your word?" the cop asked the tramp.

"Yeah, just like you." He handed the cop his pistol and his nightstick. "Take me in, Officer," the tramp said.

"And you ain't gonna tell Chistopher Hampton?"

"Naw," the tramp said. "I was just shitin' you. I don't even know him. I just heard he was a pretty good lawyer, and that he's got you cops scared to fuckin' death."

CHAPTER 2

Laramie, University of Wyoming, One Week Later

PROFESSOR HAROLD P. Johns's skin was as pallid and lifeless as his voice.

He exhibited a large head of straight black hair bent on escaping in a variety of directions. He was equipped with a nose that had no anatomical excuse for its inordinate size, and squinty eyes that appeared as colorless slits behind a pair of horn-rimmed glasses. His words rolled out in a muddy mumble. He paced in small, uncertain steps.

Often he stopped his short, staggering shuffle, gazed through his glasses in the direction of the class to see if the students were still there, and, discovering they were, a surprised look invaded his face, after which he returned to the laborious text printed across the tomes of his mind.

Ringo sat in the back of the classroom, slouched down in his chair as far as possible so as to disappear from the professor's line of sight, but Professor Harold P. Johns saw no one and spoke only to the muted stratosphere.

"Economics," he began, "is the science concerned with the production, distribution, exchange, and consumption of goods and services." He stopped, sniffed, as if he were allergic to his words, and then bravely carried on, all the while peering over the top of his students' heads. "I doubt that any of you will ever become economists. A couple of you will wander out of this university, go into business, and luck into money. One or two of you will inherit from a rich relative. But intelligence and knowledge have nothing to do with any of that. Someone—it makes no difference who—said, 'We are what we know; we knew nothing, for, in the end, there is nothing to know.'"

He offered a painful look to the classroom. "Frankly, I'm wasting my time here. You get credit toward your graduation. I get my salary, the quid pro quo, which, as you will discover, is an economic principle revered in a capitalist state." His mouth puckered at the distasteful flavor of his words. "Most of the affluent in this country don't know Adam Smith from Donald Duck."

Ringo clutched at his pencil. He had to write sometime. *Something.* He stole a look at the notes of the kid on his left. In careful, backward-leaning script he'd written, "Adam Smith and Donald Duck. No difference."

The woman on Ringo's right suddenly spoke up in a rich contralto. "If we're all wasting our time here, why not give us all A's, and we'll have a party every day instead. I'll bring the beer for the first day."

Scattered, hesitant laughter.

Ringo ventured a quick glance at the woman. She was just shy of exotic, with full lips, like the woman in his fantasies. She wore her long, black, straight hair tied in the back with a black velvet ribbon. Her eyes were large and dark and amused.

He remembered Arturo's advice. "Don't fuck schoolgirls. They wanna fuck and have babies. Then they wanna get married, and want the man to feed them."

Arturo had laughed. He always laughed. "Schoolgirls aren't good fucks anyway. Women up in the houses, they're the best. And when you're done, they don't cry. They don't wanna get married. You get what you want and they get what they want. And wash the prick good, muchacho, or you'll get clap."

Professor Johns scowled in the direction of the woman who'd offered the party. He took a handkerchief from his pocket, wiped his forehead, blew his nose, and returned it to his pocket. "Yes, we could have a party every day and learn as much useful information from carousing and debauchery as from this so-called science loosely labeled as economics, and this incomprehensible collection of garbage generously referred to as a text." He struggled as he picked up the weighty book. Then he let it fall with a thud on the tabletop in front of him. "I wrote this thing," he confessed. "The university sells it at a profit. I make a pittance known as a royalty, enough to quell any accusation that my employer is exploiting me beyond the acceptable limits of slave labor."

Professor Johns continued to suffocate the room with verbiage that fell in dull clods of sound. Ringo tried to concentrate, to sort through it, but the professor's words clogged his brain. The woman on his right obviously had this course pegged. She wasn't intimidated by the professor. He noticed something else: Her beauty was different from his mother's.

The professor continued to chant the liturgy of Adam Smith, all the while desperately grasping his lapels, as if to prevent himself from falling through his jacket into a bony heap on the floor.

"Economics can be divided into two major fields," the professor mumbled. "The first, microeconomics, tells us how the interplay of supply and demand in competitive markets creates a plethora of individual prices, wage rates, profit margins, and rental changes. The other field . . ." The professor cleared his throat and looked around to see if any were listening.

The woman on Ringo's right slammed down her pencil and threw herself back in her chair, her hands clasped behind her head. He stole another look and saw that her pad was empty. She'd stuck her pencil over her ear. She was tightly fitted into a pair of blue jeans, and when he followed her legs down to the floor, he saw her beaded Indian moccasins. How might a painting of her naked legs be, her calves in the foreground and her thighs retreating into a rising sun over the prairies?

Then the woman leaned over and whispered to him, "Economics is simple. You either fuck or get fucked. You can call me Meg, or you can call me Isabelle."

"My name's Ringo," he heard himself say.

CHAPTER 3

Bear Creek Ranch, 1940

LITTLE BEN, THEN eleven, went with his father, Ben Eckersly, the ranch foreman, to the shearing barn. The workers cursed in Spanish as they wrestled the sheep. The smells were the musk of shorn wool and men sodden in sweat.

Little Ben stayed close to his father. His father was tall, with good muscles and an early streak of gray through the center puff of his black hair. Little Ben wished his hair was black like his father's. He was a man the workers respected. Little Ben felt pride when his father smiled at him. His father didn't often smile, not even at his mother.

"Hey, this ol' ewe is for Little Ben," Arturo hollered as he pushed a ewe up against the pen and pinned her there. "It's time, isn't it? Make a man of him. You don't want him to grow up a whimp."

"What do you say?" his father asked Little Ben. "You want to ride that old ewe?" The shearers were laughing and shaking their heads as if they knew.

Little Ben shook his head no.

"Make a man of you," Arturo said. "You afraid like a whimp?"

"You're old enough to ride an old ewe." His father lifted the boy up on the ewe's freshly shorn back, one shearer holding her head and another her hindquarters.

Arturo strapped a length of leather around the sheep's neck. "Grab hold here. Be a man."

The boy looked at his father. He was not smiling, and Little Ben began to cry. He was not brave like his father. When Arturo let the old ewe loose, the boy closed his eyes and held on, the men whooping and laughing and slapping their legs.

After two jumps, Little Ben landed on his back in fresh sheep dung. He jumped up and went running toward the house. Eckersly grabbed the boy by the back of his collar. "Gotta get back on, son. Can't get bucked off by an old ewe and go running for your mother."

Then the shearers caught the ewe again, and his father lifted the boy up on her back. "She's a snotty old she-devil," his father said. With a kick on her rump, the men let her go, and they laughed and hollered, "*¡Monte la perra! ¡Monte la perra!*" But this time, Little Ben rode her for a dozen bucks, until the ewe was exhausted. Only then did he jump off. He looked at his father for approval. His father smiled and tipped his hat.

Little Ben wanted to be tough like John Wayne, the Ringo Kid, in the movie *Stagecoach,* so he renamed himself Ringo. He'd suffered some static about his name change from the older boys, but after they knocked him down a couple of times, and he kept getting up, they finally got tired of their bullying, and even his parents surrendered, so that Little Ben Eckersly became Ringo Eckersly to all who mattered in his life.

CHAPTER 4

Bear Creek Ranch, 1945

ON DECEMBER 7, 1941, in a surprise attack, the Japanese bombed the U.S. naval base at Pearl Harbor and the United States was at war.

Roosevelt assured the American people, "No matter how long it may take us to overcome this premeditated invasion, the American people in their righteous might will win through to absolute victory."

Wool was at a premium for servicemen's uniforms. Sarah Eckersly joined the women of America in knitting caps and mittens for the boys over there. Children and women took up the work of the men who were defending the nation against the tyranny of the Japanese and the two other Axis powers, Germany and Italy. Ringo worked in the hay fields, driving teams of horses, mowing, raking, and stacking hay.

But in the far-off wilds of Wyoming, life endured, the war effort notwithstanding. The war was "over there," and few of the folks knew where "over there" was. What ranchers knew was that their work, if unattended, would pile up and smother them and all the animals that were dependent on them. One could die in the trenches or starve or freeze to death on the prairies. War was wherever the fight for life was fought.

In the late spring, hard hands cut the nuts off of the lambs in the same way that one plucked off the heads of dandelions to stop their seeding. A ranch hand slammed a lamb up on the docking table, and Arturo nodded to Ringo. Arturo, the ranch's second in command, saw Ringo as his son. "Here is what a man carries in his pocket." Love flooded the herder's eyes. Arturo handed Ringo a shiny new pocketknife for his sixteenth birthday. "It has a good blade. I sharpened it myself. Here, feel." Arturo opened the castrating blade, the shorter blade with the semi-rounded end.

Two men held the lamb down and spread its legs apart. "Your knife, muchacho," said Arturo, laughing. He always laughed.

Ringo's hand longed to retreat to his pocket, next to his own tender testicles. Arturo grabbed the lamb's nuts between his thumb and forefinger and pinched them up as if pinching up two marbles from outside a pants pocket.

"Slice him here." Arturo pointed.

Ringo sliced, and the lamb bleated in a long, wavering cry of pain that brought tears to Ringo's eyes. He wiped at his eyes. "Corral dust," he sputtered.

Arturo bit down on the lamb's slippery nuts and pulled them out one at a time, the cord coming with them, the blood of the lamb on his lips. He spit the nuts into the pail of salt water. Then he lifted the red-hot docking iron from the coals and burned through the wool, the flesh, and finally the bone, the lamb bleating in agony until its heaving sides were emptied of sound.

Ringo pinched up the nuts of the next lamb and cut. He bit down, pulled, and spit the nuts into the pail. He felt cruel and evil. He felt sick. Then with the hot iron, he burned off the lamb's tail and dropped the lamb to the ground. It ran to its mother in tiny, stiff steps, blood staining the pink flesh of its tender belly. The ewe made gentle guttural sounds, and with her long tongue licked at the lamb's face and at its burned tail. That day, Arturo said Ringo was almost a man.

In the evening, the men gathered in the bunkhouse and rolled cigarettes from their sacks of Bull Durham and drank from a bottle of cheap whiskey that they passed from mouth to mouth, and being almost a man, Ringo held the bottle to his lips longer than the others, but he took only a small swig. The vile taste of whiskey watered his eyes and burned his throat. That night, his father said he could sleep in the bunkhouse with the men.

The next morning, Arturo reported, "Them fucking Japs gave up. You don't have to go fight them. Roosevelt say on the radio it's all over." Arturo was proud. He was the only ranch hand who owned a radio.

The ranch hands, celebrating the surrender of the Japanese, passed the whiskey bottle and hollered and hooted in noisy Spanish. Ringo understood some of the words—how they were going to party up in the houses in Laramie, and the fights they'd had with the gringos, and on and on into the drunken night. Ringo lay awake, listening to the bleating in the corral, and later to the men snoring and grunting in their cots like gasping, wounded beasts. Finally he drifted off into a pit of horror where a thousand lambs joined in a chorus of eternal pain.

CHAPTER 5

Bear Creek Ranch, 1940

WHEN RINGO WAS a boy, his feet had known the change of the seasons. Each school day he'd walked more than a mile to the bus stop, and in the fall his feet kicked at the cottonwood leaves that fell along the creek. Crisp, yellow, and curled, they crunched under his bare feet, and the feel of fall felt good.

In the summer, Ringo's bare feet touched the moist green ground along the creek. The creek was cool and clear and laughing. And on the other bank, the tender grasses felt like the fingers of tiny children playing on his feet.

In the early winter, his feet went slushing through the snow. The large flakes fell lazily, yawning and wet, and to keep his feet dry, he rubbed wool grease over his boots until they were as soft as a lamb's nose.

In the deepest part of winter, the snow piled up higher than his knees and filled his boots. But by April, his bare feet met spring again, along with the buttercups that popped up between the two tracks of the old trail.

"They've waited all winter to bloom," his mother said lightly, touching a yellow blossom. "How I love these pretty little flowers. Think how glad they must be when the spring sun thaws the earth." Her voice was like distant music. When he walked to the school bus, he was careful not to step on the buttercups.

And he wondered why his mother loved the buttercups, but she never said she loved him—not in words.

But he knew she loved him.

Did she love his father? He never heard her say so.

Once, his father leaned down too hard against his mother's antique kitchen table, and when the table creaked its complaint, his mother scolded, "Don't lean on the table, Ben. It's old, you know, and brittle, and valuable." His mother kept the table carefully waxed and its top protected with a red-and-white-checkered oilcloth.

After supper, silence stole over the house. Ringo could hear the wind rattling the limbs of the cottonwood tree against the house, and he heard the jangle of the loose tin on the roof. When he peeked out his bedroom door, he saw his mother sewing patches on the elbows of one of his father's shirts, his father watching, as if to see the words she didn't speak. Then Ringo crawled back in bed and listened.

Silence.

Silence.

Finally soaked in the silence, he drifted into slumber.

RINGO HAD BEEN drawing mountains with peaks that were red and yellow, with great slashes of black, and the sky was as purple as spring iris. Mrs. Foreman, his teacher at the Bear Creek School, peered down at his drawing for a long time. Then she whispered, "You know, Ringo, that I love you." And her words swelled his heart like buttercups bursting into bloom in the springtime.

He didn't think Mrs. Foreman ever told Jamey Swanker that she loved him. And Jamey needed love. He was a small boy with a head too large for his body. He talked to the birds. He insisted the birds talked back. Some of the kids would caw like a crow when he walked by, and the girls would go, "Peep, peep."

"Birds know when you love 'em," Jamey said, "and they don't make fun of you, not even the ravens."

Ringo admired the songbirds. They were brave. They sang even though the hawks and the eagles could eat them. Jamey was a strange little bird himself. He rattled off the names of birds like the names of the kids at Bear Creek School, and his list included more than a dozen species of hummingbirds that inhabited the surrounding territory. Along the way, Ringo and Jamey became close friends.

That fall, when Ringo walked to the bus stop, the sun spread sheets of light across the distant hills, and he could taste his joy. It tasted like the fresh, crisp apples his mother put in his lunch pail.

When the bus arrived at the school, Ringo ran in to show Mrs. Foreman his new drawing. And there she lay on the floor in a pool of dried blood.

Ringo stood blocking the doorway. "Don't go in there!" he hollered to the kids behind him. "Mrs. Foreman is dead." He said the word: *dead*.

Dead.

The knife blade was buried in her chest.

"Somebody stabbed her," he said.

The children were too shocked to say that one word about their teacher on the floor. *Dead.* Ringo stood frozen in the doorway, staring down at the corpse. The body looked even smaller than Mrs. Foreman. Perhaps if he waited, she'd blink, slowly rise up, smile her loving smile, and tell the children it was a bad joke and that she was sorry. Ringo pulled the knife from her chest. He dropped the knife on the floor and wiped his hand on his pant leg.

Then Jamey began his awful sobbing. Some of the children joined in with him.

Others, too terror-stricken, stood mute as stone.

"Ham killed her," Jamey cried. "Ham didn't come home last night. Dad's out looking for him now. And Dad's gonna whip him good." Ham was Jamey's older brother, Hamilton Swanker, age fourteen and in the eighth grade. Everybody, including Mrs. Foreman, said Ham was a genius.

A few minutes later, George Swanker drove up to the school-house in a new black Cadillac. He wore half a month's growth of black whiskers, an expensive fringed leather jacket, and fancy cowboy boots. Swanker ran Thoroughbred racehorses—claimed the high altitude gave them an edge in conditioning—and they'd won a lot of races. The Swankers lived out there in nowhere in a fancy house with one of those white board fences around the home property like the ones on the horse farms in Kentucky where the racing world hung out.

Jamey ran to his father, hollering, "Ham killed the teacher!"

George Swanker jumped out of his car and pushed through the children. He saw the corpse and the knife on the floor. He ran to the teacher's desk, grabbed the wastebasket, ran back to the corpse, picked up the knife with a piece of paper, and dropped the knife in. Then he dumped the wastebasket in the trunk of his car, got in, and slammed the door. He grabbed Jamey by the shirtfront and shook him. "You tell me straight, boy. Where's your fuckin' brother?"

"I don't know where he's at. He had to stay after school for smartin' off, and he killed her."

Swanker spun out of the schoolyard, with Jamey sitting straight and stiff as a scared stranger. When Swanker got to town, he called the sheriff's office.

"Better get out to the Bear Creek schoolhouse. There's been a killin'."

That's all he said and hung up.

CHAPTER 6

Bear Creek School, 1940

TEN MINUTES PAST noon, Sheriff Bill Diggs and two deputies arrived at the Bear Creek schoolhouse. The sheriff bragged he was the youngest elected sheriff in the history of the state—twenty-eight at the time. He claimed that most sheriffs were worn-out political hacks who never solved a crime. Now at thirty-five, he was already in the fourth year of his second four-year term, and he boasted a perfect record of murder convictions—three murders and three convictions, and in just seven years. He intended to keep a perfect record.

The coroner arrived in his pickup.

The children were crowded together back some distance from the schoolhouse door. They ran to meet the sheriff's car, hollering, "Mrs. Foreman is dead. Mrs. Foreman is dead."

Some of the children were still sobbing and holding on to one another, and some were still too stunned to cry. Sheriff Diggs, a tall man with loose, swinging joints and a beak that minimized his remaining features, called for the school bus on his radio. When it arrived, he sent the younger children to wait in the bus while he interrogated the older ones.

The sheriff's chief deputy, Harv Jaycox, was a lizard-faced, scaly-skinned, hairless-headed man of indeterminate age with slow-blinking yellow eyes. His lips stayed wet from constant licking.

"Well, one thing for goddamn sure, Harv, this ain't no suicide," Sheriff Diggs said. "Wonder who had it in for this lady?" He lifted up the skirt of the corpse with his nightstick to reveal her plain white underpants. "Damn sure ain't no rape, neither."

"I could've told you that without even lookin'," Jaycox said. "She sure as hell wouldn't win no beauty contest. Old, too."

The sheriff moved alongside the corpse, careful not to step in the blood.

"Done some worser than her. Them older ones can be damned glad for a hard cock now and again."

"Looks to me like she got stabbed," Jaycox said. "But whoever done it kept the fuckin' knife."

"There ain't no sign of a struggle," Sheriff Diggs said. "Her clothes ain't torn. She ain't scratched or nothin'."

Jaycox began rummaging through her desk drawers. Then he hollered, "Look what I found!" He handed the paper to the sheriff.

"Well, I'll be go to hell," Diggs whispered.

The drawing was of a figure with the gnarled hands of an old man but the face of a boy. A herd of bleeding lambs was visible in the background. The artist's signature was clearly legible: Ringo.

"Who's this Ringo kid?" Diggs hollered.

"It's me," Ringo said. He'd been standing near the door.

"Come here," Diggs commanded. He was sitting in Mrs. Foreman's chair behind her desk. He leaned across the desk and snapped at the boy. "You draw this picture?"

Ringo nodded.

"Now this here person—that's you, ain't it?"

Ringo shook his head no. He could smell the man, and the smell made him shy away.

"Now don't you lie to me, son. You know goddamned well that's a picture you drew of yourself. You think about it before you lie to me again." Diggs waited. "Well?"

Ringo stood mute.

"If it ain't you, who the fuck is it?"

Ringo's mind froze like the broken gears in the old tractor.

"I thought so. You can't figure out another lie, can you? Why were you mad at the teacher? She give you bad grades or somethin'?"

Ringo shook his head no.

As the sheriff leaned farther forward, the chair squeaked ominously. "In this state, we send lyin' little sumbitches like you to the gas chamber. You wanna go to the gas chamber?"

Then Diggs gave Ringo a tinny smile. "You come over here and sit down on the sheriff's lap." He patted his knee as if calling his dog. When Ringo stood his ground, Diggs pulled Ringo toward him, but the boy pulled back.

"You oughta slap the lyin' little son of a bitch," Jaycox said. "If you don't want to, I'll do it for you." He started for Ringo.

"Now, son, you can trust me," the sheriff assured the boy. "I can help you. You're in a lotta trouble, and you need a friend. But you gotta help me. Friends help each other, right?"

Ringo stood staring at Diggs with wide eyes, his teeth clenched.

"Now this here teacher, she musta stepped out of line, right?"

Ringo didn't answer.

"And I, for one, don't like it when teachers step outta line. Now you and me are gonna be friends," Diggs said, smiling, "and you're gonna tell the old sheriff what that teacher done to you. Right?"

Ringo stood silent.

"Well, the cat got your tongue? I ain't got all fuckin' day."

Then Diggs called in Beverly Goodson, who sat across from Ringo. She was blond, had those long legs, and could run faster than most of the boys.

"You know this Ringo kid?" Diggs asked.

"Yes," she replied politely.

"He had trouble with the teacher, didn't he?"

"I don't know."

"You know who I am, don't you?" Diggs pointed at the star on his chest. "Did the teacher ever get after this Ringo kid?"

"I don't think so." She began to cry. "She was good to all of us."

"Now, now," Diggs said. "I got a girl about your age. Don't cry. You just tell the sheriff. What kind of trouble did this Ringo kid have with the teacher?"

"I don't know," she whimpered.

"Well, you were here in this room with him and the teacher every day, weren't you?"

Finally she said, "The teacher whispered in his ear."

The sheriff's hard eyes demanded more.

Then she said, "He was about to cry. I could tell."

"So they had a secret, huh?"

"Yes," Beverly said.

"And the secret made him cry?"

"Just about."

"When did the teacher tell this secret to Ringo?"

"Yesterday."

"Who else seen it?"

"Everybody seen it," Beverly said.

Then Diggs turned to the coroner, a small, nervous man named Jessie Cruthers. "Let's get this lady out of here." The sheriff took the corpse's shoulders and the coroner her feet, and they hauled her to the coroner's pickup, the corpse dripping a trail of blood behind them. "On three," the sheriff said, and they swung the body over the side of the pickup bed. The coroner climbed into the truck bed, spread an old army blanket over Mrs. Foreman, and tucked her in.

Then Diggs pushed Ringo up against the schoolhouse wall. "Why'd you kill that teacher?"

CHAPTER 7

Laramie, University of Wyoming, 1947

PROFESSOR JOHNS DUMPED a reading assignment of twenty pages on the defenseless class and retreated to his study in small, staggering steps. Meg slammed shut her empty notebook.

"This is all so much caca," she said, as if she'd known Ringo all her life. She slipped into her black leather jacket.

"Caca?" Ringo asked.

"Bullshit," she said. "A plethora of bullshit." She took in the young man standing in front of her, a fence post of medium height, his short blond hair needing a trim. Something attractive about the way he held himself, a sort of washed-over arrogance that wouldn't surrender. "Well, what did you make of the good professor's offerings?"

"I couldn't understand what he was talking about."

She seemed amused.

"What does *plethora* mean?" He wished he hadn't asked.

"A plethora is a whole fuckin' bunch of bullshit."

If only he could say something clever. Finally he said, "You from New York?"

"Do I talk like a New Yorker?"

"I don't know. I never been there."

There he stood, that square, stubborn chin and those wide blue eyes, and his hat in his hand, old and sweat-stained. His tight, muscular body wasn't bulged out in useless places like the weight-lifting jocks'. And something about his eyes: He didn't look at her as most men did. He took his eyes away, maybe to guard against being impolite. In a suit and tie, he'd probably come off handsome if something could be done with that hair.

"Why did you pick Wyoming?" he finally asked. He had a soft voice that touched the ears in a friendly way. His mouth was serious.

"I want to find a rich cowboy and marry him." She saw his overturned boots. "Are you rich?"

"No."

"Well, you'll do for the moment. At least you're a cowboy. Come on, I'll buy you a Coke."

She led him to a far table in the Student Union through a blur of bodies emitting waves of discordant noises as they pushed and shoved and hollered while ordering soft drinks and doughnuts.

What would he say if she stopped talking?

She brought a couple of Cokes to their table in those small glasses and raised hers as if to toast. "So, cowboy, what are you taking, and why, and what are you going to be when you leave this place, and why are you here rather than on the ranch where you belong, and why do you cut your hair like that? I'd like an answer to my questions all at once."

He started to speak. She interrupted. "I'd also like to know why you're so skinny. Don't they feed people on those Wyoming ranches?"

"Never could put on weight." His pride began to show in a small wrinkle of agitation at the edge of his eyes.

"And do all cowboys wear their hair so short?"

"Sometimes there's a long spell between trips to the barber."

He was far too serious. Perhaps she ought not agitate him further.

"I'm not a cowboy. I come from a sheep ranch. But I ride horses," he quickly added.

"You're different from most of the jocks here."

Then he heard himself say, "I like to draw." Why had he told her that?

"A sheepherder who likes to draw? I'm an artist, as well."

"What kind of art?"

She lifted her glass and took the straw into her mouth and leisurely sucked on it, her head tipped back, her eyes closed. When she opened them, she said, "I'm a lost little lamb," and he couldn't tell if she was mocking him or if she was on the frayed boundary of tears.

CHAPTER 8

Bear Creek Ranch, 1940

ECKERSLY AND HIS son, Ringo, were standing near the sheep barn when the squad car drove up. Fear drove up with it.

"Sheriff wants to ask your boy a few questions," Deputy Hullberry said to Ben Eckersly. The deputy was of average height and boyishly plump, and when he spoke, his voice was soft for a deputy sheriff. "Get in, son," he said to Ringo, pointing to the squad car.

"I'll take him in," Eckersly said.

"Sheriff wants him now."

"I'll take him in soon as he finishes his chores." He turned Ringo to the barn, and they walked away.

Ringo milked Old Boss, strained the milk, ran the milk through the separator, and fed the calf half a gallon of the skim. His father put on his town boots and his silver beaver cowboy hat. Ringo changed his shirt and pulled on his own town boots.

"I want to go," Sarah Eckersly said. "A mother should be with her son."

"No, this is man's business," Eckersly replied.

"You haven't had your supper," she said.

"We'll have supper when we get back."

Eckersly, headed for the highway, was steering this way and that to miss the rocks and chuckholes. "What's this about, Ringo?"

Ringo's eyes were wild, as if seeing it again. Sometimes he

stopped in the middle of a sentence, not finding the next words. "And I thought she was lookin' at me. But she wasn't lookin' at nothin', and she was all bloody, and the sheriff said I killed her, and I never killed her."

THE SHERIFF'S OFFICE was upstairs in the courthouse, next to the jail. The phone was ringing, and loud-talking men with hard faces were crowded in the room. The photographers' cameras were flashing, and a reporter hollered at Ringo as a deputy led the boy and his father through the crowd, "Hey, kid, did you do it?"

Eckersly started for the reporter, but the deputy stepped in front of him and led them to a small room with barren white walls, where Sheriff Diggs was waiting. From under his brown cowboy hat, his hawk nose threatened like an unsheathed weapon, and his gray eyes were small and close together. Ringo sat next to his father on the wooden bench. Chief Deputy Harv Jaycox stood near the door. Eckersly looked at Sheriff Diggs and measured him as men do before they strike.

"You see this murder?" Diggs asked.

Ringo didn't answer.

"Well, kid, did you see it?"

Deputy Hullberry came into the room with a fingerprint pad. Ringo jerked his hand back, but the deputy held it firm, one finger at a time on the pad.

"He never saw it," Eckersly said. "He was on the bus yesterday, comin' home with all the other kids. You know that."

"Let the kid talk for himself," Diggs snapped. "You kill her, son?"

Ringo's fingers were wrestling.

"Well, did you kill her? I ain't got all day, you know."

"Ringo came home on the bus. He was with us all night. He got on the bus this morning. You know all that."

"Somethin' pretty fuckin' screwy here," Diggs said. "And what the fuck is this if it ain't a smear of blood on his pants!"

"Fuckin' interesting," Jaycox said.

Ringo had seen that look in his father's eyes when there'd been trouble between his father and the government man who was threatening to run their sheep off the range, and his father had grabbed him and slammed him to the floor.

"What did you do with the knife, kid?" the sheriff demanded.

Eckersly got up from the bench. "Come on, son, I'm taking you home." He turned Ringo toward the door.

"We ain't through with our interrogation," Diggs said. "And the way I got it figured, you mighta had somethin' to do with this yourself."

"You're through talkin' to my son." Eckersly and Ringo walked out the door. When they were back in the pickup, Eckersly asked Ringo, "Do you know where the knife is?"

"I saw it in her chest," Ringo said.

"Did you touch it?"

"I pulled it out of her chest."

"What did you do with the knife?"

"I left it on the floor."

"You've never lied to me, Ringo."

"I ain't lyin', Daddy."

Twenty minutes later, two officers in a squad car stopped Eckersly with a lot of siren noise. Jaycox pointed his revolver at Eckersly and ordered him out of his pickup. He pushed his gun into Eckersly's belly. "Why don't you resist arrest?" Jaycox laughed and licked his lips. He shoved Eckersly up against his truck and snapped handcuffs on him. Then Jaycox pushed Ringo into the car next to his father in the backseat.

"You remember how this sumbitch in the backseat resisted arrest?" Jaycox asked as they drove back to Laramie.

"Yeah, I remember," Hullberry said.

"Had to put the gun to the motherfucker's head," Jaycox said, "and he was a true hundred percent fuckin' coward. He put that kid in front of him and was hollerin', 'Don't shoot me! Don't shoot me!' Remember that?"

"Yeah," Hullberry said. They both laughed and went on smoking.

Sheriff Diggs was waiting in the outer office. Eckersly was still in cuffs. Diggs swaggered up to Eckersly and stuck his beak in Eckersly's face. "I got you charged with obstructin' justice and resistin' arrest. Maybe when you wanna cooperate, we can talk again—maybe, if I got time."

Jaycox pushed Eckersly through the door of a vacant cell. Ringo started after his father, but Hullberry grabbed him by the collar.

Eckersly yelled, "Don't tell 'em anything, Ringo. Nothing!"

Then Ringo heard the sound of steel on steel as the jail door crashed closed behind his father. Diggs grabbed Ringo by the arm, jerked him into the interrogation room, and slammed him down on the bench.

Diggs pushed his nose into Ringo's face.

THE OLD JAILER, Henry Plowman, wore thick horned-rimmed glasses and a small, sad smile. His old hide was prune-wrinkled, and his hair on top had mostly fled. He walked down the corridor between the prison cells with the heavy steps of a man grown weary of bearing the belly that hung over his pants and the burdens that hung over his life. He'd worked as a switchman on the Union Pacific Railroad for over thirty years, and he still wore his high-topped, round-toed black safety shoes.

"Ain't seen you at the card room lately, Chris," Plowman said to the lawyer, Christopher Hampton. Plowman gave a friendly nod to the prisoners as they walked through the cellblock.

"I figured I'd better pay the rent before I joined you boys again. You're a little too swift for me."

The old jailer stopped at a six-foot-by-six-foot concrete box that emitted the foul smell of stale urine, and unlocked the cell door. Eckersly was sitting on the edge of the lower bunk.

Before Hampton could introduce himself, Eckersly said, "I don't know what they're tryin' to pin on Ringo. He's just a boy."

Hampton was tall, in his late fifties, with a head of reddish hair. He wore an old brown tweed jacket with leather patches on the sleeves and a blue work shirt open at the collar. His cowboy boots were scuffed, and one leg of his faded denim pants was carelessly caught in a boot top. His eyes called to mind the tired eyes of a draft horse that had spent its life tugging at its traces.

"You better not get me out of here right now," Eckersly said.

"Why?" Hampton asked.

"I'm likely to kill some son of a bitch."

They sat on the steel bunk and spoke against the noise of the prisoners, whose laughter and sobbing were indistinguishable. Some shouted obscenities. "Ringo never did anything except work and go to school. I want you to take care of my son first."

"Who's going to put up your bail?" The lawyer spoke in a slow, heavy voice. Eckersly's bail was set at fifty thousand dollars.

"William Hansen and Rubert Longley own the ranch, and neither of those old boys wants to pull on his overboots again, tromp through sheep shit, and fight this late-fall weather. I've been running things for more than ten years. They'll bail me out."

THAT NIGHT IN the card room on Front Street, William Hansen said, "Nobody thought Eckersly could make bail." Hansen had just won a hand and was pulling in the chips. "But me and Rupert know the man's good for his word. We never hesitated a minute to put up his bail. Twenty-five grand each." Rupert Longley hung to his silence and his scowl but nodded in agreement.

"And I'll tell you another thing," Hansen said. "We hired Christopher Hampton to represent him and his boy. Nice, hard-workin' kid. Ten, eleven years old. Never been in trouble in his life." He stopped to light his cigar, having already chewed it half-way to the end. "I always said loyalty is one of them streets that runs both ways. When Hampton comes in here the next time, I'll win my money back. Them lawyers may be smart, but I never met one that was worth a damn at playin' poker."

THE LABORATORY REPORTED that the scrapings from under Ringo's fingernails as well as the blood on his Levi's matched the blood type of the deceased. With his confession in hand, Sheriff Diggs thought he might get a conviction against the kid in juvenile court. But he shared the concerns of his chief deputy, Jaycox. The whole damn busload saw the Eckersly kid get on the bus with the other kids, and the teacher was alive at that time.

"There's probably some kid who actually saw the Eckersly kid pull the knife out of the teacher's chest. Just the same, we'll get us a warrant out for the arrest of the little fart and hold it in the event we can't find some other solution for the case. A conviction is a conviction when votin' time comes around," Sheriff Diggs always said.

CHAPTER 9

Laramie, 1947

THAT SATURDAY MORNING, Ringo awakened in the cramped-up concrete basement room he'd rented in Laramie. A half window in the foundation wall provided the only source of natural light. His view of the earth above was the sparrow's view as it searched the ground for the scattered seeds of summer. The cottonwoods that lined the street were barren of leaves, their gray trunks the wrinkled hide on the legs of old elephants. Ringo was lonely.

The woman on his right in his econ class had noticed him. She seemed disinterested in the other men on campus, who laid long, lustful looks on her, and some said raunchy things as they passed.

When he spoke, she fastened her eyes on him. Why should she be interested in a sheepherder who'd confessed he wanted to paint? But she was the only person on campus he'd met. And how could a man be a friend with someone who caused those wild purple urges that muted his tongue and pushed his mind into dangerous places?

"You must, and I mean *must*, begin to paint."

"You'd laugh at what I'd paint."

"Trust me," she invited.

One day, they were bravely enduring the endless, all-but-mumbling drone of Professor Johns as he wandered into the history of economics. His eyes were fixed on the empty ceiling as he carried on in his usual burble of multisyllable words.

"I'd rather shovel sheep shit the rest of my life than listen any longer to that guy," Ringo whispered. He was drawing the face of a student chained to a chair in mortal pain.

"Jesus save us. Let's get out of here," Meg whispered back. She slammed her notebook closed. "Follow me." She walked to the front of the room in an unsteady gait. When she got to the professor, she whispered in his ear. He stopped long enough to nod in the middle of a sentence and then continued: ". . . a school of economic thinkers known as physiocracy that arose in France during the second half of the eighteenth century who believed that all wealth originates in agriculture, but . . ."

Ringo followed her. She seemed to stumble her last two steps before they reached the door. Once in the hallway, the door shut behind them, she broke into high hilarity.

"What did you tell him?" Ringo asked.

"I told him I was suffering a sudden onset of neocoital claustrophobia, and that I had to leave, and that you'd help me home."

"What kind of a disease is that?"

"It meant I had to get the fuck out of there now! The disease is catching. You got it, too."

Once more they retreated in a back booth of the Student Union, drinking Cokes. She bought again. "This is for saving me," she said, lifting her glass to him.

He tried to smile back.

"Why are you so serious?"

"I'm not serious," he said. "I'm just not good at talking."

She babbled happily on about her apartment, how she'd had the walls repapered with a darling design of rural French figures, and how she was furnishing it with French antiques. "Do you like French antiques?"

"Don't think I ever saw one. My mother had an antique table."

"You want to see some French antiques?" She knew she was sitting with a young sheepherder so innocent, you could box up his innocence and sell it to the nuns.

Instinctively, he knew her invitation contained more.

When he didn't answer, she said with a come-on smile, "It's my way of inviting you to my apartment."

"Well, I was wondering how I'm supposed to pass econ if I don't go to class."

"Why don't you drop it and take art?"

"I'd like to, but I can't get any credits for law school by taking art courses. My adviser told me I gotta take econ and poly-sci and logic and psychology and a bunch of English and writing courses—lotta stuff like that."

"Why don't you become an artist instead of a lawyer? One should follow one's passion. I love what you draw."

Only his eyes spoke back.

"I said I love what you draw."

"Do you love *me*?"

His words stunned him.

He got up to leave.

She pulled him back. "You're so funny sometimes." She reached for his notebook and tore out the drawing of the student chained to a chair. "Thank you for this wonderful drawing. I'll keep it forever." She tucked the paper inside her notebook. "Come on, we might as well get to know each other. You got wheels? Mine's in the garage."

He steered his jalopy in a storm of excitement. He was actually alone with her and on his way to her apartment. What would he say? He couldn't just sit there like a tongue-tied idiot.

She pointed to the driveway. When she got out, she slammed the old wreck's door several times. The door hung open like the mouth of a panting dog. She shrugged her shoulders and left it hanging.

Ringo followed her up the stairs to her apartment above the

garage of an old Victorian house. His legs felt weak. The door was unlocked. They entered into a small living room. The roof boards were exposed and painted a pale yellow. The floor was covered with a bloodred carpet. "Have a seat." She motioned to the divan, a red flowered thing with thin carved French legs. It looked too flimsy to hold two people.

The room was heavy in his discomfort. She was gaily jabbering about the French artists she'd studied, and about the Dutchman, van Gogh, and how he'd been influenced by Millet. "Of course you know all that."

She went to a small refrigerator. "Want a beer?" Before he answered, she opened a couple of bottles. "Van Gogh made paintings of potato eaters. You should paint what you know about—sheepherders."

"My high school art teacher told me my paintings reminded her of van Gogh. I made this painting of a lamb with a bunch of eyes and a big hand, bigger than the lamb's head, and the hand was all crooked and cracked and dripping with blood."

"What do your folks think about your painting?"

"My dad said, 'You can't make a livin' painting pictures, and van Gogh never sold a painting. Gotta cut your ear off and shoot yourself. Then they'll give more money for a painting of a vase of sunflowers than you can get for a champion Hereford bull and a thousand acres of good bottomland.'"

Ringo took the bottle she offered and sat down on the divan. Finally he asked, "How come you know so much about van Gogh?"

"Sometimes, when I feel worthless, I think of van Gogh. If only he had known how beautiful he was." Her eyes were wet. "It's so painful when you don't know that you're beautiful."

"You're beautiful," he said.

She sat down beside him. "Have you ever drunk beer at nine-thirty in the morning?"

"No."

A painting of a two-faced woman vaguely after Picasso hung on the wall across from the divan. "I don't understand it," he said. "But then, nobody understands what I paint, either." He examined the brushstrokes, the paint thick and uncontrolled on the canvas.

"This painting was given to me by a friend," she said. "It's supposed to be a portrait of me."

"He shouldn't let the paints on his palette run together. Makes mud. Van Gogh's strokes were pure color."

"How is it that a sheepherder likes to paint?" Her face was kind.

"I don't know."

"Could we be friends?" she asked.

"No," he said.

"Why not? We have something in common. We must escape the agony of Professor Harold P. Johns."

When he looked up, he saw she was wiping tears from her eyes.

"I didn't mean to say anything to hurt you," he said.

She ran to the bedroom. Shortly she came back. Her smile had returned. Once more she sat beside him. "You don't need to tell me about your friend," she said. "I know what happened to him. He died."

Ringo stared at her.

"I'm sorry," she said.

A long silence.

"How did you know?" he asked.

"I have my sources."

"They found his body at the bottom of a cliff," Ringo said. "His father claimed he was chasing after a bird, that he wasn't watching and fell. His name was Jamey."

"What do you think?"

"His father hated him."

"You were hurt."

"Yes," he said.

"Friendships are dangerous," she said.

AROUND RINGO, SHE wore the plainest, boyish clothes, jeans and those sweaters that called all the more attention to what was hidden. She treated her sexuality as a person dealt with a birthmark—it was there through no fault of hers—and if it affected others, well, they'd have to deal with it. It wasn't that she was guileless. She could switch her seductive power on like flicking on the bedroom light. Her frighteningly kissable lips. He couldn't sleep until his fantasies of her had been wasted.

CHAPTER 10

PROFESSOR JOHNS HAD just taken a long draft from his thermos, which some suspected contained an evil potion that fueled his endless, near-death ramblings. He was groaning on about classical economics, which he claimed began with the greatly venerated Adam Smith. "Smith's notion that the individual pursuit of private profit inures to the public good was as incompetent then as it is today. Nothing changes," he mumbled to himself. "Nothing."

"Not even the sound of his voice," Meg whispered. "This guy couldn't get excited if you rammed a hot poker up his ass."

When the bell sounded ending the session, the students fled the classroom like bats from a flaming building. Then the girl who sat directly in front of them turned to Meg. She was a smallish blonde with tight little breasts that jutted out unsheathed against a blue-striped cotton blouse. Her tight little fanny was contained in a tight little skirt that filtered down to a foot below her knees, which she kept tightly clenched. With undisguised contempt, she said, "You are so vulgar! I heard what you said about the professor. I think he's the smartest, most darling man. I ought to tell him what you said."

Meg decided in the moment if the tight little twat deserved a response. Then Meg said, "You been sucking his dick, or what?"

The prissy little bitch whirled around, stumbled, recovered herself, and stomped out of the room in tight little steps.

Meg continued to sing her praises of Ringo's drawings that

he offered in defense of Professor John's torture. She'd begun a collection. She said she was going to see that they were published. "The book will be dedicated 'To the loving memory of Professor Harold P. Johns, who inspired these drawings,' which would be highly hilarious. You draw and I'll take the notes that'll get us through this class."

Delighted at the bargain, Ringo drew with a fury. He created images of Professor Johns burning at the stake while children danced around the flames as if playing ring-around-the-rosy, and one of his drawings was of the prissy little bitch being nailed up on a Jesus cross by hooded miscreants while in the background a trumpeter in a jazz band was tooting his solo.

"How can you draw such horrifying images?" Meg asked. "Who are you anyway?"

"I've seen quite a bit," he said, and that's all he'd say.

He said he loved the peaceful heart and loving brush of Claude Monet.

She bought him a book of Monet's paintings for his birthday. He turned the pages, not wanting to leave one page for another and taking nearly two hours to absorb the paintings from cover to cover. Even when he'd reached the last of the *Haystacks* series, *Haystacks in Evening Sun,* he turned to the first page and began to move slowly through again, like a man who'd gorged himself at a feast but was still hungry.

Meg put hamburgers on to fry, cut the sweet white onions in slices, set out the dill pickles and yellow mustard, and after she'd toasted the buns on the open skillet, she called him.

He'd been captured by the paintings of Monet's water lilies rendered in both the morning light and in the evening glow, as if the sun had grown weary. "Look!" he exclaimed like a child discovering a beautiful shell on the beach. He pushed the book across to Meg and stuffed the hamburger into his mouth, bit off a large chunk, and while still chewing, he tried to tell her that

Monet's *Rouen Cathedral* paintings were fastened to the earth but were flying. "And they're aglow. They're so beautiful!" He wiped at his eyes. "It's only the onions," he said, his joy lighting her kitchen.

"I have a surprise for you," Meg said. "Follow me." Still holding his hamburger and chewing as he went, he followed her to the bedroom door. With a wave of her arm, like a master of ceremonies, she presented her gift. In the center of the small room stood a wooden easel bearing a prestretched gessoed canvas, and on the chair next to the easel sat a large wooden paint box and a palette.

"Here, Mr. Picasso," she said. "Here's your new studio. You can paint to your heart's desire. Now we shall see your great art."

He cautiously lifted the box's lid. He saw the tubes of oil paints in an entire spectrum of colors, and the larger tubes of titanium white and midnight black. He saw the array of sable and bristle brushes lying like restless children eager to burst into play.

"Here," she said, rushing to him with a bottle in each hand, one of turpentine and one of linseed oil. "I've forgotten nothing." She ran to the closet and returned with a handful of white cotton rags. "And here are a couple of palette knives," she said, testing their flexibility against the seat of the chair. "I even brought you charcoal for sketching. What else could you possibly need?"

He stood shaking his head like a blind man granted the miracle of sight.

"Now you can paint me," she said. She pulled her sweater over her head, dropped it on the floor, and stood in front of him in her bra and jeans. Lifting one leg at a time, she gracefully slipped off her jeans, balancing herself first on her left foot and then her right. She wore purple panties.

"Where shall I stand? Or do you want me reclining, like in the paintings of the old masters?"

He stared.

"Naked skin won't hurt you," she lightly chided.

As she walked past him, she took off her bra, not in the way of a stripper, but as if to rid herself of a bothersome undergarment. She dropped it on the floor.

He looked away.

"You men are so funny. You've seen endless paintings of nude women, and you never so much as blink an eye. But if one in the flesh stands in front of you, you turn into a speechless drip."

Oblivious that her naked breasts brushed his arm, she handed the palette to him and began squeezing dabs of color from the tubes. Then she removed her panties and stretched out on the blue bedspread. She raised her head and rested it on her elbow. "Do you like this pose?"

She was more than his fantasies had provided. Her lines were clean and long, her skin clear as wild morning glories before they closed in the sun. "I don't like the blue bedspread very much."

She jumped up. "Aha! The artist is emerging. Pray tell, dear sir, what background shall we fabricate?"

"Maybe you could stand over by the door, maybe lean against the door and look down." His words surprised him.

She walked like a geisha girl in small, quick steps that held her legs together and her buttocks firm. Her breasts, not ponderous, but full, bounced lightly as she moved, and her nipples were erect, as if listening.

She leaned against the threshold. "How about this?" Her nakedness mocked him. He took the brush and jabbed at the paint. His hand shook like that of one suffering a senile disease.

He thrust his brush into the Mediterranean blue and began to mix it with the cadmium red. His brush stabbed at the canvas like a libidinous knife, penetrating deeply into the canyon of his wounds.

"How about a break?" she asked. "I've been standing here for over an hour. I'm not just a marble statue, you know."

He felt swallowed in shadows. He squeezed out more black. He painted on the wings of ravens.

"Hey, my Picasso. Is it possible for us to take a break?"

He was trembling.

She walked to him and touched his arm. "Is this me? Where am I in this magnificent mess?"

He stepped back from the easel and saw what he'd committed.

She saw the brush shaking in his hand. "Are you nervous or something?"

She thought he nodded yes.

"Well then, why don't you take off *your* clothes? That way, we'll be the same. I won't look, I promise."

He attacked the canvas again. He felt foolish. Embarrassed. He set the palette and brush on the table. "I can't finish it."

"Of course you can finish it, darling boy. How dare you quit now?" Then she came to him and touched him there, touched him softly and touched him again.

"I shouldn't be here," he said.

Something dark had grown out of his humiliation. She felt sorry for her brazen assault and quickly slipped into her panties and bra. His unclothed naïveté had disgraced him, as if the clothes of self had been ripped from him. He grabbed his hat and pulled it down low. "I gotta go."

She stood watching. Sadness stole over her face.

"Don't you want to take your paint things with you?"

"No."

"Will you ever finish the painting?"

"No."

She watched him walk the way men walk when they're running from danger, or into it.

Men suffer a transient insanity, she thought. The most cultured of the species sometimes risked their good names, their fortunes, even their lives for a couple of animal minutes between the legs of a woman. They called it "pussy." They lied for pussy. Even killed for pussy. And after they doused their flame in pussy, they instantly regained their sanity. Men did not love. They knew nothing of love. They knew only of pussy.

Ringo seemed different. She hadn't discovered a kernel of the usual strutting macho in him. With most men, the less they had to brag about, the more they bragged about the little they had. But she knew that she and Ringo would never return to the childlike play they'd once shared.

She didn't want to change him. Nor could she. It was his unaffected, open self that ignited the part of her that was also real. He possessed no fund of experience to deal with her. It had been so charming and dear. They could never go back.

He'd been a blank canvas. Not a stroke had yet been laid on it. But he wouldn't stumble through life for long without learning something of the man-woman thing. He might learn it as an animal learns it, blindly blundering after his raw instincts and never discovering the fire that ignites a woman.

Or along the way, he might be captured by a woman who'd teach him a set of clever tricks so that what was painted on his virgin canvas would be only a compendium of her twisted needs. Or he might never be introduced to his own beauty, and waste it, and grow to despise it because some narcissistic female criticized him for his fumbling and clumsiness. He could be injured. Or spoiled. He was worth saving—this man, this artist in early bud. But then, she was an artist, too.

CHAPTER 11

Bear Creek Ranch, 1940

SARAH ECKERSLY WOULD never sleep until her child and her man were safely home. Past midnight, she heard the distant rumble of the vehicle. She parted the kitchen curtains and saw its headlights bouncing over the prairies like fireflies in the night. She heard the crunch of gravel as the car pulled up in front of the house, and she saw her son stumbling through the door, the deputy swaggering behind him.

"I brung your boy home to you, ma'am," the deputy said. Ringo pushed past his mother and ran to his bedroom. The deputy named Jaycox squeezed a smile from his wet lips. "Ain't you gonna invite me in for a cup of coffee? Long ways out here. It's late, and I brung your boy back."

"What did you do to my son?" Sarah demanded. "Where's his pants?"

"He killed that teacher, you know."

"That's nonsense."

Sarah Eckersly started to slam the door, the deputy's foot in the way.

"Sheriff woulda throwed him in jail 'long with them other pukes if it wasn't for me. I told the sheriff I'd make sure he gets to court when he's supposed to." He pushed past her and onto her freshly waxed kitchen floor.

She stepped in front of him. "You better leave."

"Well now, ain't you really bein' a little bit unfriendly? I told the sheriff I'd stand good for your boy." He hooked both thumbs into his front pockets and pushed out his pelvis as if to capture the room with it. "So as long as you're friendly to me, I'll stand good for your boy. That's fair, ain't it?"

"Where's my husband? And what did you do to my son?"

"Well, ma'am, I got bad news for you, and I got good news for you." He struck a match across the top of the kitchen stove, lit his cigarette, blew out the first puff, broke the matchstick between his fingers, and let the pieces fall to the floor.

"I brung your boy back. That there's the good news. But your husband weren't too cooperative. However, he's restin' safe in the county jail. Don't expect you'll be seein' him right away soon." He sat down and lifted his boots up onto her table.

His lecherous smile frightened her. "You leave right now, or I'll call the law." She started for the phone.

"Well now, why don't you just do that, sweetheart?" he said, wetting his lips for a new smile. "The sheriff's gonna be disappointed big-time, 'cause I told him you was gonna cooperate so you could keep the kid at home. Guess I better go get the little sumbitch and take him back to jail. But you know what them pukes do to kids like him." He got up, grabbed her, and with both hands on her buttocks, he pulled her to him. "Tell me somethin'. How did an ugly sumbitch like your ol' man get a pretty like you?"

She struggled and pulled back.

"I'll be back tomorrow to see how things are goin'. We got our responsibilities. Got a little murderer on our hands." Then he swaggered out the door.

She locked the door behind him. Her breath came in short, hard spasms.

Ringo could hear his mother on the telephone, telling the lawyer to please get his father out of jail, that she needed him, and please, she would pay him somehow. "You have to help us, Mr. Hampton. And they claim that Ringo killed his teacher, and he was home with us all night."

Ringo heard her rummaging in the back closet, where his father kept their twelve-gauge shotgun. He heard the gun's breech open and slam shut as she injected a cartridge into the chamber. Then the silence. The noisy, screaming silence.

Fear came stealing in. Fear was a monster dressed in black shadows that ate up the light. Fear was black wind with black fingers, and its smell was the smell of Mrs. Foreman's blood on the floor next to his desk, her eyes glazed over, staring at the ceiling, her mouth hanging open, the knife buried in her chest.

THE NEXT MORNING, Ringo boarded the school bus. The nightmare of the day before with the sheriff's knife at his things had carved raw slashes across his mind, and he struggled at the brink of exhaustion. The usual wild babblings of the children had also been silenced.

When the children got off the bus, they would be greeted by a frail, nervous little woman past sixty. Nellie Sheehan was her name. She had flylike arms and legs. Her hair was hennaed. She was older than Mrs. Foreman, and the years had pinched up her face, but she had good smile wrinkles. She'd taught school for more than thirty years, but she was forced to retire when the board of education required that all teachers, even those in one-room rural schools, be state-certified. She lacked a college degree, but her experience qualified her as a substitute

When Mrs. Sheehan opened the unlocked door of the Bear Creek School, she was greeted by a two-by-three-foot half-dried pool of blood. She found a mop and bucket, filled the bucket in the creek, and in a fury scrubbed at the dried blood. When only the blood's stain remained, she placed the mat from her car over the floor where Mrs. Foreman had lain.

A few minutes later, the school bus arrived. As usual, Ringo, last on, was the first off. When Mrs. Sheehan opened the schoolhouse door, they ran, but the woman, nearly as small as the sixth-grade girls, called out to the children in her high, quivery voice, "I'm your new teacher, children. My name is Mrs. Sheehan. You children come on in now. Everything is all right." As she spoke, she moved her head in quick side-to-side jerks, like a small bird watching for the first hint of danger.

Ringo held back with the rest. Then with tentative steps, one of the sixth-grade girls ventured through the door, and like the first sheep to start across the creek, the rest of the small herd followed. But when Ringo saw the mat on the floor by his desk where Mrs. Foreman had lain, he stopped short.

"You can come in and sit down now," Mrs Sheehan said to Ringo with her quick, staccato smile. "There's nothing here to harm you." She took him by the wrist to lead him to his desk. He stared straight ahead, followed her, and sat down.

The room smelled of death.

Mrs. Sheehan was taking the roll of students when the patrol car drove up and Sheriff Diggs and Chief Deputy Harv Jaycox came stomping in. Big boots. Big hats. Big voices.

"Excuse me, ma'am, but we gotta do a little more work here," Sheriff Diggs said. "Won't take but a minute. Have any of you seen Ham Swanker?"

The children sat silently, staring at the sheriff.

"Don't gimme them blank looks." Diggs was standing so close to Ringo that all he could see was the brown pants of the sheriff's uniform and the gun hanging from its holster below the sheriff's waist.

Fear grabbed Ringo. Suddenly, he jerked the sheriff's gun

from its holster and jumped to the other side of his desk. He held the gun on Diggs, the gun heavy and swaying in his hand.

"You let my daddy go," Ringo shouted in his high-pitched boy's voice.

"Why, you little sumbitch." Diggs hollered. "I shoulda throwed this kid in jail when I had him. Gimme that gun."

"Shall I shoot the little bastard?" Jaycox asked, his gun pointed at Ringo.

Mrs. Sheehan came running to Ringo. "Give me that gun," she ordered. The gun in Ringo's hand was in her belly when she grabbed it from him. She dropped it on the floor, her arms around the boy like those of a panicked mother.

"Harv, throw that kid's ass in the squad car, and put the cuffs on the little bastard," Diggs said. "We got a vicious little sumbitchin' murderer on our hands."

"You are *not* going to take him," Mrs. Sheehan said, still holding on to Ringo. I know his parents, and he is a very good boy."

"Let loose of him," Jaycox said, pulling at Ringo's arm. "You heard what the sheriff told me."

"You are *not* taking him," Mrs. Sheehan hollered in her high-pitched voice. "No. You are *not*. You leave him with me." She took Ringo by the hand and led him to her desk. "You sit here." Then she said to the children, "This is recess. You go out and play, and stay out of the creek."

Mrs. Sheehan turned to Diggs. "You and your deputy go sit in your car. I'll call you when I'm ready."

Diggs stared at the little woman for a moment. He picked up his gun, holstered it, and looked over at Jaycox. "What the fuck," he said. "Let's have us a cigarette."

After the two men left, Mrs. Sheehan pulled up a chair next to Ringo. "Why did you do that?"

"He's hurting my daddy."

"Your daddy will be okay."

Then she asked Ringo about Ham Swanker. Everybody said Ham was a genius, including Ham. At fourteen, he was smarter than all the kids and the teacher put together. Once when he got bored, he'd offered to teach the kids something called calculus.

Ringo told Mrs. Sheehan how once at recess Ham put his knife to Jamey's throat, and how Ringo jumped on Ham's back and was holding on when Mrs. Foreman came around the corner of the schoolhouse and saw it all. Mrs. Foreman made Ham give her the knife, "and right now!" Mrs. Foreman said she was going to tell the bus driver to have Ham's father come fetch him, and Ham was scared, and he said his old man would beat him for sure. The next morning, they found Mrs. Foreman lying faceup in that pool of blood, staring with clouded eyes at the ceiling.

After Mrs. Sheehan heard Ringo's story, she called for Sheriff Diggs and his deputy. Before she'd let them in, she made them put their cigarettes out. "You know better than to smoke in a schoolroom," she admonished. She told them what Ringo had told her. "You should be ashamed of yourselves for the way you threatened a little boy. You'd better leave him alone, or I'll call the authorities." They both laughed.

Then the two stomped out of the Bear Creek schoolhouse.

Mrs. Sheehan waited for the children to settle in their seats. They were still shocked and silent. She thought it better if the children discussed death together. She turned to a third grader, a blond boy with freckles, who seemed more composed than the rest.

"What's your name?" Her smile turned down at the corners.

"Donald." He was a rancher's son on Prairie Dog Creek.

"Donald, what is death?"

He thought for a moment, his frown in assistance. Finally he said, "Death is when you get stabbed and they haul you away in a pickup."

Some of the children began to cry again. After that, she called the bus driver, and at about ten-thirty in the morning, she sent the children home for the rest of the day.

Then Mrs. Sheehan called Arnold White, the superintendent of schools, and told him that in her opinion the children at Bear Creek needed psychological counseling.

"How would you know that, Mrs. Sheehan?" the superintendent asked politely.

"Well, I could tell. The children were very upset. They saw their teacher hauled out of the schoolhouse dead and bloody and dumped in a pickup truck and hauled away."

"These are all country children who see death all the time, Mrs. Sheehan," Superintendent White said. "Most of the families out there do their own butchering. They shoot deer and antelope and prairie dogs and coyotes and Lord knows what else. They don't need babying. They need to forget this horrible thing and get on with their schooling."

"But they don't see the teacher they loved all bloody and dead every day—murdered, no less. I've seen how upset they are."

"I've seen children upset over having to face a substitute teacher," Supertindent White said. "But they'll soon get over that, as well. I appreciate your concern. Those parents will be much more appreciative of the tax dollars I save them rather than my hiring some psychologist who'd probably just stir things up, and cost the district a potful of money."

That same day, Jaycox stomped up the walk to the Eckerly house. Sarah was alone.

CHAPTER 12

"THAT LITTLE SON of a bitch says that Ham killed their teacher," George Swanker hollered as he kicked open the door of their mansion. "You hear me, woman?"

His wife was leafing through the pages of *Good Housekeeping*. Swanker grabbed the magazine, threw it on the floor, and shouted in her face, "I said, Jamey is fingering his own brother. Says his own brother killed the teacher. Hear me?"

Martha Swanker mumbled something.

"Jesus Christ, can't you say anything?" he hollered in her face.

"Jamey is a good boy," she muttered. "He loves birds."

"The little son of a bitch is good for nothing," Swanker said. "He was out bird-watching this morning and left the men to clean the horses' stalls. And now the little bastard is fingering his own brother for murder." He started for the door. "He hasn't got anything in his fuckin' head but birds. Something the fuck's wrong with him."

Swanker charged into Jamey's room on the second floor. He shoved the wide-eyed, terror-stricken boy up against the wall. "You know how Pete puts those chickens' heads on the chopping block and cuts their heads off?" Pete was one of their hired men. "Well, I'll cut your fucking fingers off one at a time if you don't tell the sheriff that you killed your brother, Ham. You got that?"

Later that same day, Swanker pulled up in front of the sheriff's office, ordered Jamey out of the pickup, and walked ahead of the boy, as if not to claim him. The child was hiding both hands in his pants pockets.

"Come in, seventy-seven," Sheriff Diggs was hollering on his radio. "I never can find Jaycox when I want him." When he saw Swanker at the counter, he said, "Mighty glad to see you, George. What can I do for you?"

"My boy Ham's been killed. Didn't come home on the bus last night. This little son of a bitch killed his own brother." Everyone knew Swanker had a drinking problem.

"Whatcha talkin' about, George?" Diggs asked.

"Ask him," Swanker said, pointing at Jamey. "He knows."

The sheriff aimed his long nose at Jamey. Jamey shied back.

"Well, tell him," Swanker hollered. He grabbed the boy and shook him. Jamey's jaw moved silently up and down, and tears welled up in his eyes.

"You maybe had a couple too many this mornin'? This kid couldn't kill nobody," Diggs said. "We've been friends a long time, George. You better not be fixin' to send me on some wild-goose chase. Why don't you go home and sober up, and we'll talk about this in the mornin'?"

"Well, the kid says he done it, and the kid never lies."

"How did you kill your brother?" Diggs asked Jamey.

Swanker answered for him in slurred words. "He killed him with a knife."

Swanker handed the paper sack to the sheriff. Cautiously, the sheriff opened the sack and pulled out a large knife covered with dried blood.

"Whose knife is this?" the sheriff asked as he examined the knife carefully.

"It's his," Swanker said, pointing to Jamey.

"Where'd you get a regulation police knife?" Diggs asked Jamey.

Jamey didn't answer, his eyes rolling in terror.

"Then maybe you can tell me where the fuck your brother's body is," Diggs said to Jamey.

"He told me he followed Ham out behind the school, and he stabbed him there," Swanker said. He dug his hand into Jamey's arm, and Jamey nodded.

Diggs slowly shook his head, grabbed his hat, and pulled it down low over his eyes as if to assure all present that he meant business.

Swanker stumbled and caught himself before he fell. "Hurry up," he yelled at Jamey, who was bringing up the rear.

SHERIFF BILL DIGGS arrived at the Bear Creek schoolhouse with George Swanker in the front seat of the sheriff's car and Jamey in the back. Swanker took a swig from the flask he kept in his coat pocket. "Get out," Swanker hollered at Jamey. "Now show the sheriff where your brother's body is."

The boy headed for the creek. At the creek's edge, Jamey jumped across, holding on to the willows, Diggs close behind. Swanker half fell into the shallow water as he waded across. The men watched while Jamey carefully parted the willows. The boy stood staring down.

"There ain't nothing here," Diggs said. "I thought you said he was out on the prairie."

"He musta rose from the dead," Jamey whispered.

"The fuckin' kid lied to me," Swanker said. "Sorry to cause all the trouble. One thing for sure: I'll teach that kid how to tell the truth."

"You better quit drinkin'—at least in the mornin'," Diggs said. "I got more to do than follow you around all day on a drunkin' goose chase."

On their way home, Swanker said to Jamey, "I'm getting Ham the fuck outta here. Where's he at?"

"I don't know."

"Remember what I told you about your fingers. I'll cut 'em off for sure if you don't tell me straight."

"Teacher made Ham stay after school. I never saw him after that. I just got on the bus and come home."

"Remember, I told the sheriff you killed Ham. And you stick to that story."

"I shoulda killed him," Jamey said. "He killed the teacher."

Swanker yanked Jamey out of the car and stumbled into the house. "Never say that again, you worthless asshole." He slapped the boy and knocked him halfway across the room.

"Hey, woman, where you at?" Swanker hollered for his wife. "Their gonna put this little bastard away for good for killing his brother. I say let the fuckin' state feed him. He's no good to us. All he does is chase a bunch of fucking birds around. The worthless little shit can't even shovel horse shit."

CHAPTER 13

Laramie, Conrad Hotel, 1947

RINGO FOUND A job no serious student would have considered—as night bellhop at the Conrad, the town's only hotel. But Ringo needed work. The job began at eight at night and ended at two in the morning. His job included sweeping and dusting the lobby, sifting the cigarette and cigar butts from the ashtray stands that stood by the elevator at each of the hotel's four floors, after midnight mopping the floors of the lobby and the men's and women's toilets and swabbing the toilets with Lysol, and if he could get all of the work done before two in the morning, he was free to sleep the remaining half hour or so before quitting time. His pay was a dollar an hour, plus tips, which were rare, since most of the hotel guests had already checked in.

The night clerk, also the hotel's accountant, was a short, fat man with pure white hair, thick glasses, and skin that hung from his jowls like the wattle under the bill of an albino turkey. He was riveted to his thick ledger with its carefully penned numbers. Occasionally, he eyed Ringo with undisguised disdain.

A night never went by that the old curmudgeon couldn't find something wrong with Ringo's work—the most minute specks of dust in the corners of the lobby, visible only from behind the clerk's magnifying spectacles; end tables that didn't sit quite straight; and he pointed to the dust on the windowsill, which could be seen only if one cocked one's head at a severe-enough angle to gather the ambient light creeping in from the hallway.

It was two in the morning. Ringo was asleep on the old black leather couch that faced the reception desk.

"Hey, kid, stop that damnable snoring," the clerk hollered in his scratchy old voice. "It's quitin' time. Go on home with it."

Ringo jumped up, blinked, shook his head, gave the clerk an apologetic smile, and staggered toward the door. He was just about out when he heard the clerk pounding the hand bell at the reception desk.

Bling bling.

Bling bling.

"Show this man to his room," the clerk said.

The guest gave Ringo a doubtful once-over—the kid's Levi's unraveled at the bottom, his lopped-over boots and faded shirt. "You the bellhop?"

"Yes, sir," Ringo said. He grabbed the man's small black leather suitcase and his smaller salesman's display case and started for the elevator. Room 437. He knew the room—on the left at the end of the hall, the fourth floor. Every room on the fourth floor was vacant. And as Ringo could have predicted, the clerk had assigned the guest to the room farthest from the men's toilet located at the other end of the hall.

The guy who'd be staying in room 437 had a small potbelly and wore a wrinkled business suit with a tie that looked like a rescued rag from a rummage sale. The elevator moaned up the four floors at a pensioner's pace. The guy cleared his throat. Ringo knew what was coming. The salesman didn't need him to haul up a couple of small bags.

"Where can a guy get a little action around here?" the salesman asked.

"No girls staying here in the hotel," Ringo said. He set the man's bags on the rack at the foot of the bed. The ceiling in the small room was as high as the room was long. A porcelain washbasin with two rusting faucets hung from the wall. Next to the basin stared a dark oak dresser, its mirror reflecting the starkness of the room, and across from the dresser stood a double bed with its brass and iron-post headboard.

"It's been a long dry spell. Gotta be some action in this fuckin' town." He handed Ringo a fifty-cent piece.

"I been told there's some houses on Front Street by the railroad tracks—two blocks down."

"Thanks, kid," the guy said. He handed Ringo another quarter.

Ringo said good night to the clerk, who acted as if he didn't hear him. Then he walked out into the cold fall night, the starlight sifting down through the tiny worn holes of a black celestial blanket.

As ordered by the night clerk, Ringo had parked his truck a half block down the street from the hotel. A bellhop wasn't entitled to take up a valuable parking place near the hotel. He mounted his truck, turned on to Front Street, and slowed his truck to a crawl. Then he lowered his head and peered up the fifteen stairs, where the small red light was inviting through the darkness, and he saw 437 walking up the stairs.

"You're a sniveling coward," Ringo said out loud to himself. "You'll never be a man."

Ringo stood looking up through the small ground-level window of his basement room in Laramie. In the late fall, the edge of dawn was silent, but in the silence he could hear Meg's gaiety. He'd been right. They could never be friends.

Never.

Through the early yellow light, he saw Meg standing there naked, her breasts inviting, her eyes laughing, her lips, luscious and lewd, and offering. But her immaculate heat had transformed him into something abysmally absurd.

He should have proclaimed that his smears on the canvas were the greatest work of art of the fucking century. *The* fucking century. He should have spoken in a slow, authoritative voice: "I've released the secrets of an enchanted psyche that have come bursting wet and dripping onto this canvas." And when she exclaimed in a breathless whisper how his painting was perfect, he should have said nothing. He should have cocked an eyebrow, vaguely smiled at her, put his paints back in the box, and walked away.

Forever.

But no.

He, "her Picasso," ended up as little more than an ant dragging its emptied shell across her living room floor. He could never be the lover of a woman who mocked him. Nor could he be her friend.

No. Never.

That morning, Ringo walked up the basement stairs and out through the stiffened stems of old weeds and dead grass. He felt his loneliness like a man meandering lost on an uninhabited desert.

The time had finally come.

CHAPTER 14

Bear Creek Ranch, 1940

WHEN THE BUS driver let Ringo off, he walked slowly along the creek toward the house, the water low and lazy in the late fall, the ice beginning to gather at the creek's edges.

Maybe he'd climb up on Old Paint and rest his face against the horse's neck, feel the warmth of his new winter coat and smell the good horse smell. Maybe they'd go exploring. Perhaps they'd never come back. He'd rounded the last bend of the creek and had just reached the back door of the house when he saw the white car coming.

Jaycox drove up to the house, parked his squad car, turned the rearview mirror to examine himself, wiped the corners of his mouth, got out of the car, unbuckled the belt holding his revolver, knife, and cuffs, and tossed them into the front seat.

He threw his left leg slightly to the side as he walked, a habit acquired as a youth to suggest that his parts were of the size requiring such an accommodating maneuver. His waist was small and round, like a log. His narrow shoulders were widened by the padding in his officer's jacket, and a shiny silver star glared out over his heart. He stomped up to the door.

Sarah Eckersly answered the deputy's knock. He walked in without a word.

Her hair was still mussed, her mouth barren of lipstick, and her once succulent lips seemed wilted and were wordless.

Jaycox pulled an oak chair back from the kitchen table and sat down. He could smell the woman, not sweet, not musky, but a good woman smell. "Where's the kid?" He tipped his hat back and looked Sarah up and down with an unbridled leer.

She didn't answer.

The man's presence caused a catch in her throat—the blatant evilness she'd felt from him the night before had left her feeling weak and vulnerable.

The deputy licked his lips and lifted his boots up on her precious table. The table groaned its objection. "You got the kid hid somewhere? And where's the coffee?" He twisted his mouth into a salacious smile.

She lifted the blue porcelain pot from the stove, took her husband's cup from the cupboard, and filled it. She put the cream and sugar in front of him. He sipped at the coffee. "You rancher types like it strong," he said. "Remember, I could've put the kid in with them pukes in the county jail. And like I asked you, where the fuck's the kid?"

She felt light-headed. "He's at school." Why hadn't she said he was coming in from the barn, or something like that? With the timid arrival of courage, she said, "I talked to our lawyer this morning. He told me that if you thought Ringo killed his teacher, you wouldn't let him go to school that way."

"Your lawyer don't know shit."

"You needn't use that language."

"Juveniles are treated different from adult criminals. Your lawyer probably don't even know that." He sipped again at the coffee. Over the top of the cup, his eyes were steady on her.

She felt as if she were dissolving into the rushing stream. She had no power against its current. His wet, revolting mouth. She backed up to the wall and stood next to the Jesus calendar. His vulgar animalism was like the rams in the breeding pasture. She tried to conceal her rapid breathing. "Our lawyer says he's going to get my husband out of jail today. He'll be home any minute."

"Your old man ain't goin' nowhere. Did you miss me last night, darlin'?" When she didn't answer, he said, "You gonna treat me right, or what? I took care of your kid."

She stayed standing next to the Jesus calendar, staring at the floor. Then the deputy got up from the table.

CHAPTER 15

Casper, Wyoming, 1925

THE WAYFARING WOMANIZER who'd fathered Meg claimed her mother, Marsha Mendleson, was an ignorant bitch. She hadn't taken the first precaution against the onslaught of the spermatic horde. One of its numbers punctured her egg. He argued that if she hadn't been so fucking ignorant, she'd have washed away the leavings of their folly in a solution of nonoxynol-9, and, absent that, she could have gone to Madam Belemy for an abortion. He even offered to lend her the money. But Marsha had taken neither precautions nor his offer, the result of which was Meg Mendleson.

Marsha had longed for a child as far back as she could remember. She wanted a real, living doll, and she was going to have one. She didn't care if she was married or not. She didn't care what her father, Richard Mendleson, thought about it. She had her own trust fund left to her by her doting paternal grandfather, Buck Mendleson, who'd scooped up a bundle in the oil business.

When Marsha gleefully announced to the world that she was with child, the sire of whom was, as her father phrased it, little more than "some pussy-chaser passing through," he loosed a mournful diatribe of despair:

"I raised this daughter, loved her, took care of her for more than eighteen years, played Santa Claus for her when she was a baby, got her teeth straightened, stayed up at night thinking she was going to die when she had her tonsils out, and I attended those god-awful boring parent-teacher meetings.

"I sat through her school plays, bought her first formal gown for the prom, and worried into the wee hours of the morning when she wasn't home from her date. I sent her off to college, and all I did was raise a piece of ass for some son of a bitch who met her in a bar, had no investment in her, and probably didn't even buy her a drink. All he wanted was to shove the meat to her. Then when she got pregnant, he was off fucking some other man's daughter. If I could get my hands on the worthless son of a bitch, I'd kill him."

Richard Mendleson had grown up in the big house that his father, Buck, bought to impress the men at the Petroleum Club. Buck sent Richard off for an education at Harvard Business School, where he romped with the best of the country's rich men's sons. Buck bought the kid a fancy car to buzz around in, enjoying vicariously what he'd never experienced firsthand. All he ever did was work. But Richard never worked a day in his life. His hands were as smooth as a newborn baby's butt.

Soon after Richard trickled out of Harvard, he touted a bunch of ideas the old man didn't understand and didn't give a shit about. Richard took the company public, bought up oil-servicing equipment and seismograph trucks. He formed marketing companies, bought the old Pluto Oil refinery in Casper, and modernized it to the tune of ten million.

Then the oil depression descended, the consequence of cheap Arab oil, and Casper went belly-up. Richard's companies, all of them, were garbaged. He hung around the house for months, moping and cursing the politicians and the big oil companies and claiming it was a worldwide conspiracy of a bunch of damned Arabs who put him out of business. He also blamed his wife for spending too much money. One day, the bank foreclosed on their home.

At last, desperate and hanging on the edge of suicide, he decided to go begging to Buck for help. But he didn't have the courage to face the old man, so he sent his wife, Eloise, Marsha's mother. She, too, had never worked a lick in her life, unless one defined working as driving herself to the country club for lunch.

Eloise could make the old man laugh, and she cooed over him. It touched Buck to be told that someone loved him. "Papa, you know that I'd never make a very good peasant. We are about to become peasants, Papa, *peasants*." She was on the tipsy brink of tears.

"I know," Buck said. "It takes skill to be poor and survive." He wrote her a check for a hundred thousand that he'd stashed away. He felt guilty. He said, "Parents like me who deprive their kids of the lessons taught by hard work have to pay the price." He was talking while he was writing his check for Eloise. "Richard and you never sweat except in a sauna."

He handed her the check. "And you never learned somethin' I learned workin' out on the rigs. Sweat, hard work, and disappointment fertilize the gardens of joy and growth." The old man claimed he finally sounded like a damned philosopher of some kind. But all Eloise heard was the music of the check being ripped out of his checkbook.

"Now this is all there's gonna be," he said. "When this is gone, you're gonna learn how to wait tables, and Richard is gonna learn how to shovel shit."

"Yes, Papa," Eloise said. She took the check from the old man and kissed him and told him that she loved him. After two years, the money was gone, and she was back again. Hard luck. The oil business was still on its ass. "On its *ass,* Papa," she said again. And the old man, still feeling guilty, wrote another check. He was getting low on funds himself, but he said his aim was to die broke.

He put some money in a trust fund for Marsha, and it was just before the old man died that Marsha came home that day to joyfully announce to Eloise and Richard that she was pregnant. By that time, the last of Buck's money was gone. Richard had finally found a low-paying job at the bank as an assistant cashier.

Richard and Eloise moved into a small apartment on lower Durbin Street, still a decent address, but it was a minimal abode that reflected little social wattage. There, Marsha brought home her daughter, Meg.

Marsha, with her new baby, was exorbitantly happy in that house of otherwise dire depression. Marsha had dipped into her trust fund sparingly, with one overriding objective: to fulfill every need, every whim, every fleeting desire her child, Meg, might command. She needed nothing more than to love her child, and for her child to love her. She read her *Alice in Wonderland*, *The Wizard of Oz*, and half of the New Testament before the she could say "Mama." She dragged the child with her wherever she went and took no leave from the inexorable bliss of her motherhood.

When Papa Buck died, he'd kept his promise: He died broke. For Richard and Eloise, it was as if their world had ended. No money, no standing in the community. No money, no respect. No money, nothing that represented human virtue.

But soon little Meg brought new life to the house. Her mere presence made people laugh, where before they'd lolled away in moldy gloom. A certain magic pursued the child. She became the personification of joy.

Richard and Eloise were soon caught up in the life of little Meg. Mother and grandmother argued about whose turn it was to read Meg her good-night stories and her napping stories. Marsha showed the child how to tap-dance at four, to bake a chocolate cake, to grow pansies in a wooden box, and how to sew button eyes on her rag doll.

Meg was a beautiful child. She had coal black hair—probably a gift from her sire—and the dark eyes of her mother. Eloise proclaimed with glowing pride that her grandchild had been born happy. She insisted it was nearly impossible to render little Meg unhappy.

When Meg was barely eighteen, she graduated from Natrona County High School, in Casper, where she'd done well in history, art, and poetry. Richard had died the year before of a heart attack. Eloise played bridge once a week with her oldest friends and was living on Social Security. Marsha, now an irretrievably reclusive spinster, had no interest beyond her daughter, Meg.

One morning early, Meg came to her mother's bedroom door carrying a small suitcase that had once belonged to old Buck. Her mother was still in bed, her eyes glued to the television.

"I'm leaving, Mother," she announced.

"See you later," her mother said, without realizing that Meg meant forever.

When she hadn't heard from Meg by three the next morning, Marsha called the police in high hysterics. Shortly they discovered Meg had taken the bus out of town. The ticket agent knew the girl and remembered she'd boarded the 11:00 A.M. Greyhound for Denver. She'd purchased a ticket all the way to New York.

From there, Meg, by unspecified resourcefulness, had taken a ship to London, and after that, gathering money from further unidentified endeavors, she spent the following three years in Europe. She wrote home occasionally. Marsha's monopolizing hope for even a sparse note from Meg provided Marsha's consuming reason for life.

Meg lived for six months in Paris in an artist's colony on the Left Bank, where she took up residence with a wild-eyed sculptor named Paul Caruth. He skimped by on a fellowship, completed over thirty nude studies of Meg, and seduced her after each as her only pay. Not much pay, she thought. Not from Paul Caruth. From Bobby Helburn, the painter, maybe. But Caruth's interest in her body cost her little and provided her a place to stay and, on most evenings, something to eat.

Meg gave up writing poetry when she was presented her forti-
eth straight rejection slip, the last from *The New Yorker*. She said,
"That magazine must only publish the stuff from those who are
fucking the editorial staff. No fucky—no publish. Listen to this
shit." She read a verse aloud to Caruth while she was posing.

> the orchid is a lily or a hand-painted
> hunk of wallpaper in the parlor which
> in the midst of green moonbeams
> drives men to bury gardenias in the kitchen.

"Push your pussy out a little farther," Caruth said. "Push it out
like it's a hungry cat begging for a scrap."

"Fuck you," she'd heard herself say. Her words surprised her.
But she'd already given too much to the miserable bastard for
too long. She said she left Caruth with his sculpting knife in one
hand and his dick in the other. What she needed was a piece of
paper—a degree from a university. Any university.

Meg thought the University of Wyoming was a bump on
the totem pole of higher education. But she could claim Wyoming residence, and compared to what she'd have to spend at
other schools, she could cheap it through. Then along came that
painter-sheepherder, Ringo, and she had to decide what to do
with him. He'd awakened something she'd kept locked down,
something that had dared not surface to stare out at her and to
make its demands of her.

The painter-sheepherder hadn't been in her plans. She told
herself he was a mere complication along the way, and she'd shake
it off like a pestering housefly. What exactly he'd taken from her,
she didn't know. But whatever it was, she wanted it back.

CHAPTER 16

Laramie, 1926

SARAH, RINGO'S MOTHER, had been in her second year at the University of Wyoming—a music major—when she thought she was pregnant. She could sing like the meadowlark, her mother said, and her father would sit back and smoke his pipe while she sang, her mother at the piano. At such times, her father seemed the happiest, his eyes soft and aglow with his love.

Sarah dreamed of being onstage in New York City, on Broadway, singing and dancing and dazzling the crowd—a girl from Wyoming making it big.

Her mother discouraged her. "A woman must make choices. Are you going to run off to New York and compete with a thousand other pretty girls? The few who make it work their way up, man after man in bed after bed, and when they can't get in bed with the director, they end up dancing at some striptease joint, sleeping with most anybody to pay for their fancy clothes and to support their drug habits."

"I'm not that kind of girl, Mama," Sarah protested.

"Just remember: You've only gone to the University of Wyoming. People in New York think Wyoming is some little hick town in Montana or some such place."

"What kind of a woman do you think I am, Mama? I could

get a job as a waitress and work my way up. Remember, I waited tables at the Campus Café."

"It's different in New York. You'd be lucky if you weren't gang-raped on the streets. New York is no place for a Wyoming girl." Her father added, "They'd eat you up like hogs on fresh corn."

"Thank God I married your father. He always made a decent living. He never ran around with other women, and we are blessed with you." Her mother cast a loving smile at Sarah. "But whatever you decide, your father and I will give you our blessing. You're the author of your book of life."

One Friday night, Sarah and some of her girlfriends had decided "to whoop it up," to celebrate their survival of the semester's finals, when Jim Skaggs, a roughneck from the oil fields, swaggered into the bar with all his macho manners.

That night, Sarah was half drunk, and Skaggs had taken her in a hard way in his pickup. She'd bled. And she'd cried. Later on, she told him she thought she was pregnant. She said he had to do the right thing—the baby and all. And he said he'd marry her if she'd just stop her goddamned crying.

After that, they drove his new Chevy pickup to Cheyenne, and they were married by a justice of the peace. Skaggs wore his black leather jacket, and she wore a matching one. They thought it very hilarious—a protest against all that big wedding hoop-de-do of her parents.

"Nothing will change," Sarah promised. "We'll always be wild, even after the baby is born. We'll name him Tarzan, and call him Tar for short." Then she threw herself into his arms and kissed him out of pure primordial passion.

Sarah's father, a decent but predictable man, was a conductor on the Union Pacific Railroad. He'd warned her not to run around with Skaggs. "That kid is wild and no good," he said. "All he wants out of life is beer and pussy. I never raised you to be just a passing piece of ass for some roughneck."

Sarah's mother asked her if she wanted a drunken oil-field worker to father her children, and said that she should think about that long and hard. And Sarah had thought about it.

But Sarah thought Jim Skaggs was "sooo cute," his tough look, his boots, and his new Chevy pickup, and he was "so different from her father, so brutish, so marvelously animalish."

Sarah lived with Skaggs for more than a year. But the marriage proved to be founded on a mistake of fact. The psychologist called it a "hysterical pregnancy," one that disappeared once the panic of pregnancy faded. "See it all the time in young girls in response to their loss of virginity."

When Sarah visited her parents, her father would greet her with "Welcome home, Mrs. Skaggs," and she'd say, "Please, Daddy, don't call me that. Skaggs is such an ugly-sounding name."

Sarah's father wasn't an ugly man, nor was he ignorant. At least Jim Skaggs wasn't ugly—his shiny black hair, his full mouth and small ears, his belly beginning to slip, but ever so slightly. Still, he was ugly in the way he treated her, his hands with dirty fingernails all over her, pushing, pinching, probing, his bestial copulation, like that of a frenzied cur in the street.

One night, Skaggs came home staggering drunk and smelled of some sickening perfume, and he admitted he'd been with the whores on Front Street. In the morning, his eyes were red-veined and bleary, and he denied all he'd confessed. "Just drunk talk," he said. But the divorce was easy. Skaggs had grown tired of supporting her "hotsy-totsy ways."

The night their divorce became final, they celebrated at the Purple Sage Saloon. "Here's to our new lives to come," Skaggs toasted.

"Here's to the best of our old days," Sarah toasted. Why was her excitement for him revived? When they went to the hotel, Skaggs made a big scene at the reception desk. "This is my ex-wife. Got any problem with a man goin' to bed with his ex-wife?"

"Couldn't care less," the old clerk said. "Twenty bucks."

In the early hours of the morning, when their wildness had finally been quenched, Skaggs pulled on his pants and said, "It's too fucking bad you couldn't be that way while we were married." He slapped her across her bare buttocks. "You're still one hell of a piece of ass if once a year can do a man." After that, she put on her clothes and went home to her mother.

SARAH MET BEN Eckersly when he was mentoring some 4-H boys with their fat lamb entries at the Albany County Fair in Laramie. Sarah was assisting the eighth-grade girls at the home economics booth next to Eckersly's. The girls had baked a pan of brownies, and after the judging, Sarah offered the handsome man and each of his boys a brownie. That evening, he invited her out—not for dinner, not even for a drink, but to see a drive-in movie.

She felt an unsettling anticipation with this quiet, handsome man who was careful in choosing his words and who was nearly ten years her senior. She moved close to him in the front seat of his pickup truck, and he put his arm around her shoulder, but he didn't otherwise touch her.

Eckersly was unfailingly courteous and thoughtful. She found herself thinking his kind would make a good father for her children. He had a powerful body, but his gentleness and sparse words were offered as a precious gift. After a year of benignly tender courtship, during which Eckersly not once approached those places, even when she'd wanted him to, he asked her to marry him.

They'd been driving in his pickup truck through the Snowy Range, those high, craggy mountains that rose up as if the land had awakened after having lain slumbering for eons. On that early-summer day, the forest meadows danced with lupine, the color of alpine skies. The red willows budded along the creeks, and small patches of snow still hung on in the shade at the edge of the timber.

"I love you," Eckersly said, his eyes fixed on the road. "And I promise to make you happy every day of your life, and I'm a man of my word. We can have a good life on the ranch. It's peaceful there. No one will bother us. I'll remodel the house and put in a new kitchen stove. And someday we'll own our own place."

Later that summer, they were married in the Lutheran church in Laramie by the Reverend Charles Schmidt. Sarah threw her arms around her new husband and kissed him in front of their friends, and at that moment she felt a soaring joy she'd never felt before.

Then he drove her to the ranch, with her mother's wedding present in the back, the family's Early American antique table. He lifted her over the threshold of the small white house, and went back for the table. She asked him to set it in the exact center of the kitchen.

What Sarah felt for Eckersly wasn't that blind, burning, breathless insanity, the product of those devilish chemicals the body produced to ensure the propagation of the species. She'd already been down that road with Skaggs. Eckersly was a strong man, straight and true as any hero, a man who was a gentleman even when he made love—and a man who'd be a fine father for her children.

But over time, his handsomeness had grown common in her eyes. And his dependability, his utter predictability, made living with him like living in a convent, in which every occurrence of the day had been preset by centuries of precedent and nothing was left for discovery.

Once, he said that one cannot love a person without respect coming first, and she'd remained unfailingly respectable. And, yes, she wanted his child. That one overriding desire overrode her other feelings. Her mother said she'd never meet another man as decent, dependable, and handsome as Ben Eckersly, no matter how long she looked. "Life is about choices. You make your choices, and you stick with them, for good or for otherwise."

Sarah accepted the daily drudgery of a ranch wife without complaint—the predictable meals for the men, the small vegetable garden that required predictable attention and matured predictably, the predictable housekeeping chores, and, at the end of long days, the predictable prayer at mealtime offered by Eckersly, followed by their predictable conversations—about the sheep, the herders, the weather, the absent know-nothing owners, the markets, the coyotes, and the invading neighbors on their range.

She lived with Eckersly in that small white house that bravely clung to a protruding knoll on the otherwise uninhabited prairie—a place so tedious that over the ages even the prairie became bored with itself and grew nothing but sage, short fescue grass, and scrubby cacti. The harvester ants scavenged much of whatever dared grow, and built their hills, wide as a bushel basket, wherever they pleased, so that the prairie looked like a pockmarked hide that stretched to eternity.

The birth of their son provided small gifts of joy, and budding hope—hope for what, Sarah never asked herself. Her life was with her handsome husband and their beautiful son, whom they called "Little Ben." He looked for all the world like his father, except his eyes were blue, and his hair was blond, like hers.

She admitted that at certain times she was snippy and ill-tempered. She thought their marriage reflected the isolation of the prairies that surrounded them in a kind of spiritual despair. But one thing Sarah Eckersly was always proud of: She lived with her choice.

CHAPTER 17

Bear Creek Ranch, 1940

THAT NIGHT, SARAH hadn't slept, and before the sun was up, she slipped into the same cotton dress she'd worn the day before and prepared breakfast for Ringo—the usual, bacon and eggs, and pancakes—then packed his lunch and sent him off to school. She hadn't spoken to the child of the stabbing death of Mrs. Foreman, nor did she ask him any questions about his treatment at the hands of the sheriff. She thought it better to let it go, to hope that the horror would fade as her own demons had. She watched him walking slowly toward the bus stop, and after he disappeared from sight, she went to the window to look in the other direction.

She kept her vigil periodically, until she saw what she expected and feared.

Even before Jaycox parked his white squad car at the back door of the house, she'd seen the dusty line across the prairies marking his approach. She walked to the bathroom and looked in the mirror. She made no effort at makeup. She straightened her dress. Then she threw a plain blue cotton shawl over her shoulders, pulled it around her bosom, and walked to the door.

The deputy was in their kitchen. Ringo turned the front door knob slowly. The door was stuck. The deputy would hear the slightest creak. Ringo pushed on the door and, at the same time, pulled back on the knob to hold it quiet.

He was breathing hard.

The front door broke loose at the bottom with a small scraping noise. Ringo waited.

Frozen.

Listening.

Slowly, Ringo pushed the door open and slid sideways into the living room. He eased the bolt silently back. The curtains were drawn, the room almost dark. He waited for the sudden charge of the deputy. Fear grabbed at him. He tried to hold his breath and to hear beyond it.

Silence.

He took a tentative step toward the kitchen door. He heard rhythmic sounds, the table groaning. He heard loud breathing. Moaning. Then with his heart pounding, his breath coming in short gasps, he peered around the door into the kitchen.

He saw the man's naked white butt on top of his mother. His pants and shorts were bunched around his boots, and he saw the man's hairy legs. The deputy was pounding at his mother. She was moaning, and the legs of their precious table were grinding into the linoleum. His mother's moaning grew louder. Her mouth was open, and her eyes were staring at the ceiling like the eyes of Mrs. Foreman on the schoolroom floor. The man was hurting his mother in that terrible way.

He ran to his parents' bedroom and threw open the closet door. He reached through the clothes until he felt the cold steel of his father's twelve-gauge shotgun, the one he'd fired last winter while they were hunting cottontails. With the shotgun in his hands, he cocked the gun, slipped up to the kitchen door, and peered in.

The man was still hurting his mother on her precious kitchen table. The red-and-white-checkered oilcloth was on the floor, along with his father's great cup, which lay broken. His mother's underpants were draped from a chair. Her bra hung over the chair post.

"Get off my mother!" Ringo hollered. He lifted the shotgun to his shoulder to shoot.

"Jesus Christ!" Jaycox shouted, jumping off of Sarah Eckersly. "Where the fuck did he come from? I thought he was in school."

Sarah struggled up from the table. Her dress was unbuttoned. Her breasts were bare, her nipples raised and red. She reached for her underpants, and with both hands she tried to step into them. But the front of her dress gaped open, and her breasts escaped. Frantically, she began buttoning her dress. The two top buttons were torn off.

"Oh, Ringo," she cried. "He made me do it."

"Whatcha talkin' about?" Jaycox said. He grabbed at his own pants.

The Jesus calendar on the wall stared down with forgiving eyes.

Then holding his pants half up with one hand, the deputy started for Ringo. Jaycox reached out to grab the gun. Ringo fired and slammed another shell into the receiver. The charge ripped into the kitchen floor, leaving a gaping hole at the deputy's feet.

Jaycox jumped back. His pants fell to his boot tops. "Jesus Christ, kid! You tryin' to kill somebody?" He began pulling at his pants. "You're under arrest for murder. You murdered that school-marm, and I'm takin' you in."

Ringo stood his ground, the gun pointed at the deputy's belly.

"Jesus Christ, you want me to charge you with resistin' arrest, too?"

"Ringo, put the gun down!" Sarah screamed. "Ringo, don't shoot anybody!"

The deputy got his shorts and pants all the way up, zipped his fly, and started for the boy again.

"Get back," Ringo hollered, aiming down the barrel.

"Gimme the gun, boy, and I won't hurt you." He reached out in Ringo's direction. Ringo fired and slammed another shell into the receiver. The blast left a second hole at the deputy's feet.

"Goddamn you, you murderin' little motherfucker," Jaycox hollered.

The hole in the floor at the toe of the deputy's boot was large enough to drop a grapefruit through. Then Sarah said in a mother's commanding voice, "Ringo, give me the gun! I won't let him hurt you." She started for her son.

"Get back, Mama, or I'll shoot him."

She held out both of her arms, pleading. "Ringo, honey, listen to me."

"No, Mama, I'm gonna shoot him. He was hurtin' you." He tried to steady the shotgun on the chief deputy.

"Give her the gun, son," Jaycox shouted. "If you give her the gun, I'll go, I promise, and I'll never come back. Please, kid. Give the gun to your ma."

"What do you want, Ringo?" Sarah asked.

"I should kill him for hurtin' you."

Jaycox turned and started for the door. Suddenly, the deputy whirled around and grabbed the shotgun.

Ringo pulled the trigger, and then pulled it again. The blasts from the twelve-gauge blew away all of Chief Deputy Harv Jaycox's left ankle. His boot, with the severed foot inside, hung by a couple of stubborn tendons like a church bell strung in hell.

CHAPTER 18

Laramie, County Jail, 1940

WHEN HANK PLOWMAN, the jailer, unlocked his cell, Ben Eckersly grabbed his hat and walked out ahead of the old man. Plowman clopped along, talking to one inmate and another, giving them the news and taking messages they wanted passed on to their wives and families. When Eckersly got to the perimeter door, he waited without patience for the old jailer to catch up.

"Ben, if you wanna wait 'til noon, we'll be serving lunch," the jailer said. "Don't never say there ain't no free lunch." He smiled and unlocked the steel door.

"The old boys bailed me out," Eckersly said, referring to the ranch owners.

He tipped his hat to the jailer, checked out, and paid the twenty-five-dollar storage fee on his pickup.

In jail, he'd had time to think things through. Sarah wasn't meant to be a rancher's wife. She was the sensitive sort. She had no friends there except him, and a husband consumed with sheep and sheepherders and the endless issues of sheep ranching couldn't be much of a friend to a woman.

Although you can get used to the beauty of the sunrises that glorify the mornings with their dazzling displays, and all you see is the early light cast on the day's work ahead, Eckersly never got immune to Sarah's beauty. Some days, hers was the only beauty he saw. Not much to treat the eyes under the hood of a pickup, trying to get the rattletrap started when the temperature had dropped to thirty below. Not much in splinting an old ewe's broken, pus-swollen leg, or pulling the bulging, bloody ticks off a sheepdog, or riding out into a blizzard, the blowing snow plastering a man's face white and his feet so frozen that he couldn't take the first steps off his horse without the risk of falling.

Once, he'd saved up some money, and they'd gone to Denver to see a play and take in a nightclub. They'd rented a room in the Brown Palace, the hotel that Mr. Hansen said was the place to stay. But when they'd gone to bed, she seemed strangely preoccupied. He'd tried to kiss her, but she turned from him.

"What's the matter, honey?" he asked.

"I don't like to sleep in hotels," she said. "They give me the creeps."

"Why?"

She was silent.

Up on one elbow, Ben persisted. "Well, why?"

"I don't know," she finally said.

"We could rent us a motel room. Do motels give you the creeps?"

She didn't answer.

They lay quiet for a long time, her back still to him. Finally she said, "We can't afford to rent a motel room, too."

He put his arm over her to reassure her. He felt the warmth of her back against him. He knew that he loved her. Perhaps one day he'd own a small spread with a few sheep on good range, and perhaps one day they'd have a son. What more could a man want? Finally he'd drifted into sleep.

AFTER RINGO WAS born, Sarah focused her attention on the child, and Eckersly understood. But at times he felt lonely. And he thought his feelings were a mirror of hers. He spoke of it once.

They were sitting at the kitchen table after supper, the boy in bed. "Are you feeling a little lonely, maybe?"

"Why do you always ask questions like that? Of course I'm not lonely. I have the two of you." She was mending the hole in one of his stockings, the stitches of black mending thread sewn across the hole in the same direction, then across in the other direction.

"Sometimes I feel lonely," he said. He wished he hadn't said it.

"How could you, of all men, be lonely? You have Ringo, and you have me, and you have those men. You're with someone all day long." Her needle was going in and out, her fingers moving fast.

"It isn't the same with them," he said.

She locked the thread with three quick stitches, lifted the stocking to her mouth, and bit off the thread with white teeth.

"I don't get much of you," he heard himself say.

She rolled the mended sock into its mate and dropped it in the basket.

"I do everything I can for you and Ringo. What more do you want?"

"You're a good woman. I couldn't make it without you."

Then she took another sock out of the basket.

ECKERSLY HAD BEEN lying on the hard, filthy mattress of his cell. The sounds of desperate men had surrounded him. He'd thought of killing Jaycox. Why deny it? Every man, if he were a man, had at some time premeditated a killing. Men get drenched in hate. They fall into it like they fall through thin ice in early winter, but most men pull out of the deadly waters, and good sense takes over.

Still, a man can lie awake at night and see his .45 punch a pretty hole between some bastard's eyes, and he crumples into a pile of worthless crap, and the killing feels good. Jaycox and the sheriff were lying bastards who were willing to destroy a mere boy with a false charge of murdering his teacher. To lock Ringo up in some reformatory would be as good as killing him. But Eckersly would kill neither Jaycox nor Diggs.

No. Never.

Ringo had a trait Eckersly envied—that sensitivity thing Sarah talked about—to be attracted to something other than the business side of life. In the spring, the boy had a choice between working the sheep with Eckersly at docking time or wandering with his mother over the prairies in search of the early wildflowers. Eckersly tried to deny it hurt him that his son chose his mother. He wished he could take Sarah by the hand, roam across the land, and share the joy of new life, of a prairie flower that comes timidly peeking up through the winter's hard prairie floor. But bluebells weren't flowers to Eckersly. They were feed markers. You could predict when the grass would follow by how early the bluebells bloomed. And sheep ticks also came with early prairie flowers.

Ringo had those long fingers of Eckersly's grandfather, who'd been an artist, pitiful though he was—a man who couldn't make a living. Nobody respected him. Eckersly thought genes were like sheep. They mostly followed the flock of other genes in a person's herd of genes. Now and then a stray escaped, and that stray, say the artist gene from his grandfather, had found its way to Ringo.

When he was still a boy, Eckersly's father brought home what ranchers called "a bum," a lamb without a mother, the poor creature running from ewe to ewe, stealing a couple of sucks until the ewe discovered that the lamb wasn't hers and kicked the hungry little beast from her teat.

Eckersly's father also brought a Pepsi bottle and a nipple, and Ben filled the bottle with cow's milk and fed the lamb as his 4-H project. His lamb won a blue ribbon at the county fair. Then his lamb was sold to the highest bidder and sent off to be slaughtered. He cried when he said good-bye to the fat little bundle of wool with the innocent eyes and the soft, wet, pink nose. "A heart washed in enough tears usually hardens," his grandfather used to say.

Eckersly's father warned him to stay as far away from the railroad as he could—dirty, cold, miserable work around those coal-burning locomotives. Brakemen and switchmen froze to the bone in winter, and in the sweat of summer, a few minutes in the shade alongside a boxcar provided their only respite. And they were covered with soot, which filled their pores from their ankles to their eyes. Eckersly took a degree in animal husbandry at the University of Wyoming, and straight out of school he got a job with Longley and Hansen as a ranch hand.

By the time he'd been through three full seasons at that ranch, he knew as much about sheep ranching as the old hands, and he was smart, steady, and responsible. The workers liked him because their hard labor, their blistered hands, and long hours were his, and even a year before he became foreman, it was common knowledge that he was the man for the job.

IN THE EARLY afternoon, when Eckersly drove into the ranch from a distance, he saw the squad car at the back door. He had the power to kill in his hands. He could feel it. He'd knocked men down before, and they usually didn't get up, not until he backed off. He'd never killed a man, but a man knows how to kill without being taught. And if the man inside his house was Jaycox, Eckersly would want to kill him. The bastard had mocked him and called him a coward while he'd been handcuffed and helpless in the backseat of the squad car. No, he wouldn't kill the son of a bitch. He wouldn't even demand that he apologize—only that he dismiss the charges against him and leave Ringo alone, and forget it. That was the sensible position to take. And Eckersly was a sensible man.

CHAPTER 19

Laramie, University, 1947

THE EYES IN the class were locked on Meg as she strutted to the back of the room. She took her seat next to Ringo.

"Hi. Where've you been?"

He pretended not to hear her. It was over. He tried to focus on the professor.

He had read the goddamned book and sorted through the language the professor was mumbling—something about the physiocrats who were proponents of free trade and laissez-faire, whatever the hell that was. He wrote "fizziocrats." He wished Meg would disappear.

Her perfume.

She slid down in her seat just short of prone, as was her habit when she was bored to the bone. When the bell rang, he started for the door. As he passed her, she stuck her index finger over his belt in the back and pulled him to a stop.

"Hey, aren't you going to speak to me? I've been worried about you. I went over to your place, but your landlady said you hadn't been home for the last two nights."

He stared straight ahead, like a wooden soldier.

"Can't we be friends?" Her voice sounded sad.

He started for the door, her finger still over his belt in the back, the warmth of her finger against his skin.

"Are you mad at me?"

As she followed, she held on with that finger. "I didn't mean to embarrass you," she said. "We could go to my place and talk about it. We at least owe each other that much, don't you think?"

He stopped, his back still to her.

"Besides, your paint things are there." She stepped around in front of him. Her eyes were soft and sad.

"Don't cry," he said suddenly. Why in hell did he say that?

"I promise I won't ask you to paint me. I promise I won't take my clothes off in front of you. I promise I'll give you a beer and make you your favorite hamburger at nine o'clock in the morning."

CHAPTER 20

Bear Creek Ranch, 1940

RINGO DROPPED THE shotgun, his eyes wide and unbelieving. Jaycox was wildly thrashing on the kitchen floor, holding his left leg with both hands. He drowned the house in his horrible shrieking. "Jesus! Jesus! Jesus! God A'mighty Jesus!" His blood poured out into the boot in a terrible torrent.

Sarah Eckersly screamed, "My God, Ringo, what have you done?" Her face was speckled with splatters of blood, and small pieces of bone were stuck to her dress.

"Get me a doctor! Get me a doctor!" Jaycox cried through blasts of his hideous shrieking.

Ringo ran to the kitchen cabinet, found a white cotton dish towel his mother had fashioned from a flour sack. He grabbed a paring knife from the knife holder, slit the towel, and ripped off a long piece of cloth.

"You goddamed bastard, I'm gonna kill you," Jaycox cried.

Ringo looked down at the chief deputy, as if deciding his fate. Then he tied the strip of cloth tightly above the deputy's left knee, as he'd seen his father do to stop the bleeding of a ewe whose leg had been ripped by a coyote. After that, he put on his coat and walked out.

"Ringo, where are you going?" Sarah ran after him. "Please, Ringo, don't leave me with him."

"He won't hurt you anymore, Mama."

"Oh, Ringo, please don't tell your father what you saw. Ringo. Please, or he'll kill the man, and they'll put your father in the gas chamber, and we'll be out in the cold."

Ringo turned from his mother and walked toward the barn. Sarah started after him, but the chief deputy's screaming turned her back. "Jesus Christ, woman, get me to my car and drive me in! Jesus Christ, help me!"

She looked at the man bleeding on her clean, waxed kitchen floor. She saw the shotgun lying where Ringo had dropped it. She picked up the gun. She felt the power of it. It felt right. She stood over the deputy, the gun pointed down at him.

"Don't shoot me. Jesus, God, please don't shoot me."

She should kill him. It was the same as rape. Then she saw his agony. She felt sick. She leaned the gun against the wall, grabbed the mop and bucket, filled the bucket with water and poured in the soap.

When Eckersly opened the kitchen door, he saw the deputy rolling in agony, holding his left leg. He saw the blood on his wife's face and on her dress. He saw the shotgun standing in the corner and the holes from its blasts through the kitchen floor.

Sarah ran to Eckersly. He held her, and looking over his shoulder, he saw his cup lying in pieces on the floor, the spilled coffee, the checkered tablecloth crumpled in a heap. He saw her underpants on the chair and her bra hanging over the chair post.

"I shot him," she said. "He was raping me."

"Jesus God, get me to a doctor, man, a doctor," Jaycox cried in gasps.

"Where's Ringo?" Eckersly asked, still holding his wife.

"At the barn, I think."

"Did he see this?"

"I don't know," she said.

Eckersly lifted Jaycox up over his shoulder like a sack of wool, hauled the chief deputy to the squad car, and dumped him into the backseat. "Take my pickup and follow me in," he said to Sarah. Then Eckersly took off, the squad car bouncing wildly over the prairies. What duty did he have to save the life of a man who'd just raped his wife? He should let the raping bastard die. Jaycox would probably brag that he'd traded his foot for the best piece of ass he'd ever had. The forks in the trail were ahead. One led to the highway, then to Laramie and the hospital. The other meandered for endless miles into the desert with its graveled slopes and blowing sand.

His vision of the bastard in the backseat dying seemed correct, as when justice is recognized beyond the law. And if there were any meaning in life, it had to begin with justice. Now he had the power of justice in his hands.

"Your fuckin' kid shot me," Jaycox mumbled through his moans.

"My wife shot you."

"No, man, your kid shot me. Your wife's just tryin' to cover for your kid. Jesus, hurry up!"

"You're a lying son of a bitch."

"I ain't lyin'. She never done nothin' to me."

Maybe Ringo had shot Jaycox. Sarah, the eternal mother, would take the blame. If he'd been Ringo, he'd have blown a hole through the bastard's belly. And what had he done to Sarah? He could never touch her again without touching the scar.

When Eckersly got to the forks of the trail, he turned into the desert.

"Jesus Christ, man, I'm bleedin' to death," he cried. "I got kids. They're good kids. Mikey, he's fourteen. He writes poems, and he's a good artist. He can draw horses that look better'n real horses." Jaycox howled when his leg bumped up against the side of the squad car. "An' Marianne is twelve. She wants to be a nurse like her ma. Her ma's workin' at the hospital. Jesus Christ, man, take it easy."

Looking in the rearview mirror, Eckersly saw Sarah a couple hundred yards back, following in their pickup. He braked the squad car to a stop. Then he walked back to their pickup. "Wait for me here."

"Where are you going with him?" Sarah asked.

"I said, wait for me here." With that, he drove off through the sagebrush toward the far bluff, with Jaycox moaning in the backseat.

CHAPTER 21

Laramie, Meg's Apartment, 1947

MEG'S POWER HAD reduced Ringo to little more than her plaything. He felt the shame of it. He felt defeated. Then he'd gone with her to her apartment. He sat straight and stiff on her small coach.

The smell of frying hamburger.

The book of Monet's paintings sat on the coffee table, but the paintings were of no interest.

"Can't we be friends?" she asked, flashing her showy smile.

How could he be angry at a woman who bore no shame for her body? He should have taken her as he'd taken her alone under the safety of his bedcovers.

Meg brought him the hamburger on a large red plate. "Now we can be friends again." She sat down beside him.

He picked the burger up with both hands, but when he felt her hand, he stopped chewing. Her eyes invited. She'd been put on this earth to torment him. But he knew truth in the way a ram in the breeding pen knows truth. He got up from the couch.

"You're so beautiful," she said. "Put your arms around me. I can't stand it without your arms around me." They stood staring at each other, as if readying themselves for an attack. Her breath smelled of her heat, and his breathing was hard and rapid.

"You're the one who likes to strut around nude. Take off your clothes," he commanded in a voice to which there was no reply.

She'd never heard that voice. And his eyes belonged to the man who'd been hidden within the child. She hadn't understood that when the man emerges, the boy is at his service. She took off her top, then her bra, and at last she stood naked, and he watched as a man watches. Then he pulled off his clothes as if they were flaming, and he saw her hungry eyes, and he felt no embarrassment.

She took his hands and used them for her pleasure. And the battle was launched in a storm of wild purple daisies, and the sounds were of birth and of dying, and the pounding was deep into the flooding, and at last the floodwaters were joined and emptied their worlds.

On the floor at that moment, he heard himself say to her, "I love you," and his words were strange to his ears—that love should be born of fire.

CHAPTER 22

Bear Creek, 1940

ECKERSLY, HIS JAW set, his eyes dead ahead, herded the squad car over the sage, the brush scraping its bottom, the wheels spinning, the car bucking like a loco horse.

Jaycox's agony seeped out in rhythmic groans. "You don't have to kill me. I'm gonna die anyways." Then barely above a mumble, he said, "One thing I want you to know before you kill me. I'm sorry for what I done to your wife, an' it seems to me that I've paid the price for it. Seems to me we're square."

Then the low-riding car high-centered on a small rise. Eckersly slammed it into reverse, gunned the engine, and released the clutch. The wheels spun helplessly—the smoke, the smell of burned rubber. He opened the trunk. No shovel. He found the jack, but no rocks, no chunks of old wood to slip under the jack or the tires.

Fate had spoken.

Sarah was out of sight. He lifted the deputy's sawed-off shotgun from its rack on the dashboard, checked the gun, saw it was loaded, and walked about twenty paces from the car.

Eckersly wiped his prints off the gun, dropped the gun on the ground, returned to the car, lifted Jaycox onto his shoulder, and lowered him next to the gun, his face in the dirt.

Jaycox struggled to turn his head. "Jesus, man, please don't leave me here." His breathing came in labored gasps. "Tell my wife I'm sorry. She works hard. Tell her I've always loved her."

Eckersly felt no pity. But a weary sadness filled him. No matter the choice he made, things would never be right. He looked down at Jaycox. He was nothing. He had always been nothing.

He broke off a stem of sage and brushed away his tracks. Then he took careful steps—a foot on a small clump of sagebrush, a foot on a mound of fescue grass—so as to leave no evidence.

Sarah was waiting in their pickup. She saw him come into sight. She watched her husband hopping this way and that down the slope, a man surely gone mad.

When he arrived at their pickup, he saw his wife's face shrouded in horror. For a moment, they stood silently staring at each other, afraid of what each saw in the other.

"My God, Ben, what's the matter with you?"

CHAPTER 23

ONE THING THE boy Ringo knew: Shooting a deputy sheriff would get him the gas chamber. The deputy called Jaycox had said so. And no one could save him from the gas chamber, not even his father. He had to save himself. The water was low, and clear as tears. At the creek, he crossed on the protruding rocks. No tracks. Then he headed for the open prairies.

He could hear his mother begging, "Please don't tell your father what you saw," and what he saw was his mother staring up from the table, the deputy on her, her eyes like the dead eyes of Mrs. Foreman.

He walked on without looking back. In the distance he saw the schoolhouse standing straight, stark, and stubborn on the prairie. He was a lost comma moving across a gray mottled page. He walked toward the distant peaks as if seeking to be taken into the land by his walking. He walked until the sun was threatening to set.

When he topped the brink of a long ravine, he saw a broken down, caved-in homesteader's cabin.

The cabin was the size of a couple of horse stalls. Its walls were of ax-flattened cottonwood logs. The roof of logs no larger than fence posts was covered by sod and had collapsed at one end. The door was so low, an average-size man would stoop to enter. On the south, a glassless window stared at the emptiness, and a rusted stovepipe jutted out of the roof. The ground surrounding the cabin, nearing a century in repairing, was still barren where thin iron-rimmed wagon wheels drawn by a team of horses had borne the weary to this small blister on the prairie that those, now lost to history, called home.

Nearby oozed a small spring. The mud surrounding the spring was marked with the sharp tracks of antelope and by the smaller prints of badgers, mice, the meadowlark, and the spastic ground-running noisy bird, the killdeer.

Ringo saw a fresh set of human tracks in the mud.

All of a sudden, as if its duty was to alarm all prairie creatures of his intrusion, the killdeer began bobbing along the perimeter of the seep with its fast-running dance and its shrill two-noted warning.

"Killdeer! Killdeer!"

"Killdeer! Killdeer!"

Ringo surveyed the prairie in every direction. Whoever authored the tracks was in the cabin. He approached the cabin, one careful step at a time, until he was within a few feet of the door. Tensed to run, he edged forward. He held his breath and felt the thumping of his heart as he inched up and peered in.

He saw the dirt floor thick with dried dung where livestock had taken refuge from the blinding storms of winter and the blistering sun of summer. Gazing at the far corner opposite the south window, he saw what appeared to be a figure. He squinted his eyes against the darkness. It was only an old brown cardboard box with flaps.

Then the box moved.

He pulled back to run. Who was this creature huddled in the shadows? Probably an escaped convict. But what if it were an old man who'd wandered away from home and was lost? He held his breath to listen. At last, he gathered up his total courage. His high boy's voice pierced the silence.

"Who's in there?"

Then Ringo saw the face lift slowly up from between the figure's knees. His hair was long and matted with clinging dung.

"Whatcha doin' in there, Ham?" And Ringo took off running.

Ham Swanker stumbled to the door. "Hey, come back. I'm not intending to harm you in any way whatsoever. That is my word of honor."

Ringo, already half a football field from the cabin, stopped. Slowly, a small step at a time, he started back toward the cabin.

"I've refused to return home," Ham said. "My old man will beat me until I am de-boweled."

"You killed our teacher," Ringo charged, still poised to run.

"The most incriminating evidence sometimes fails to reveal the truth," Ham replied. "I suppose you have nothing whatsoever to eat. I'm approaching the threshold of death by starvation."

"We can kill us a sage chicken," Ringo said, poised to flee. "They've been watering at that spring. They'll come down to drink. Maybe you can hit one with a big rock."

"And I have matches."

"Maybe we can discover some good throwin' rocks up there," Ringo said, still wary of his companion. They began exploring the barren ridge above the cabin.

"Here's one," Ham said. "Let's employ rocks such as this." He held up a rock about the size of a small hen's egg. "And why, my dear boy, are you out here?"

"I shot a deputy."

"My good God!" Ham exclaimed. He took a good look at Ringo. "You are a top-drawer criminal! Did you kill the deputy?"

"I shot him with my dad's twelve-gauge."

"My good God! That would kill a cow. Why did you kill him?"

"He was hurting my mother."

"My old man beats my mother constantly, and I never shot him. I should have." Ham lifted his shirt in the back. "Look here." The scars were jagged tracks across a white desert. "My old man beat me once with his quirt so severely, I couldn't get out of bed for two days."

"How come he beats you so much?" Ringo asked.

"It's because he hates people who are more intelligent than he, and he's plain mean. My mother says if he can't beat somebody, he's unhappy. Doesn't your old man ever beat you?"

"No," Ringo said. "He doesn't beat my mother, either."

"Well, a man ought to beat a woman occasionally, or she'll get out of sorts."

"My mother never gets out of sorts."

"She must be some woman," Ham said.

By then, the boys were standing side by side at the edge of the seep, watching, waiting. Ham started to speak, but Ringo put his finger to his lips. "Shhhh." Then they heard scratching sounds.

The mottled gray sage chickens blended into the surrounding brush. The largest in the lead peered and pecked as they moved toward the water. She was the size of a barnyard hen, the half-dozen smaller ones the size of young fryers.

Ringo saw them first. "Don't move," he whispered. "They'll think we're stumps." When the birds were about ten feet away, Ham let fly with a rock. He missed the hen, and with a loud, exploding, clucking commotion, she flew off. The young ones squatted to the ground.

Ham let fly with another rock. He missed again. This time, the entire flock flew.

"Well, there went supper," Ringo said. "Maybe we'll get somethin' in the morning."

The boys gathered dead sagebrush limbs on their way back to the cabin.

Ham watched as Ringo shredded the dry, curly bark. Then he bunched the bark into a small cone, took Ham's matches, and lit a fire. Ringo fed the flames with small pieces of sage until he had a fine blaze burning in the old cracked stove.

Ham broke the silence. "Why didn't you try to kill one of those sage chickens?"

"I'm not good at rock throwin'."

"It takes courage to kill." Ham poked at the fire with a limb of sage. "However, you did kill that deputy." He sat down in the dried cow dung. "I'm so hungry, I could devour the ass off of a dead man."

"Well, don't be thinkin' about eatin' me," Ringo said. "If you do, they'll put you in the gas chamber for sure." Ringo glanced at Ham and saw the light of the fire reflecting across his face, and the lines were wild and weird. "How come you killed Mrs. Foreman?"

Ham didn't answer.

The fragrance of the burning sage made the small cabin smell clean. Ringo remembered how his mother told him that the Indians burned sage to rid them of their evil thoughts. When the fire seemed right, he asked again, "How come you killed Mrs. Foreman?"

Ham was still silent.

"Don't you want to talk about it?"

Finally, Ham said, "One must learn that trust is a fundamental weakness of the human species."

"What do you mean?"

"One cannot trust what one believes. One cannot trust what another believes. One cannot trust what one sees, or hears, or even knows. To trust is to convert the trusting into a fool."

They were silent again. The yapping of the coyotes sounded like the dead in lamentation.

"To trust your friend is to set your friend up for his betrayal of you," Ham continued. "Or your betrayal of him. Friendship cannot endure itself."

The fire had retreated to lazy embers.

Then Ham said, "But predestined powers sent you to me. You're the only friend I've ever had."

After the fire was nearly out, the boys lay down in the dried dung and watched the glow of the embers fade on the ceiling until at last they slept.

CHAPTER 24

Laramie, Belle June's, 1947

IT WAS A Saturday night and the whorehouse was bustling with business. The cowboys and sheepherders were in town, and college kids, with allowances that could be stretched to include an occasional visit to those chambers of carnal sin at ten dollars for a "short time," were tittering in the waiting room with wide eyes and fire in their jeans.

A preacher might sneak in early on a weekday evening to avoid exposure to his parishioners. But the clergy, and any wayward members of their congregations, were secure knowing that the exposure of one was the exposure of all, and, therefore, all were safe.

Mertle Jepperson of the Methodist Ladies Bible Study proclaimed she could demonstrate that Laramie, because of the town's well-regulated houses of prostitution, had the lowest rape rate of any city its size in America, "for which," she said, sighing, "we can thank the Lord."

The prevailing wisdom held that even a "short time" could release what might otherwise bloom into harm—bored husbands leaving their bored wives for fresher pastures, and those with creepy fetishes taking risks that were rendered unnecessary when they were liberated in those secret chambers, not to mention that randy sheepherders and ranch hands had a place to release their animal urges.

The madam at 213 Front Street, who answered to the name Belle June, a blond, large-boned farmer's daughter from Pierre, South Dakota, claimed she'd acquired her education in "the school of hard cocks." Ten years earlier, she'd opened her first palace of pleasure in the small boomtown of Gillette, Wyoming. When the boom went bust, Belle June moved to Laramie. The houses in Laramie—four in operation—all did well, but Belle June's was reputed as the best of the bunch. She provided what her johns longed for—busty, young, wild things who'd put out a good go and make a man feel like a man with a minimum of guilt, and, from Belle June's perspective, in a minimum of time. As with doctors and lawyers and all other professionals, time was money. The madams indulged the university professors in their obsessions, which were especially freakish among the "brain trust," as Belle June called them. She had a rule of thumb: "The brainier they are, the creepier they are."

Monthly, the madams met to discuss matters of mutual concern, such as threatened competition. After all, as Belle June argued, "there's only so many hard-ons to service in one small town." And one thing for sure: They had to make certain their girls were free of disease, because, as Belle June often warned, "all you have to do is give a dose of clap to one college kid and his old man will be all over the city fathers like flies on shit." That meant trouble for everybody.

Nor was Belle June beyond magnanimity. She funded the Woodrow Wilson Chair in World Peace at the University of Wyoming. She said the organization didn't have the first idea about the kind of *piece* she was talking about, a great joke that old Woodrow would have appreciated. Although her morality was supple, her most ardent goal was to encourage men to make love, not war.

All the madams gave generously to the churches at Christmas and supported the Salvation Army and the Red Cross. They were members of the Laramie Chamber of Commerce and paid the same dues as were extracted from other businesses, even though their identities were not expressly carried on the rolls of the Chamber.

The madams in the houses were celebrated for their meticulous honesty. A sheepherder could leave his season's earnings on deposit with the madam and be assured that when he returned to his herd, she'd refund whatever balance remained after honestly deducting for the services of her girls and the herder's accumulated liquor bill. After the bars closed, any thirsty man could get a drink in one of the houses, and, if he were a regular customer, on Sundays as well. Servicemen in uniform were given a 10 percent discount and a drink on the house. Businessmen often held meetings in those upper rooms, the women serving them drinks and favoring them with their scantily clad presences to add flavor to their otherwise dreary labors.

One day, Meg Mendleson simply walked up the fifteen steps in broad daylight, rang the bell, asked for the madam, and said she wanted to go to work. That was before she met Ringo in Professor Harold P. Johns's econ class.

CHAPTER 25

Laramie, 1940

ECKERSLY OPENED THE pickup door on the passenger side, slid into the seat, and sat in sightless staring. Sarah, horror stamped on her face, began shaking him.

"Ben, what have you done?"

No answer.

She shook him and shook him, as if to awaken him. "Did you kill him?"

Finally he answered: "No, I didn't kill him. The car got stuck in a gully up there."

She grabbed at his jacket and began shaking him again. "You killed him, didn't you?" Her teeth were clenched, her jaw muscles tight.

"No." Suddenly, he saw his woman, *his,* shaking him to save her lover. He turned from her.

"Is he dead?" she asked.

"No."

"Then go back for him," she screamed. "We have to get him to the hospital."

"You want me to save your lover?"

"Are you crazy, Ben? He raped me."

"Then I'm going back and kill the son of a bitch." He started up through the sagebrush toward the stuck squad car.

"Ben, come back," Sarah cried. "It wasn't rape. I had to save Ringo."

The bastard Jaycox had used Ringo to force Sarah into it. He should kill the bastard. Any man would. He could step on his throat and watch the life fade out of him. He could rip off the tourniquet and let him bleed to death. He could leave him there, and whoever found him would see it as a self-inflicted accident.

He heard his wife screaming.

And in his mind's ear he could hear Christopher Hampton's admonition: "A premeditated killing can get you the gas chamber." But he wasn't premeditating the killing of the man. He was simply *not saving* the raping bastard. Surely no law required him to save a fiend who'd forced his wife into sex to save their child.

He hurried to where Jaycox lay dying. He was still breathing those slow, shallow, terminal breaths. Eckersly looked down at the pitiful pile of flesh. He'd felt more sympathy for a fatally wounded sheep. He'd at least put the animal out of it misery with a merciful bullet through its head.

Maybe the son of a bitch had paid the price. If he lived, which was doubtful, he'd bear evidence of his crime every step, every day, for the rest of his life on a peg leg—a life in perpetual pain.

So this was the miserable, no-good bastard Sarah wanted to save. But did she want Jaycox saved, or did she want to save her husband from a charge of murder? He'd carry the son of a bitch down, and after that, whatever happened would be in the hands of fate. He lifted Jaycox up onto his shoulder again. The man's head flopped against his back; his hanging foot flopped against his chest with each step as he found his way through the sagebrush to Sarah, waiting in their pickup below.

When he arrived at the pickup, he shoved Jaycox into the truck bed. He took off his jacket to create a pillow and slipped it under his head. Without a word, Sarah climbed into the truck bed and sat down with her back to the cab. She lifted Jaycox's head to her lap and held it.

"Hurry," she said. "There still may be time."

CHAPTER 26

Casper, Wyoming, 1946

MEG MENDLESON RETURNED to Casper to oversee her mother's funeral. Her grandparents, Richard and Eloise, had passed years earlier. No more than a dozen townsfolk attended the services, and those included the mortician and his assistant. Mr. Newhouse, the grocer who delivered her mother's groceries, and the presiding preacher from the Methodist church, the Reverend Hepburn, as well as the organ player, were there, along with two older women whom Meg didn't know but who openly wept at appropriate times. After the short ceremony, she gave both women a decent hug and a brushing kiss on the cheek, and thanked them for coming.

One of the matrons in a black dress and who wore round-toed, low-heeled black shoes told Meg between sniffles that when their reading group was studying Hemingway's *For Whom the Bell Tolls*, Meg's mother opened the meeting by vigorously ringing an old cowbell she'd found somewhere, and with held-back laughter and great aplomb proclaimed, "It tolls for you."

"Your mother had a wonderful sense of humor," the woman said. "She never attended another of our meetings before her death. It was as if she heard the bell."

Meg came upon her doll in her toy box. Yes, her mother had loved Meg. But she thought she'd been loved like a pretty doll is loved. She kissed the doll on its cold ceramic cheek and gently laid it back with the rest of her toys.

The two small rooms of her mother's apartment were crusted in filth, choked in clutter, and smelled of unremitting pain. Meg threw out a stack of *National Enquirers* that nearly reached the ceiling at the southeast wall of the bedroom. Her mother's wardrobe consisted of several faded, dust-covered dresses, a worn pink chenille bathrobe, a pair of ragged pink cloth slippers, and a pair of black shoes with thick heels. She threw them in the trash with the *National Enquirers*. She boxed up the toys and the doll and sent them to the Salvation Army.

Her mother's scrapbook included numerous photographs of Meg, along with a newspaper clip showing Meg as Julia in *Julia Comes Home*, the junior class play, in which she'd won the leading role. Meg's birth certificate was folded in the center of the scrapbook like a bookmark. She stuffed the certificate in her purse.

Meg found a shoe box with the letters she'd sent to her mother, the envelopes bearing numerous postmarks of cities in Europe. A photograph in a gold-leaf frame of the family patriarch, Buck Mendleson, sat on a small table next to the bed. Buck was leaning against an oil-well derrick, wearing breeches and knee-high lace-up boots. His wide smile stretched his mustache into handlebars, his Stetson slanted rakishly. The King James Version of the Holy Bible sat next to the photograph. In the table drawer she found a small gold heart-shaped locket with a diamond chip at its center, containing a bleached-out photo of Meg as a baby.

The television with its fifteen-inch screen produced only fuzzy black-and-white images. The cupboards were barren except for three cans of Campbell's tomato soup and an unopened box of Kellogg's cornflakes. The milk in the refrigerator was long soured. A stack of dirty dishes lay crusted in the sink. She threw it all out.

Guilt attacked.

She hadn't been there for her mother. But her mother, in keeping with her resolve to devote her life to the happiness of her child, had never hinted in her numerous letters to Meg that she was ill, much less that she suffered alone and would die in those filthy rooms without medical care. In a resolve against her frivolous past, Meg had enrolled at University of Wyoming for an education she could afford, since she was a Wyoming resident.

Throughout her life, she'd followed a simple formula for survival: She got what she wanted by providing others with what they wanted. Such is the professional formula of doctors and teachers and carpenters. Meg needed money for school, and her decision to go to work in one of the houses was merely an extension of her earliest times, when, in exchange for a smile and wet kiss on her grandfather's cheek, she could extract from him anything her tiny heart desired.

In her bohemian life in Paris, Meg had lain with men for pleasure—theirs, yes, and hers. She'd lain with them to be accepted, to feel a part of another person's life. In that world, people lay with people whose names they didn't know. You'd better not look at someone with more than a blink or you'd get invited for a lay. And if you could do it for fun, like golfing for fun or playing tennis for fun, what was so wrong about going professional with sex, like golfers and tennis players go professional?

Most people sold their lives—*sold* was the word. Most worked long, hard, boring years, often doing what they hated in order to eek out a bleak existence. She could see no soul-damning immorality in a fair trade of sex for money. She argued that women, especially the snobbishly sedate, had always sold themselves to men for what they wanted. Women who married for money were scheming whores. Women who endured cruel marriages to support their children were desperate whores. Women who hung on in humiliating jobs and suffered the harassment and abuses of their bosses were frightened whores. Women who worked their way up the corporate ladder by fucking the men on the rungs above them were ambitious whores.

The worst of the whores were those snooty churchy types who spread their legs out of matrimonial duty, and who looked down their Presbyterian noses at the workingwomen up in the houses who fucked for the money they needed and made no pretenses about it. The one woman Meg knew who was not a whore—her dear dead mother—had bedded her father for one purpose: to achieve motherhood, and thereafter she endured her lonely, desperate life, asking for nothing more than the joy of being a mother.

Meg thought she could probably work part-time in one of the houses on Front Street and make enough to go to school. She'd need time to study. She couldn't be lying on her back all night every night with john after john between her legs and hope to keep up with her schoolwork.

She had a plan. She'd work in one of the houses before school started. After she was established in the house, she'd announce that she had decided to attend classes. No one would dare object that a girl from one of the local houses was going to college to better herself with an education.

ON AN EARLY-JUNE evening, Meg climbed the fifteen stairs at 213 Front Street. The black maid, brushing down the wrinkles of her dress, opened the door.

Meg smiled at the maid. "Looking for the madam."

"And what would your business be, honey?"

"Same as yours."

"Lordy, honey, I only serve the drinks and clean up around here," the maid said with a deep, good-natured chuckle. "Just a minute. I'll see if I can find her."

Meg stepped inside. Then she walked down the dark hallway to the waiting room.

The walls were covered with red flocked wallpaper. Opposite a couple of straight-backed chairs sat a black leather couch. The floor was covered by a burgundy carpet with scattered burn holes like black freckles.

The ten-foot ceiling of embossed tin had been painted to match the walls, but the ensuing years of smoke had turned it to umber. The light from small red bulbs in candlelike wall sconces provided a heavy rosy glow to the room. The room smelled of stale tobacco smoke, old booze, and a convention of perfumes.

A massive woman the size and shape of a sumo wrestler entered the room in slow, lumbering steps. She was wrapped in a quilted yellow bathrobe and wore a pair of bunny slippers, the yellow fleece cuddling her thick ankles. Her peroxided hair was bound in curlers the size of large sausages, and her face was smeared with white grease given in aid of smoke-cured, middle-aged skin. She inhaled from her cigarette, blew it in Meg's direction, and looked the young woman up and down like a fussy judge at a dog show. The madam saw the clear skin, the dark eyes, the black hair causally embracing her shoulders, and the obvious contents of Meg's tight sweater and skirt.

"Whatcha want, honey?"

"Looking for work," Meg said.

"We don't hire children here."

"I'm no child."

The madam watched Meg walk across the room, inspecting the place as if she were an interior decorator considering a remodel.

"I could help you brighten things up here," Meg said. "I've had some experience."

"What kind of experience, honey?"

"Been in Europe the last three years. Give me a try. You don't like what I do and the business I bring, you won't lose much."

"Whatcha want?"

"I'll take mine like the rest of your girls."

"Good," Belle June heard herself say. She didn't know why she said it. She didn't want to cross "the association" that got its cut in exchange for the girls it provided the houses along the Union Pacific rail line, and Belle June got the best, the youngest, and the prettiest. But this walk-in was too good to turn down. She'd tell Affonsi, the guy from the association, the truth: Fifi, the wild one from Ireland, said she had to go home to Boston—her mother was sick—and that left Belle June short-handed. She'd pay the association its cut on this new girl, as if they'd furnished her in the first place.

"What's your handle?" Belle June asked.

"Everybody calls me 'Happy.'"

"Go see Dr. Simmons on Garfield Street. Get your clean papers, and you can go to work Saturday night. Come early, 'bout this time. I'll show you your room and introduce you to the other girls." With that, Belle June shuffled her bunny slippers back down the hall.

Meg went to work at 213 Front Street starting in the middle of June, and by early September she was ready to approach Belle June about her plan to go to the university. Already she'd established herself as the favorite in the house, and in ways, Belle June had begun to see Meg as a daughter. Belle June was all for college. "You gotta better yourself, honey. If you don't do it yourself, nobody's gonna do it for you."

Meg listened.

"There ain't any future in this business," Belle June said. "You gotta run it like I do, or you gotta marry out of it before you're too old to catch a man. Most girls drink it up, or some bastard sweet-talks 'em and steals their pussy, or they get sick and have to quit." She puffed on her cigarette and coughed. "Whatcha wanna be, honey, a goddamned doctor or lawyer or somethin'?" Her voice sounded like rats in a pile of tin cans.

"I want to be a schoolteacher."

"Jesus, honey, that'd be funny as hell. The school board would shit little green apples if they knew one of their teachers had been a working girl." Belle June thought Meg had been properly nicknamed Happy. She brightened the house with a perpetual presence of joy that permeated the place. At that time of month when a girl suffered "the flowers," as they called it, and might be depressed, she'd often turn to Meg. She was always happy.

Some of the girls were homesick for their families. Some had kids they were putting through private schools and hadn't heard from in months. Some had johns who were harassing them. Some suffered a sense of self-disgust. Often tears flooded the kitchen, "the wailing womb," as Meg called it, where the women shared their fears and loneliness like unsung requiems. Meg attacked the doldrums. She had a way. Some claimed her being there seemed to smear happiness all over the place.

That fall, Meg Mendleson enrolled at the university, and from then on she worked only on the weekends, when the house was the busiest, the college boys the horniest, the sheepherders the drunkest, and the cowboys the wildest—the same weekends that Ringo Eckersly worked his late double shift at the hotel.

CHAPTER 27

Bear Creek, 1940

THE NEXT MORNING, Ringo and Ham, shivering in the freeze of dawn, waited silently, stones in hand, but the sage chickens failed to return.

"Means there's water someplace else within a mile or two," Ringo said. He looked out across the prairies and saw the distant rumps of the antelope like white dots on a gray page. "Antelope don't drink until the middle of the day. They walk through their supper and can eat whenever they're hungry. Guess that's why they got four stomachs, like a cow."

"Who gives the first flying fuck about stomachs, except mine is empty. I'm utterly starved. You seem to know a mammoth amount of useless information." Ham had begun to look gaunt. "I'm so hungry, I've begun to understand the origins of cannibalism."

"You wouldn't eat your best and only friend, would you?"

"No." But Ham didn't sound convincing.

As they walked back toward the cabin and stepped through some tall grass, a cottontail rabbit skittered ahead.

"Watch where it goes," Ringo said.

"It is concealing itself in that hole," Ham reported.

"Put your foot over the hole so he can't come out. I'll find us somethin' to dig with." In a few minutes, Ringo returned with a couple of rusted triangle-shaped sickle teeth from a horse-drawn mowing machine he'd found in the junk pile behind the cabin. On hands and knees, the boys started scratching at the dirt like hounds after a burrowed fox.

"Good God Almighty," Ham said. "Perhaps he's retreated to China."

"Reach down there and see if you can feel him yet."

"I have no tactile contact with the creature." Ham's arm was in the hole up to his shoulder.

"Think how you'd feel if you were the rabbit and you knew some giants were diggin' their way down to you, and you could hear 'em gettin' closer and closer, and you knew that pretty soon one of 'em would grab you and pull you out and eat you," Ringo said.

"I have serious doubts that rabbits think in such a fashion," Ham said. He reached down into the hole again. Suddenly, he let out a scream and jerked his hand out. "The accursed creature bit me!" He inspected his bleeding index finger, which suffered a gash half an inch long. "I'll retaliate against the little beast!" He ran to the junk pile and returned with a five-foot length of one-inch rusted pipe and jabbed the pipe into the hole over and over.

They heard the squeal of the rabbit and the thudding of its feet against the side of the hole. Finally, when all was silent, Ham reached slowly, down and down, until he felt something furry. He pulled the rabbit out by a hind leg. Some of its entrails were hanging outside the carcass, and its head was bloody and smashed in.

Ringo turned away.

"Well, we've obtained ourselves some breakfast. I've been saved from eating you. Only joking, of course," he said with the first smile he'd offered in days.

Ringo pulled the heart from inside the animal's diaphragm, separated the liver from the string of guts, flung the guts aside, carried the heart and liver to the cabin, and laid them on the stovetop. Then they heard the approaching airplane.

"Get down," Ringo hollered. They lay flat on the floor of the cabin. A Piper Cub flew low over the cabin.

"They're lookin' for us," Ringo said. They held their breath.

The plane flew just above the roof of the deserted cabin, circled, flew over again, and then flew on.

"Do you think we were discovered?"

"Don't think so," Ringo said. "But one thing for sure, we aren't gonna build a fire 'til tonight. They'll see the smoke."

"I'm famished, and I'm tempted to take my chances." Ham stepped out into the emerging sun to gather its warmth. "We should consider taking a blood oath, like Tom Sawyer and Huck Finn did."

"What do you mean?"

"We're closer than even blood brothers."

"Well, you didn't treat your own blood brother too good," Ringo said.

"That's because Jamey hadn't achieved the high state of criminality that you have. He never killed anybody. We must cut ourselves and let our blood join so we can achieve true blood brotherhood."

"We haven't got a knife," Ringo said. "Maybe we could just promise."

"No. Mere promises are made to be broken." He put his arm around Ringo.

"You're my brother. That rabbit already bloodied my finger." He handed Ringo one of the sickle teeth they'd been digging with. "Cut yourself with this. Then we'll mix our blood and thereby we'll become brothers by blood."

Ringo grabbed the sickle tooth and scraped the end of it hard across his arm. When the blood didn't come, he scraped across it again, and then again.

When Ringo's arm finally bled, Ham said, "Good God, you

are a brave young urchin." He pinched at his finger to bring back his own blood and pressed his bleeding finger against Ringo's bleeding arm. His eyes grew soft, and a smile crept onto his face. "We are hereby reborn as blood brothers." Ham suddenly hugged Ringo, and Ringo found himself hugging Ham.

At last, Ham spoke again. "So, dear brother, what are the current demands that beckon us?"

"We gotta wait 'til dark. Then we'll cook this rabbit. After that, we'll kinda figger it out as we go."

CHAPTER 28

Laramie, Hospital, 1940

SARAH ECKERSLY WAS still holding Jaycox's head in her lap when they arrived at the hospital emergency room. Eckersly called for assistance. Shortly, two nurses arrived with a gurney. A gray-headed nurse pushed the gurney alongside the pickup, and the other nurse, a thin, plain-looking woman with early gray in her hair and with strong arms, climbed into the bed of the truck, and while the dead man's head was still resting on Sarah's lap, she sat down next to Sarah and put her fingers to his throat in search of a pulse.

"It's too late," Sarah said. "He passed almost as soon as we started."

The light of the emergency room reflected on the sagging skin of the corpse, the open eyes, the hanging mouth, as if all of the body's orifices had opened to release whatever soul the man possessed. The nurse turned the dead man's face toward her.

"Oh my God! Oh my God, it's Harv! Oh my God!" Betsy Jaycox cried.

Frantically, she felt at his throat again for a pulse.

Betsy Jaycox pulled her husband's head from Sarah's lap and held it to her breast, crying, "Oh my God! I knew this would happen one day. Oh my God!"

Eckersly stood silently at the side of the truck.

The gray-headed nurse pulled off the bloody rag that covered the dangling leg. She shook her head in disbelief and dropped the rag back in place. She looked over at Betsy Jaycox, who was sobbing and rocking her dead husband.

Sobbing and rocking.

Sobbing and rocking.

"We can leave him here until the coroner comes," the gray-headed nurse said.

"I want him out of my truck," Eckersly ordered.

The gray-headed nurse took a hard look at Eckersly, but when he gave no suggestion that his demand would be withdrawn, she returned shortly with another nurse, who pushed a gurney into position at the end of the pickup bed to receive the corpse.

Sarah felt guilt burrowing in. She put her arm around Betsy Jaycox's shoulder. Surely the woman had endured endless pain from the man, and still she must have loved him. Sarah saw her own man standing at the side of the truck.

Compared to Jaycox, he was a saint. And she'd questioned her love for her husband? She felt a gnawing sense of shame.

Then, in horror, Sarah witnessed the women pull the corpse out of the truck by its right foot, the left foot dangling.

Sarah hugged Betsy closer, and Betsy, not knowing who Sarah was, and not caring, held on to Sarah. Then Sarah saw herself only hours before with her arms around Jaycox. Surely she'd been fighting him. Yes. Surely.

The gray-headed nurse climbed into the truck to help Betsy down. When Betsy reached the gurney, she threw herself across her dead husband and wouldn't let loose of the body as the gurney was pushed through the emergency room door.

Sarah climbed down from the truck, and a young nurse with a friendly face, seeing Sarah's pain, took her hand. "How did this happen?"

Sarah thought she should say the man was raping her, but she was afraid that Betsy Jaycox was still within earshot.

"It was an accident," Sarah said.

"You'll have to come in and fill out some papers, and we will have to call the sheriff."

Eckersly threw Sarah a stern sideways nod, and she quickly got into the truck. "We didn't come here to answer questions," Eckersly said. "We came to make a delivery." Then he rolled up the window and drove away.

The young nurse shouted after him, "What's your name?" As the truck turned the corner, she said, "We don't even know his name."

CHAPTER 29

SHERIFF DIGGS THOUGHT he'd find his chief deputy, Jaycox, at the Eckersly place—that Eckersly woman, of course. He couldn't rouse the horny bastard on the squad car's radio, and that meant Jaycox had hit the jackpot with the bitch. The thought pissed off Diggs. Why should an ugly son of a bitch like Jaycox get all the goodies? But when no one answered the door at the ranch house, and both the squad car and the Eckersly family's pickup were gone, he became concerned.

Only slightly.

Probably Jaycox and the Eckersly bitch were trying to avoid her kid and had run off somewhere to get a little. Seen it more than once with Jaycox. The sheriff tipped his hat back and scratched at the top of his head as if to awaken long-dormant brain cells. But maybe something else was going on. Then the sheriff got a call from the hospital emergency room. Jaycox was dead.

"Dead?"

"Yes. He'd been shot."

"Well, some sumbitch is gonna pay hell for that, and goddamned soon. And I mean goddamned soon."

ONCE ON THE highway, Sarah Eckersly finally broke the silence. Her voice bled through the deep-throated rumble of the truck and the whine of the tires on the pavement. "He died in my lap," she said, staring straight ahead.

She'd never held his head on her lap, Eckersly thought. Not once. And because Jaycox was dead, was he supposed to attach some respect to the scumbag like people do when a worthless bastard dies, and people say only good things at his funeral, even if what they say catches in their throats?

They rode in silence for a long while. He tried to sort through the thoughts that were savaging his mind.

"He said he was sorry," Sarah finally said. "Then he died."

"I suppose that made it all right."

"You'll never understand," she said.

"What's to understand? He raped you. It was the same as rape. I should have killed him."

A jackrabbit jumped from the side of the road and ran in front of the headlights. Eckersly made no effort to miss it, and they heard the thump of the animal hitting the truck's underside.

How had it been for her? Eckersly knew she'd never say. Surely it must have been a horror, the repulsive son of a bitch. His eyes were locked on the pavement.

Why try to explain it? she thought. Things are not so black and white with a woman, not so violent, so bursting with hatred and lacking in human compassion. The man died with his head in her lap, and he'd said he was sorry. And her man—yes, Eckersly was her man—would never understand. Perhaps he'd never forgive. She should have fought Jaycox to the end. Then she said, "They'll be coming after us."

"For what?"

"They'll say we killed him," she said.

"He bled to death, for Christ's sake."

Her silence.

He knew she was right. There'd been that bad blood between

the sheriff and him. Diggs would charge that Eckersly had the motive to kill and did kill Jaycox. There'd be no reckoning for such a killing except another killing—the death penalty. Death was in the service of justice.

"What about Ringo?" Eckersly asked, still speaking at the road ahead.

"He's just a child," she said.

Eckersly knew Diggs would abuse Sarah with hard questions and break open her wounds. The truth was locked behind the lips of this woman he loved—and he loved her despite the tight, cold place where she stored her heart. She couldn't speak the truth—that she had lain down for Jaycox to save their son, or that she'd lain with him for reasons she wouldn't admit and that Eckersly didn't want to know.

"What are you going to tell the sheriff when he comes for me?" Eckersly asked.

"What do you want me to tell him, Ben?"

"I want you to tell him the truth."

"You want me to tell the sheriff how you dumped Jaycox out there on the prairie to die?" She turned to hear his answer.

Finally he said, "Well, I guess we'd better have our stories straight, or it'll all be over, especially for Ringo."

"Why do you claim it's Ringo you're protecting? What about yourself?"

What was his woman saying? As his wife, wasn't it her duty to protect him? Or did she want him punished? Had she actually cared for the rotten bastard?

"You wouldn't lie for me, would you?" he said.

"You're the one who always says a man, if he's a man, should never lie," she replied.

"So you want me to tell the sheriff that Ringo shot him, that I hauled him off to die, that you wanted him saved, so I tried to save him, and that he died anyway? You want me to say that?"

Finally she said, "I'll tell the sheriff I shot him, that he was trying to rape me."

"And what are you going to tell him about me?"

"Can't you lie for yourself?"

Then silence.

Miles of silence across miles of emptiness.

At last, Eckersly broke the silence. "Ringo's probably home waiting for us."

"We'll have to talk to him about this," she said.

"You want to make a liar of our son?"

She didn't answer.

When the wind stopped for an instant to catch its breath, they could see through the dust where the ranch buildings stood. No lights.

"Maybe he's gone to bed," Sarah said.

"He probably wonders where we are," Eckersly said. "Probably scared to death and has the doors locked."

The house door was unlocked. Sarah rushed in, turned on the lights, and charged through the house, calling his name. She searched in every room, in the closets and under the beds.

Outside, Eckersly continued calling. Maybe the boy couldn't hear him against the wind. He grabbed a flashlight and walked to the barn. The horse, Old Hard Head, stomped in his stall. He searched the full length of the sheep shed, calling.

Back at the house, he found Sarah had already mopped the kitchen. He saw the two holes in the floor left from Ringo's shotgun blasts. A few stray pellets were embedded in the linoleum. The red-and-white-checkered tablecloth was nowhere in sight. In its place she'd put down the hand-embroidered linen tablecloth her mother had given them for a wedding present.

"Where did you put my shotgun?" Eckersly asked.

"Back in the closet," she replied. "Where's Ringo?"

"The gun has Ringo's fingerprints on it."

"I wiped his fingerprints off the gun," Sarah said.

Eckersly sat down at the table. The damnable table knew her secret. It held her nakedness and joined in the conspiracy to sully their marriage. And there it stood on its four ancient legs—and still honored. He put his boot against the table and shoved it away from him.

Silently, she straightened up the wrinkled tablecloth where his boot had struck. "The gun has my prints on it," she said. "You have to find Ringo."

"I'll track him down in the morning," he said.

"What about the wind? It can wipe away his tracks?" She started for the door. "I'll find him myself."

He stepped in front of her, put his arms around her, and held her. She began sobbing softly, her arms hanging at her side as if paralyzed.

"I'll go soon as I finish my coffee," he said.

She left the table and rushed to the bathroom. In a fury, she began cleaning herself—then again, and again, and when she realized that the stain of Jaycox could never be washed away, she ran a tub of water and let the water soak into the places. After a long while, she prepared herself for bed, but she would not sleep until her son was home.

This man, her husband, whom she knew like a book that she'd read from cover to cover countless times, and whom she hardly knew at all, had wanted to kill Jaycox. Men were like that. Sometimes their utmost need was to kill. But she'd changed her husband's mind, and he'd gone back for Jaycox. Yes, she'd tried to save Jaycox. Even under the best circumstances, a man with that much blood loss, with that kind of shock, and after that long, hard ride to the hospital probably wouldn't survive.

Suddenly, she wanted to hold her husband's head as she'd held the deputy's. She wanted to tell him that she'd lie for him, that she loved him, not in the way he wanted her to love him, but in her way. She'd say that the man raped her. It was the same as rape. She'd been afraid of him. She was alone. Her child was in danger—and what it had been for her, she wanted to sweep from her mind.

Eckersly sipped slowly from the strange cup. Before he left to find Ringo, he should tell his wife that she'd been very brave. Maybe she didn't understand what had happened to her. But he loved her. And she loved him with an affection that seeped through like cold air under the storm door in the winter. Yes, it was love.

He sat at the damnable table, the half-empty cup his only excuse for not trudging off into the night with the threatened storm spitting in his face. He couldn't leave this thing unsettled with Sarah.

And the sheriff: What would they tell the sheriff? Eckersly lifted the strange thin cup to his lips. He spit out grounds that had escaped from the bottom of the pot. How could he ever again go to bed with this woman whose body surely held the bastard's sperm and whose lap had held his head, the lap where Eckersly's head had never rested?

He needed her.

He started for the bedroom to tell Sarah that he loved her. Then he lifted the window shade, and he saw the headlights approaching from a long way away off, and he knew they were coming for him.

CHAPTER 30

THE SUN WAS down, and the long evening shadows had disappeared into the invading darkness. The antelope, fear of the human species imbedded in their genes, had surrendered the water to the boys, as had the prairie dogs, the badgers and rabbits, the sage chickens, the red-tailed hawks, and even the great golden eagles. The boys drank from a rusted can they'd lifted from the junk pile.

"Pigs wouldn't drink this urine," Ham said. Then he drank until he'd emptied the can.

"If it was poison, the coyotes wouldn't drink it." Ringo pointed to their tracks in the mud. "They're too smart to drink poison water."

"This water tastes like urine," Ham said. He handed the can to Ringo.

"Tastes bad," Ringo said. "Probably has a lot of animal piss in it."

That night, the sagebrush fire in the broken stove lit the cabin's darkness with an eerie dancing light, and the merciless attack of their hunger assaulted. They roasted the rabbit and its heart and liver on the stovetop, and before the cooking was half done, they were ravenously ripping the remaining morsels from the bones. Then they broke open the bones with rocks and sucked the marrow, and they chewed the tender ribs, as well.

"If they catch us, they'll lock us in the gas chamber," Ham

said. "My old man told me that it required the last victim half the night to die. We must escape before we're captured here."

Ringo was still sucking at the rabbit's thighbone. "We'll figure it out in the morning."

They sat gazing into the slowly dying fire. Ringo tossed another piece of sage on the embers, which soon exploded into flame. The boys huddled together to keep warm. At last, the flames nodded, and the boys nodded until both the fire and they drifted into slumber.

ECKERSLY SAW THE lights of the distant vehicle bobbing over the prairie like a firefly. "They're coming," he said. "I'm out of here. I'm gonna find Ringo." He grabbed the flashlight from the shelf.

Sarah followed him to the porch. Alone, she steeled herself for the oncoming peril.

Eckersly gave a whistle to Buster, the dog, who soon understood his assignment. Some of Ringo's tracks were visible behind clumps of sage, where they'd been sheltered from the wind, and when Eckersly lost them, either Buster picked up the scent or, following in the same direction, they soon came upon the tracks.

They'd never come after him—not at night. They'd be afraid of an ambush. Men, without eyes for the night, are fearful of the dark in unfamiliar places. He hadn't wanted to leave Sarah alone, but Ringo was out there someplace. Later, when his son was safe, he'd handle the sheriff. Somehow.

Buster's nose fastened to the trail. Eckersly's feeling for Jaycox had been pure hatred. But Jaycox's last, futile struggle to hold on to life had left Eckersly hoping Jaycox would somehow make it, and, in the end, Eckersly had been glad they'd at least tried to save him.

Yet his feelings of unrequited anger kept returning when in

his mind's eye he saw the son of a bitch on top of Sarah. Then he wanted the man dead. And the one thing he couldn't forget—Jaycox's head had been on Sarah's lap when he died. He'd thought of stopping the truck and pulling Sarah out from under the bastard. *Once* under him was enough. She could put the man's head on his coat for a pillow—more than he deserved. He'd imagined how she was protecting him from their jarring ride across the prairie, as if the filthy prick were her man. He'd wanted his wife up in the cab with him. But he'd driven on.

Old Buster was tight on Ringo's trail. Eckersly was pressed to keep up. Where had Ringo been headed? Perhaps he was scared and got lost. Thank God for old Buster.

For Christ's sake, what did she say to Jaycox on their trip to the hospital? She must have been stricken with horror when the man bouncing on her lap died. And he'd left Sarah alone, and she'd had no protection from the assholes in the sheriff's office. They'd assault her with their words—or worse. What story would they twist out of her?

Eckersly didn't know how many hours had passed before he topped the crest of the small hill, and through the open cabin door below he could see the light of dying embers dancing across the logs. It was then that Ringo whispered, "Shh . . . I heard somethin'. Maybe the sheriff." The boys sat frozen against the cabin wall. Then suddenly, Buster was licking Ringo's face and Eckersly's flashlight was in their eyes.

"Howdy. Looks like you boys have already had supper." Ringo jumped up and grabbed his father, who stood stooped in the doorway, and held on to him for a long time. Finally, Ringo said to his father, "He was hurtin' Mom. An' I shot him."

"I know," Eckersly said.

"Is he dead?"

"Yes."

"I didn't mean to kill him."

"Don't fret, son. You didn't kill him. I did. Come on. Let's go home."

"Please," Ham pleaded. "I must go with you. Ringo and I are brothers."

With barely a moment's delay, Eckersly started out with the two boys for the ranch.

At times they stumbled through the sage and sand and slid down the steep banks of the washes that crossed the trail. Occasionally they stopped to rest, but not for long. At last, darkness surrendered, and the sun rose. Eckersly encouraged the boys to the edge of their endurance. At times he helped Ringo up the sides of a gully, and when the boy seemed incapable of the next step, he tried to pick him up and carry him, but Ringo refused his father's help.

Exhausted, the small party arrived at the ranch midmorning. A couple of deputies were lolling at the kitchen table, drinking coffee and smoking cigarettes.

When Sarah saw Ringo stumble through the door, she ran to him and threw her arms around him.

Then Ringo saw the deputy named Hayward snapping handcuffs on his father.

"Let my daddy go," Ringo hollered.

His father yelled from inside the squad car, "Ringo, it's all right. I won't be gone long."

The boy stood motionless for a moment, trying to decide. How could his brave father give in to them?

"Everything's going to be all right," Eckersly told Ringo.

Hullberry spun around and slapped Ringo hard across the face. He crumpled.

Eckersly struggled to get out of the car, but his hands were cuffed behind him, and Hullberry put a boot against his shoulder and shoved him back.

He cuffed Ringo's hands behind him and shoved him into the backseat beside his father.

Then Hullberry turned to Ham, who'd been standing at a distance, not knowing where to hide and too tired to run. "We're takin' you in, too. I'm plumb out of cuffs. You sit up here between me and Howard, and if you behave yourself, we won't tie you up with somethin'."

"I have something to say. This is not as it may seem," Ham said.

"Best not say anything, son," Eckersly hollered from the car. "You need a lawyer."

"You better shut up back there," Hullberry said. "You're the one who's gonna need a fuckin' lawyer, and a good one—assumin' there are any."

"Yeah," Hayward said. "When we get through with you, you'll be needin' a whole army of lawyers."

As Hullberry spun the patrol car out of the yard, Sarah Eckersly stood at the doorway. She watched for a long time until the patrol car disappeared over the far horizon.

"I smell the chamber gas already," Hullberry said.

"The last son of a bitch they gassed was that crazy bastard from Ten Sleep. Hear he pissed and puked all over the place," Hayward said.

"Hey, Eckersly, whatcha got to say for yourself?" It was Hullberry again. "You oughta know better than to kill a police officer. You get gassed for that in this state. Ol' Harv fuckin' your wife or somethin'?"

"That sure wouldn't surprise me none, knowin' ol' Harv," Hayward chortled. "But I'll tell you one thing for sure: I wouldn't blame him none."

The car bounced wildly over the prairies, and father and son, both handcuffed, were unable to protect their heads from smashing into the roof of the patrol car. Ringo's eyes were propped open wide with fear.

"Don't worry, Ringo. It's going to be all right," Eckersly said.

"That's plumb right," Hullberry hollered back. "They're gonna put this kid away for killin' his teacher, and they're gonna put you in the fuckin' chamber for killin' Harv Jaycox."

"Take her a little easy," Hayward said to Hullberry. "You're gonna break my neck on the ceiling of this fuckin' patrol car if you ain't careful."

"My daddy didn't shoot that deputy. I shot him."

Eckersly: "You be still, Ringo."

"It's the truth. I shot the deputy with our shotgun. He was hurtin' my mother."

"Ringo, be quiet!" his father ordered.

Hayward turned around and spoke to Ringo. "Right, kid. Nice try—tryin' to take the blame for your old man. He's got you pretty well trained."

"You always told me to tell the truth," Ringo said to his father.

"Ringo, I said, be quiet!"

"If you must know, I killed the teacher," Ham said. "Ringo never killed anybody. I can attest for him. He's my brother."

"You're just like your old man—plumb full of bullshit," Hayward said.

"Yeah," Hullberry said, "we already got this kid's confession, and he had the teacher's blood all over him and his prints were on the knife."

Then Eckersly said, "Ringo came home on the bus with the other kids that afternoon. Everybody knows that. You know that."

Ringo and his father were locked in separate cells, one at each end of the cellblock. Ham was taken into the sheriff's office for interrogation.

"Are you all right, Ringo?" Eckersly hollered out of his cell.

"I wanna go home," Ringo hollered back, as if across a far canyon.

"You *are* gonna go home. Just hang in there and don't say anything to anybody except the lawyer. Understand?"

Ringo didn't answer.

"Did you hear me, Ringo?"

Ringo didn't answer.

In a frenzy, Eckersly shouted for the jailer. For over an hour, he screamed and rattled the bars with a tin cup. Finally the old man waddled down the hall.

"You have to release my son," Eckersly said. "This is no place for a boy eleven years old. You know that."

"We ain't got no place for juveniles right now. An' if you'd of took your lawyer's advice, you and your boy wouldn't be here. Remember, he told you not to cause no trouble, that you could go to the gas chamber for shootin' a lawman. I heard him say it right to your face. Now just look where you're at." He laid sad eyes on Eckersly.

"Somebody else is going to get killed if you don't get my son out of this jail. He's innocent," Eckersly shouted.

"I try to help people here. I respect 'em, but I don't have much respect for a man who leads his son into crime like you done with that boy."

CHAPTER 31

Laramie, University, 1947

No LONGER WAS Meg a towering enigma who devastated Ringo at will. Now that she'd given herself to him, she'd become a goddess who'd descended to fill his nose with the fragrance of love and his mouth with the sweetness of its pleasure.

He thought that to touch another's body in that way must be like touching the soul. He'd never touched a woman that way, and now that he had, it was as if the door to Meg's soul had been unlocked, and he could enter, and the landscape he saw was wild, strange, and beautiful.

He wondered why she'd chosen him. There were all those "big men on campus"—the fraternity men and the lettermen—even the brainy ones. She could have any of them. Instead, she'd chosen him.

Her beauty wasn't the Hollywood kind. She had her own brand of beauty, which made men turn to see her again as they passed. Her nose wasn't one of those cute turned-up ducktails like the little blonde's in econ. Meg's was a strong nose, not large, but it had the classic character of the women he'd seen in the books of Italian paintings, and her cheekbones were the kind sculptors noticed.

She didn't flaunt her assets. But the big men on campus gave her the come-on, with their mouths turning up on one side and their eyes squinting into almost a wink, as if to say, I'm hot for you, baby. She brushed them off like pestering door-to-door hucksters.

By habit, he'd noticed Meg's teeth. If you were examining a good-looking horse offered for sale, the first thing you did was "mouth" the beast—part its lips and check the wear on the teeth, which provided a rough read of its age. Meg had those straight, strong, white teeth.

When they walked, they held hands. He'd never walked with a woman holding hands. At first, he felt embarrassed. But he didn't want to be with her without holding her hand. He had to touch her. How could any man walking by a prairie flower not stop and touch its petals lightly? And he felt whole and strong and connected holding her hand.

Sometimes when it got below zero on the Laramie plains, and the wind was whipping up the icy air at fifty miles an hour, and the old pickup wouldn't start, they'd walk, heads bowed into the wind, to the nearby Campus Shop for a cup of coffee. He put sugar and cream in his. She said only farmers drank sugar and cream in their coffee.

Sometimes after they'd downed the last drop, they just sat at the table, looking at each other without saying the first word. They didn't care if others were watching, the big shots on the campus and the girls staring and acting like they were amused by this hick and this magnificent woman sitting there staring at each other that way. The hick—he even needed a haircut—must have something you couldn't see—like a ten-inch dick or something.

Sometimes they told each other what was beautiful about the other, and suddenly they felt their own beauty. That's what falling in love is about.

"It's the way you say things—your innocence," she said.

For damn sure, he wasn't innocent.

"And it's the way you talk so slowly, as if you're kissing each of the words you say to me," she said.

For him, it was the way her upper lip came down over her lower lip when she said things like "baby" and "beautiful." But he didn't know how to explain that. "It's the way you look at me and make me feel beautiful when I know I'm not," he said. He loved her.

And he felt attacked by joy.

On the weekends, he had to work two full shifts at the hotel, and she said she'd miss him so much, she didn't know if she could stand it. And on Friday night, they held on to each other as if these were their last good-byes, kissed each other long and passionately, looked at each other with desperate, parting eyes because they would never see each other again, never, not until Monday morning in Professor Johns's econ class.

CHAPTER 32

Laramie, County Jail, 1940

WHEN HE CLOSED his eyes, Ringo could see his mother. They'd been walking on the prairies in the spring, and the sky was as blue as his dark blue crayon. He could hear his mother's happy voice. "Oh, I love you," she said, flinging her arms across the horizon as if she were onstage and the flowers were her audience. "We won't pick the flowers. We will always only love them." When he opened his eyes, she disappeared. He was alone in the county jail. His cell smelled of urine, and the sounds were the cacophony of noise from the drunks, the desperate, and the insane.

Sometimes Sarah Eckersly brought Ringo fresh cinnamon rolls, and her bean soup was his favorite. Both were often cold before the old jailer made the delivery to his cell. Sometimes she held the boy to her breast. Then she'd hold him out from her with both hands, look into his eyes, and with a quivery smile say, "Don't worry, Ringo, Mr. Hampton is going to get you out of here."

"Are they gonna put Daddy in the gas chamber?" he asked her one day.

"Of course not, darling." She pulled him to her breast again, and although she struggled against her threatening tears, Ringo could feel them against his cheeks. Yet she never said that she loved him.

Never once.

"Man," the big hairy inmate hollered from across the way, "I'd give ever'thing I own, includin' my pinto pony, to get a hunk of that honey."

"You ain't even got a pony," the other guy in his cell said. "Hey, honey, how's about comin' over here? I got somethin' for you."

"Don't worry, Mama," Ringo said. "I won't ever let anybody hurt you."

Sarah called the lawyer, Christopher Hampton. She admitted they were without immediate funds, but she told him her mother had money. "Please, Mr. Hampton, my son is only eleven, and he's innocent of everything except trying to protect his father, and he's in jail, in the company of common criminals."

The sound of her voice—the pain and the naked fear.

And Hampton couldn't ignore his vision of a child cooped up with common criminals. When he visited Ringo, he found the boy lying on the lower bunk without a blanket.

He sat down by the boy. "I'm Christopher Hampton, your lawyer. How are you doing, son?"

"I wanna go home," Ringo said.

"Your father sent me to help you. Do you understand?"

"Are they gonna put my daddy in the gas chamber?" His eyes were floating in fear.

"Who told you that?"

"Those sheriff guys said they were gonna put my daddy in the gas chamber for killing that deputy. But I shot him."

Hampton leaned closer. "Who did you tell that to?"

"I told that sheriff guy. I told him to let my daddy go. I told him I shot that other sheriff guy. He was hurting my mother."

"Where was he hurting her?"

"On our antique kitchen table," Ringo said.

DESPITE HAMPTON'S PRESENCE each morning in Judge Emery Foster's chambers, it wasn't until the ninth day of Ringo's incarceration that his case finally surfaced on the judge's docket.

"Good morning, Mr. Hampton. You've been a very a persistent advocate. I'll say that much. Weren't you here yesterday?"

"And the day before," Hampton replied. "And the day before that."

"You have a small boy in jail, I understand. What is this world coming to, with boys his age in jail? I've been enduring merciless lawyers in another trial, one over the bank's foreclosure of a mortgage. People are all the same. They want the money the bank loans them. They make their promises to pay it back. They put their promises in writing, and when the money comes due, they run to me, crying that the bank is doing something wrong. Something *wrong*, Mr. Hampton, and it's right there in the papers they signed."

Hampton listened, waiting.

"But who offers sympathy to a judge? We sit up on our benches alone—*alone*, Mr. Hampton—and both sides offer only their fawning and groveling, which neither flatters nor assists in the decisions we must make, and then the appeals court judges, who've never laid the first eye on a litigant, write their decisions, as if we trial judges have escaped from an asylum of idiots."

The judge found his handkerchief and blew loudly. "Then the parties bring in the wife and their kids and sit all pitiful-like in the front row of my courtroom in shabby clothes, holding on to one another, and their lawyer—old Henderson, who will talk on for at least forty days and forty nights after he's dead—says they'll all be thrown out in the cold in the middle of the winter. It's a pity, Mr. Hampton. But there are no pity clauses in their mort-gages."

Hampton offered a patient smile.

"And after that hearing, Mr. Hampton—please have pity on *me*—I had two divorces, with kids who were being pulled apart like fish worms. The wife always claims the husband beats her, and the husband always claims the wife is a lying, cheating bitch, and they both want the kids, and neither should have them. They'll be back in my court in less than thirty days, one claiming the other was drunk and left the kids in the car half the night." The judge began opening his mail, with Hampton still standing.

"And I've got two appeals from drunk-driving convictions. Drink! Drink waters the roots of evil. Do you drink, Mr. Hampton?"

"Occasionally."

"Well, I should think very occasionally, Mr. Hampton. Now, this boy who is in jail: I understand he is accused of stabbing his teacher. And I understand his father is charged with the murder of Harvey Jaycox. Is this so?"

"Yes. However, there's a just explanation for all of this."

"There are always just explanations for everything—*everything*, Mr. Hampton! I'll get to your case at my first free moment—my first. In the meantime, it might do this boy some good to sit in jail a few more days and learn a lesson he won't forget."

Hampton was at the judge's office the next morning, and the mornings after that, until the judge finally ordered the sheriff to have the boy brought to his chambers. "When I took this job, I didn't intend to marry you, Mr. Hampton. I spend more time with you than I do with Emily, and with far less satisfaction."

By law, Judge Foster, as district judge, also presided over the juvenile court. Ronald Lucas, the prosecutor, sat in a chair directly in front of the judge's desk. Christopher Hampton, with Ringo seated next to him, sat to the right of Lucas. The boy wore a clean change of clothes that Sarah had brought, including his Sunday blue plaid flannel shirt and new jeans. In her plain black dress, Sarah sat on the other side of Ringo, holding on to his hand.

The judge turned to Deputy Hullberry. "I'm told that this boy stabbed his teacher to death, and that he confessed to the murder. Is that true? Are we missing something here?"

"Well, Your Honor, I think you ought to talk to the sheriff about that," Hullberry said. "There may be somethin' new in that case."

"You'd better bring the sheriff in here, then," the judge said. "I'm not about to turn a murderer loose on the streets; I don't care if he's five years old."

Shortly, Sheriff Bill Diggs sauntered into the judge's chambers. "I gotta admit that tryin' to keep our people safe, we got a little hasty about the murder of Mrs. Foreman," Diggs said. "We got a confession out of this kid, but he was tryin' to cover for his friend, a sixth grader named Ham Swanker."

"I know the family well," the judge said.

"It couldn't have been this kid," Diggs said, nodding in Ringo's direction. "Every kid on the bus said he was on the bus when the bus left the school that afternoon. And the teacher was alive when the bus left. Only person not on the bus was the Swanker kid. We got the right kid this time."

"One other thing, Bill," the judge said to the sheriff. "I hear from some of my sources that this boy was the one who actually shot Deputy Jaycox, not the boy's father. What do you have to say about that?"

"That ain't the way the cookie crumbles in this case," Diggs said.

Sarah Eckersly sat quietly next to her son. The judge turned to Sarah. "I understand you were present when Chief Deputy Jaycox was shot. What do you have to say about that, madam?"

"Excuse me, Your Honor," Hampton said, interrupting, "but Mr. Eckersly has been charged with the murder of Deputy Jaycox, and he's entitled to the husband-wife privilege."

"Of course." The judge cleared his throat and stared at Hampton for a long time, trying to decide what to do with Ringo.

Suddenly, Ringo jumped to his feet and said, "I shot him. He was hurting my mother."

"Hush," Sarah Eckersly said. She turned to the judge. "The child is trying to protect his father. He had nothing to do with the death of Deputy Jaycox. I can at least say that on behalf of my child."

The judge turned again to Ringo. "I want you to tell me the truth, son. Were you present when the deputy was shot?"

"I represent this boy," Hampton said. "Under the present circumstances, I instruct him not to answer. He's exercising his Fifth Amendment rights against self-incrimination."

"You may have a conflict of interest, representing both the father and the son, when both may have been involved," the judge warned.

Hampton stood silent.

"Well, I'm not sending this child home," Judge Foster declared. "One of his parents is charged with murder. The other was present when these felonies were committed, and this boy may have been instrumental in all of this." The judge looked at the notes he'd made on a yellow legal pad. "We'll have a full-scale hearing down the line, when the facts in this case can be sorted out a bit better."

The judge slammed his file closed. "In the meantime, I find from the report of the Department of Children's Services that this boy was an original suspect in the murder of his teacher, Mrs. Foreman, at the Bear Creek School, that he may be prone to cover the crimes of others if he's not guilty of the crimes himself. He may have been present when Deputy Jaycox was shot, and he may have been a witness to that shooting. I find that he is potentially too dangerous to go at large pending his trial. Therefore, I remand him to the custody of the sheriff, to be kept in suitable facilities until further order of this court."

"Please, Your Honor." Sarah Eckersly rushed to the judge's desk. "Please! He's a good boy. Ask anyone."

"Yes, madam," Judge Foster said. "I wish I could ask Mrs. Foreman. Fine woman, I understand."

"If you'll give the boy over to me, I'll take custody of him," Hampton offered. "He's quite harmless, I assure the court. He's only a little frightened boy."

"Mr. Hampton, you are known for your good intentions taking over your better judgment. No, Mr. Hampton, the boy will be quite comfortable in the custody of the sheriff. I'll tell the sheriff he can send the boy's books to him, and I'll have the Children's Services worker stop by from time to time to see that he's progressing satisfactorily." Judge Foster offered Sarah the flick of a smile, and as they left, he stood at the door, watching the woman weaving down the hall, holding on to the lawyer.

The judge endured two more weeks of relentless imploring from Hampton.

Finally the judge called the parties to his chambers. "It is true, Mr. Hampton, that Mr. Eckersly has a right to declare a husband-wife privilege to prevent the state from interrogating Sarah Eckersly. And it's also true that you can keep the boy silenced with a claim of his Fifth Amendment rights. But the other side of that coin is that absent the family's willingness to come clean with all of the facts, there is little reason for me to provide them any favors."

Hampton immediately responded: "You're a fair judge, Your Honor. You surprise me that you'd hold an eleven-year-old child hostage, keep him in jail, where you know no child should be, in order to coerce information from this family on behalf of the state—and against their constitutional rights."

The judge threw Hampton a sharp scowl.

"You know I respect you, Judge Foster. But it's not proper to deprive either Mr. Eckersly of his husband-wife privilege or the child's right not to testify against himself. Those are crucial rights. In good conscious, you mustn't keep a child in prison because the mother or the boy won't talk to you. You are a judge, not a prosecutor."

"Well, Mr. Hampton, perhaps you're right," the judge said. "I never thought of it quite that way. I'll order the Department of Children's Services to place the boy in a foster home. You can draw up the order and I'll sign it."

RINGO HAD BEGUN to shrivel both physically and emotionally by the time he was placed with Mrs. Cynthia Foley, the foster mother. He rarely spoke. He refused to play with the other boys, one a Mexican-American child Ringo's age, named Hernando, who cried at night, and the other boy approximately the same age, named Billy, who was as pale as chalk.

Mrs. Foley put a large bowl of hot potatoes on the table, another bowl of steaming macaroni and cheese, and a dish of canned spinach covered with yellow margarine. Ringo stared at his plate. The other boys ate in silence, like ravenous beasts at the trough.

"Eat your food, Ringo," Mrs. Foley said with an empty smile. "You have work to do around here, and you have to go to school in the morning."

Billy eyed Ringo with suspicion. "You try to kill somebody?" His head was almost in his plate. He stuffed more macaroni in his mouth.

"We don't talk about things like that," Mrs. Foley said. "Ringo is a good boy."

"You won't be here long," Billy said.

Hernando reached for the macaroni dish.

"That's a good boy," Mrs. Foley said. "Ringo, see how Hernando finished his food?"

"They're gonna send you to the reform school," Billy said.

"Billy! You know that isn't true," Mrs. Foley scolded.

"They sent Ike, and they sent Stump."

"Well, they were bad boys. Ringo is a good boy. And so are you. Now you eat your spinach, Billy."

"Stump wasn't bad. He just stole stuff 'cause he was hungry."

That night after supper, the boys did the dishes and helped Mrs. Foley clean up the kitchen. Then in their room, Billy asked Ringo if he wanted to play cops. Ringo shook his head no.

"The cops come after my old man," Billy said. "If you wanna play cops, you can be the cop."

Ringo shook his head again.

Hernando was leaning over from the upper bunk, watching like a frightened kitten in a tree above the hounds.

"He's dumb," Billy said. "He never says nothin'. Soon as the judge gets to your case, he's gonna send you to the reform school. He sends 'em all there. He ain't gonna send me there, 'cause I'm gonna run."

Ringo was silent.

"I never done nothin'," Billy said. "Them other kids broke in, an' all I done was eat some of the candy they give me."

Then Hernando began to cry.

CHAPTER 33

Laramie, 1947

THEY CLIMBED THE rocks of Veedevoo, near Laramie, where dumps of gray granite were piled hundreds of feet above the mountain floor like beseeching arms of buried, towering prehistoric beasts. The early-spring flowers had ventured out. The alpine buttercups announced in noisy yellow that they, too, had survived the winter. And the pinkish buds of the mariposa lilies waved in the warm wind and joined in the celebration of the tardy spring.

"Everything changes in the spring. It's a certain magic," Ringo said.

"I wish I could change," Meg said.

"You're like a flower," he said. "If you were a flower, I'd never pick you."

"I wish I could change," she said again.

"How could I love you if you changed, even a little?"

Finally she said, "Maybe I should change my name. I never did like Meg. Sounds so short and hard, like bolts and pegs. I should change my name to something romantic."

"Like what?"

"I've always liked Isabelle," she said.

"Isabelle!" he cried. He gazed out over his kingdom, the granite piles turned to castles, and he and Isabelle, his beautiful queen, were in command of the world. His chest was full, a volcano of joy ready to erupt. He grabbed for her hand. Then suddenly he said, "They'll be moving the sheep out to the north pasture."

"You'll never stop being a sheepherder," Meg said.

Ringo heard her laughter like the music of a mountain stream. He'd lain at the stream's banks, the lazy clouds floating by— sheep in the sky he tended with his eyes. No one had told him about the love thing. Arturo knew nothing of it. Yes, his mother and father had shown a distant caring for each other. But this magic that he and Meg touched with their eyes, embraced with their arms, and tasted with their lips brought on a joy he could feel down to his toes, and in their parting a pain that reduced him to little more than a wilted weed.

She looked at him, and her tears welled up.

"We will be this way forever," he said.

"We'd better go." She pulled him after her. But he held back and brought her gently to him and kissed her as if his kiss must last until the granite crumbled.

Love is a dreadful disease, she thought. The disease caused the way he looked at her, his kisses gentle or wild, depending where they found themselves on the winding road of their emotions. She trusted him. And she needed him. That was the trap.

There'd been men in her life with spacious personalities. But they'd been like wild stallions who'd as soon kick her in the chest as take her for a ride. The gift came from loving someone who loved her back, the gift of the gods, and it frightened her. She thought how life would be without him. Yes, she was trapped.

"We will be this way forever," Ringo said again as they walked to his pickup. He swung her hand in a large arch as if their arms had grown together.

"Ringo, we need to talk," she said. She couldn't bear to go on with this. She picked a small white budding bluebell peeping out from the grasses. She touched the flower to her cheek. She sat down on a granite outcropping, and he sat next to her. She pulled her hand away from his and felt the coolness of the air on her fingers where once they'd been warm.

His smile beamed joy. "My mother used to say we shouldn't pick the flowers because of their pain. But if I were a flower, my life would be complete if you picked me."

"You are so dear," she said. Then tears took her, and he wondered why.

CHAPTER 34

Bear Creek Ranch, 1940

SARAH BEGGED THE ranch partners, Longley and Hansen, to let her run the ranch while Eckersly was in jail awaiting trial. She pleaded that she'd learned from her husband what needed to be done, and how to do it. And the urgency they saw on her face, joined with their reluctance to put on their boots of dirty labor and their coats of grimy sweat, supported their decision "to give her a chance at it," as they put it.

Faithfully, she made her weekly visits to the jail, where she and Eckersly talked about the lambs, the herders, and the purchase of winter hay. They avoided talking about Eckersly's case, and he refused to talk about himself. He tried to say that he loved her, but although the feeling sought escape, it was hard to talk about love when business at the ranch was foremost in her mind.

She gave him a perfunctory kiss at the beginning and the end of each visit. No tears. No whining. He felt respect for her, and sensed her desperation. Once, he tried to tell her how proud he was of her, but his words seemed shallow, and after that he let such thoughts go unspoken.

Eckersly, a man of action, could take no action. He could strike out at no one. He couldn't stand in a courtroom and shout that Jaycox, the raping bastard, got what was coming to him. He couldn't argue that justice was so much bullshit displayed in the phony trappings of a trial.

He thought of the wily coyote caught in a steel trap. The trap broke its leg, the merciless pain of it. But the beast was not as helpless as he. The coyote would chew off its leg and escape.

If only Sarah would tell him the truth. But did she know the truth, and would he believe her if he heard it? What had it been for her with the bastard Jaycox?

One thing he knew: She was a slave to duty. He both admired and despised that. Duty was a mask that hid whoever she was. Sometimes they sat without speaking, she with that faint, pained smile of endurance cemented across her lips. How could he ask her the questions that bedeviled him—questions he was ashamed to ask? Perhaps he and Sarah were like parts from different machines that didn't mesh and only ground away until the machine one day disintegrated.

Had she felt even the faintest sense of lust, of bestial wildness that might have seeped up through the horror of her time with Jaycox? It was horror. It had been rape, or the same as rape, he kept reminding himself.

He was fighting madness.

She wasn't safe in the company of the randy ranch help, especially if they were drinking. Even if she were safe, she faced them with little authority. He knew she struggled through her duties, milking Old Boss twice daily, feeding the horse, Old Hard Head, and, the most taxing of all, trying to direct the workers. Yet she hung on to the job, and without complaint.

Longley and Hansen likely saw her stay at the ranch as temporary. If Eckersly didn't get out of jail before spring, they'd hire another manager. Then what? She'd have no place to go but to her parents. She tried to be cheerful. Hope. Hope always made the threat of tomorrow tolerable. "You'll be out of here soon," she said to Eckersly. "Hampton will get you out."

How was she going to testify at his trial? Such was the monster hiding in the closet. He never asked. What difference did it make? Whatever she'd done with the bastard Jaycox on her precious antique table, she'd done to save Ringo.

Yes.

Surely.

CHAPTER 35

Laramie, Courthouse, 1941

FOR SIX MONTHS and thirteen days, Eckersly occupied his cell in the northeast corner of the jail, awaiting trial for his alleged murder of Chief Deputy Harv Jaycox. The delays, according to prosecutor Lucas, were due to the groundless motions filed by Hampton, who sought, among other relief, to discover the evidence that Lucas would be presenting against Eckersly. Hampton had also sought to change the venue of the trial to Rawlins, a town over a hundred miles west of Laramie, where the citizens were acquainted with neither the sheriff and his deputies nor the victims of the alleged crime.

But Hampton knew Judge Foster would never give another judge the prestige of trying a good murder case. Moreover, if the judge moved Eckersly's case to another county, the local paper would publish editorials raising hell, the judge's friends at their ten o'clock coffee break would raise hell, the sheriff would raise hell, the people of the town would raise hell, and Foster's wife, who faithfully watched every murder case he'd ever tried, which totaled three in twenty years, would raise hell on into the night, until she finally fell asleep from the sound of her discordant yappings.

Hampton tried to disqualify Judge Foster from hearing the case, claiming that his close association over the past decades with

Diggs and his deputies should ban him from presiding over the trial. Hampton knew Judge Foster wouldn't rule favorably on any substantial defense motion in a murder case. Murderers had to be convicted, executed, and the citizens rendered safe—and the judge reelected.

Nevertheless, Hampton had to put his motions before the court so that if Eckersly were convicted, he could never claim he was represented by incompetent counsel. And such motions had to be made and argued to preserve the record for an appeal.

Privately, the judge thought Jaycox was an ignorant know-it-all smart-ass, and an ugly one to boot. Why some women took to the scaly prick with ears, the judge couldn't fathom. But Jaycox had been around a long time, and had friends among the deputies, the hospital people, and some of the railroaders with whom he played poker on Front Street. And the townsfolk were outraged over the brutality of the killing—the man's leg blown off with a shotgun. Justice had to be satisfied. And folks hadn't forgotten that Jaycox had a couple of decent kids and a hardworking, faithful wife who never tried to steal another woman's man.

The judge worked closely with Sheriff Bill Diggs and his deputies in an effort to keep the town free of major crime. The judge had served in the infantry in World War I, although his service had been relegated to a supply depot at Fort Ord, since he'd earned a pre–law school degree in accounting. He was a member of the local country club, and his wife was a member of the Mayflower Society, its Wyoming membership boasting nine, confirming the remarkable fertility of their Pilgrim ancestors.

"I always liked Harv Jaycox," the judge's wife, Emily, had proclaimed at breakfast on the morning Jaycox's death made headlines in the town's only newspaper, *The Laramie News*. The headline read DEPUTY DIES IN MYSTERIOUS SHOOTING.

"He was always so nice to me, so courteous," she'd said.

"Yeah, he was quite a ladies' man," the judge had said. "I'll bet the church'll be standing room only for all the women he's serviced in this county."

"Why, Emery, how could you say such a thing?" his wife had replied. "He never once made an improper advance to me."

Snapping back from his reverie, the judge now lifted his coffee cup to salute his wife and laid a puckered, perfunctory kiss on her cheek before hurrying off to his chambers for another day of hassling with the local lawyers, "those gutless beguilers," as the judge saw them, "who'd kiss my ass for small advantages, those dullards with empty arguments, those boorish drones with groaning voices, deficient intellects, and defunct ethics."

Still, those same lawyers could dethrone him if he crossed enough of them too often, especially prosecutor Lucas with his big mouth and his nose up the ass of the local press. And those lawyers who represented big money could beat him—the pervasive big money of the railroad and the local cement plant and especially the ubiquitous big money of the university. Everybody in Laramie had more money than he, the price, he thought, that a judge must pay for being honest.

Every six years, he had to stand for reelection, and if over 50 percent of the voters wanted him thrown out of office, out he'd go. Then what? There wasn't much demand for a dethroned judge. He had a duty to see that the state and its prosecutor were fully protected, especially when the prosecutor was against the likes of Christopher Hampton, who'd work right up to the ethical line, and who might slip over a little from time to time.

A few weeks before Eckersly's trial, Sheriff Bill Diggs ambled into the judge's chambers, and he and the judge talked about old times, old girlfriends, old drunken parties, old hunting trips, the good old days clear back to grade school. Finally the sheriff got around to Jaycox.

Diggs told the judge how loyal Jaycox had been—and he reminded the judge how Jaycox's wife was a wonderful Christian woman who sang in the Baptist church's choir and worked hard as a nurse at the hospital, and how they had those kids who were fine students and members of 4-H, and the boy was a member of the marching band.

"Jaycox was a good man," the sheriff said, "and if Eckersly don't get what's comin' to him for his killin', my whole staff'll be pissed to the hilt. Bad people out there will figure they can kill any deputy in Albany County anytime they please and get away with it."

"We'll take a good hard look at this, Bill," Judge Foster said. "Be sure and give my regards to Harmony, and tell Mrs. Jaycox I personally send my deepest condolences. I sent flowers to the funeral."

Judge Foster listened politely to Hampton's motions, nodded to him from time to time, as if he were taking them in with a certain degree of agreement. He told Hampton he'd give his motions careful consideration and have a decision for him shortly. Five weeks and three days later, enough time having passed to support the supposition that the judge wrestled long and hard over the issues, the judge mailed Hampton his order overruling all of his motions. During that time, Eckersly languished in jail, awaiting his trial. Under the law, bond was not available to those charged with first-degree murder where the evidence of guilt was clear and convincing. And the judge had so ruled.

THE DAY OF Eckersly's trial, the wind ran wild across a hundred miles of vacant plains, and in high hilarity hurled anything loose, or that could be loosened, across the land—hats, newspapers, small dogs, and the pervasive cinders of the Union Pacific Railroad's coal-burning locomotives. The cinders beat against the faces of the people like small, sharp buckshot. The people walked with their heads bowed to protect their eyes, and leaned into the wind as if they were walking uphill. At Laramie's altitude of seven thousand feet, the air was thin and bone-chilling ten months of the year, and its citizens suffered an enduring suspicion that summer was but a fleeting fantasy.

On the streets of Laramie, one's ears were assaulted by the mournful bellowing of coal-burning switch engines and the explosive sounds of boxcars banging into one another. Added to the cacophony was the high, mournful whistling of coast-to-coast passenger trains on their scheduled runs. The town smelled of smoke. But the people of Laramie were a hardy, proud, uncomplaining lot.

The Albany County Courthouse was an imposing three-story structure of hand-cut sandstone the color of a palomino horse. The courthouse was the hub of the county's official business, the county offices on the first floor, the judge's and prosecutor's quarters and courtroom on the second, and the sheriff's office and jail on the third. In the courtroom, the American flag stood boldly behind the judge's bench. The ceiling was lofty, and the room's oaken pews were of a design to guarantee the discomfort of all.

Justice was a bustling business in Laramie. It hired judges, court clerks, court reporters, the sheriff, his deputies, dispatchers and secretaries, the prosecutor, his deputies and secretaries, along with a bevy of private lawyers and their secretaries, who, but for the business of justice, would have been relegated to selling real estate and used cars.

The business of justice required bailsmen who profited beyond usury by providing bond for an accused. The jurors and witnesses and the families of the accused occupied hotel rooms and took their meals at the local restaurants.

The business of justice provided the county a budget for the Sheriff's Department's vehicles—gas, oil, and repairs—its guns and ammunition, as well as food and blankets for the prisoners.

The business of justice required accountants to keep the books and recording clerks to keep the criminal records. The epicenter of this bustling business was the Albany County Courthouse.

The harshness of Laramie's climate drove many to treat their misery with the most widely used medication known to man—alcohol. And without drunken husbands beating their wives, drunken sheepherders fighting in the bars, drunken college students disturbing the peace, and the usual ration of hopeless drunks cluttering the streets, including an occasional desperate drunk attempting to burglarize a liquor store to satisfy his drinking habit, the lucrative business of justice would soon dry up. But only rarely was the town of Laramie favored with an honest-to-God murder case, a delight the sheriff bestowed upon the citizens when he'd filed charges against Ben Eckersly, a thoroughly sober man.

On the day of the trial, the courtroom was packed to the walls with a throng of spectators, which included a half-dozen off-duty cops showing their support for their fallen brother, Jaycox; a prim high school civics teacher accompanied by her twenty-six students, who sat grinning, giggling, and gouging one another; several grizzled railroad conductors and a couple of brakemen waiting to be called to their trains; a law professor with thick glasses and two dozen of his law students, many of whom also wore thick glasses; and a potpourri of curious townspeople who'd gathered to witness an honest-to-God murder case about to take place in Laramie, Wyoming.

Eckersly, in his "Sunday-go-to-meetin' clothes," a gray western suit and black round-toed cowboy boots, sat by his lawyer, Christopher Hampton, who was wearing his usual worn western tweed jacket with leather patches at the sleeves, a blue denim shirt, and a western bolo tie with a piece of moss agate fronting the clasp, and he'd donned his black woolen "court-goin' pants." His cowboy boots suffered without polish.

After two days of questioning by the lawyers concerning the jurors' "biases and prejudices," the jury was selected and sworn and the opening statements of both lawyers delivered. Prosecutor Ronald Lucas charged that Jaycox's killing was cold-blooded murder. Christopher Hampton's defense seemed vague and scattered, something about no crime having been committed at all.

Lucas, in his mid-thirties, with a shock of black hair a little too long for the comfort of the town fathers, wore a dark business suit that he'd lately purchased from JCPenney, and his toes pointed in as he paced in front of the jury. His thin face seemed molded in a perpetual scowl, and his raspy voice assaulted the ears.

"Now, Sheriff, when did you first meet Ben Eckersly?"

Diggs was sprawled in the witness chair like a long-legged puppet with the strings cut loose. "I first seen Eckersly the night of the day that Mrs. Foreman, the schoolmarm, was stabbed. That was the first day of October, last year. He come in with his boy. I was wantin' to question the boy concernin' the murder of the boy's teacher."

"How did that go?"

"Eckersly was plumb uncooperative," Diggs said.

Hampton jumped to his feet. "That's a conclusion of the witness. He should tell the jury what happened or what was said."

"Okay," Diggs said before the judge could rule. "I told Eckersly I was goin' to have to ask him to leave if he kept answerin' for his kid, and he got up and took his kid with him. I let him go. Didn't wanna cause no trouble with a lot of spectators around—embarrass him and all. Then I had my deputies, Harv Jaycox and Darwin Hullberry, go stop him on the highway and arrest him for obstructin' justice."

"What happened when Chief Deputy Jaycox tried to arrest the defendant?" The prosecutor tossed Eckersly an accusing look.

"Eckersly resisted arrest."

"That's obviously hearsay," Hampton objected.

"Well, it's the damn truth," Diggs said. "Harv told me, and I never knowed Harv to lie to me."

"Wait just a minute!" Hampton shouted as he stomped toward the bench. "What Jaycox did or didn't say to the sheriff is pure hearsay, and the sheriff knows that."

"Sustained," the judge ruled.

Hampton nodded agreement, but his facial expression spoke otherwise.

"Was there bad blood between them?" prosecutor Lucas asked.

"That calls for a conclusion of the witness," Hampton objected, still on his feet.

Before the judge could rule, Diggs said, "Yeah, real bad blood."

"I have a motion!" Hampton took long, angry steps to the bench, Lucas following. As was the judge's order, Hampton spoke in a whisper, so the jurors couldn't hear him. "I move for a mistrial. The sheriff has intentionally prejudiced this jury. The jury will now conclude that Mr. Eckersly killed Jaycox because of the supposed bad blood between them. The sheriff's prejudicial comment has convicted Mr. Eckersly of first-degree murder by providing testimony of malice that didn't exist until it was improperly invented and foisted on this jury by the sheriff. The bell of prejudice has been rung, and nothing Your Honor can do will unring that bell."

"I'll unring the bell," the judge whispered. "Your motion is overruled." The judge turned to the jury. "Pay no attention to what the sheriff said about there being bad blood between Mr. Eckersly and Mr. Jaycox. That testimony by the sheriff was improper."

The sheriff looked over at the jurors and smiled.

Still at the bench, Hampton whispered to the judge, "You didn't unring the bell, Your Honor. You rang it again by repeating it, and a motive has now been established for this alleged murder—and it has been *wrongfully* established."

"Well, tell me, Mr. Hampton," the judge asked, "was there bad blood between them or not? All we're looking for here is the truth."

"It's not proper for you to push me to make the state's case," Hampton said. "If my client is to be convicted, he must be convicted on proper evidence, not on the blatant errors of the court or the gross improprieties of the witness."

"I warn you, Mr. Hampton," the judge whispered back. "You'd be well advised to watch your language. I don't know a judge who'd stand for a lawyer insulting the court as you just did. If you believe I've committed error, you can tell the Supreme Court of Wyoming about it." The judge turned to the prosecutor. "In the meantime, proceed, Mr. Lucas."

CHAPTER 36

Laramie, Belle June's, 1947

"WHAT'S THE MATTER with you, Happy?" Belle June, the madam, asked, peering at Meg through puffs of smoke that she blew in Meg's direction. "You sick tonight or somethin'?"

Four other women sat around the table in the kitchen. Meg was in her "uniform," as she called it—a pair of high-heeled black slippers and her short, see-through black nightie fastened at the top with two glass diamonds. She held her head with both hands under her chin. "Something's happened to me," Meg said.

"Never seen you like this before, Happy," Marge said. She was the blonde wearing a long red dress with a low-cut front sprinkled with sparkles. The ampleness of her bosom created grave doubts that the dress could hold its contents. She wore the long dress because she said her tricks didn't like skinny legs. "You have to show 'em what they like, and they like big boobs."

"Never seen you like this, either," Carmen said to Meg. She was wearing her pink ballerina's outfit. She was thin, tiny, and little girl–like. "What's the matter, Happy?"

Mabel, the black maid, took heavy, slow steps into the kitchen. "There's a john out here asking for you, Happy."

Belle June waited.

Meg continued to stare into the distance. Marge got slowly to her feet. "I'll take him," she said.

"No," Mabel said, "he only wants Happy."

"You gonna take him?" Belle June asked Meg.

"I got to thinking about when I have grandchildren," Meg said. She spoke as if she were addressing the great unseen. "I want to take my grandchildren on a walk through the woods, and I want to show them the flowers."

"Good Jesus, should I call a doctor?" Belle June said with a cough. "Come on, honey, that john's waitin'."

"And I want to take them down by a little creek where the water's clean." Meg's voice was soft and distant. "And I want to sit there with them and hear them laughing." She turned to Belle June, her eyes still far away. "Did you ever hear children laughing?"

"I heard 'em," Carmen said. "My kids laughed all the time when I was home." She started to cry.

"Good Jesus, this has gone far enough," Belle June said. Marge went to the cupboard and came back with a bottle of vodka. "Better have a drink," she said, pouring a shot into Meg's coffee.

Meg looked out across her cup. "Someday I want to be a grandmother. Grandmothers are important, don't you think so, Belle June?"

"Good Jesus, Happy!" With effort, Belle June got to her feet and stood alongside of Mabel. Both women peered down at Meg.

"I better go tell the john Happy ain't here tonight," Mabel said.

"She sure as shit ain't here," Belle June said. "What's the matter with you, honey? You ain't never been like this before."

"When one of us is in pain, it hurts us all," Carmen said.

"Look, honey, you wanna go home tonight, or what?" Belle June asked. She leaned over to have a better look at Meg. "It'll leave us shorthanded."

"I want to be like the water in the mountain creek," Meg said. "I want to have direction, and I want to be clean."

"Clean? You pick somethin' up?" Belle June asked.

"It's a man," Marge said. "I seen it before a lotta times."

"I'm so lonely, I don't even want to be with myself anymore," Carmen whimpered. Marge poured some vodka into Carmen's cup.

"Well, I'll say one thing," Belle June said, sitting back in her chair. "We all got our troubles."

"I lost my dad," Carmen said. "He was all I had, and he loved me. I never let my mother know, because she hated him." Her tears made her mascara run into small black rivulets.

"Good Jesus, am I gonna have to close this fuckin' whorehouse down tonight?" Belle June said. "Come on, girls. We got work to do."

Then Marge said to Carmen, "You at least got kids."

"I don't have them," Carmen said. She took another drink from her cup. "The Children's Services took them from me, and I couldn't fight for them."

Mabel, the maid, came back to the kitchen. "There's a couple of johns out there. One of 'em looks like he's got a bundle a green and can't wait to get rid of it." She saw the faces of the women sitting around the table. "My, my, what *is* this? Sunday confession or somethin'?" Nobody answered. "Babe is in with an all-nighter and Georgia is busy." Mabel waited for instructions, looking from woman to woman.

"Well, girls," Belle June said, "one thing I always say. Best way to chase out the blues is to go to work."

Marge said, as if speaking to herself, "Why am I the worst person in the world? And the answer is, I am not."

"Well, you ain't makin' any money, either, honey. You gonna go out there, or what?" Belle June asked.

Meg said, "I came onto a path, and I thought, Somebody has been here before. It was a really pretty path and I took it."

"What I want is someone to share my heart with," Marge said, "and there ain't any of those kind around." She poured more from the vodka bottle.

"Come on, girls, I can bullshit with the best of you," Belle June said.

"I was married once," Marge said, "but he was a lightweight jerk, a pretty boy who turned out to be nothin' but a silly son of a bitch. I had to go to work to put food on the table, and I couldn't make it as a waitress. We'd have starved to death."

Meg was still staring into space. "Then this voice said, 'You're not just a thing like something on the shelf that's sold.'" Meg turned to Belle June. "I'm a whole human being, Belle June." Her voice sounded like the voice of a far-off child beseeching her mother for understanding.

"That's always been the trouble with a smart whore," Belle June said. "They get to thinking too much."

Carmen addressed the ceiling. "When I talk to my dad, I look up at the stars, and I say, 'I love you.' And he says back, 'I love you, too.'" Then she turned to Meg. "But he never says he's proud of me anymore." Her face was like a faintly pretty, smiling skull. When she started to cry again, she looked younger.

Belle June took a step or two toward the door, as if to herd her girls into the parlor. "Get over it," Belle June said. "It's doesn't make any sense for all of you to be this way."

"I was adopted," Marge said. "I used to ask, Who am I? Someone that two people didn't want? In high school, I used to scream at my parents and tell them I hated them. They were very loving to me. It isn't their fault that I'm here. They're both gone now."

Carmen stopped crying, took another drink from her cup, and began singing: "We are poor little lambs who have gone astray, ba, ba, ba."

Belle June slumped down in her chair. She took the bottle from the table, poured her cup half full, and pushed back. "It's hard for me to sit here and listen to you with my heart," she said. "A madam can't afford to do that." She took a long drink from her cup, made a face to match the taste of the vodka, lit up another cigarette and blew out the smoke. "A madam has to keep her distance."

"I'm not ready for this death thing," Marge said.

Belle June took another quick swig from her cup. "Lotta ways to die," she said. "Woman can die of starvation. Woman can die slaving all her life keeping house for some asshole. Woman can die snorting the shit." She sat there, breathing heavily. The silence in the kitchen let the sounds of impatient men in the parlor roll in.

"I had me a man once," Belle June said, the tears floating to the surface of her eyes. The girls at the table looked at her with surprise. "A man can fuck a girl over a hundred times worse than all the johns that ever walked into a whorehouse," she said.

Out of respect for Belle June, the girls looked away.

Then Belle June said, "I loved him, but he was a no-good son of a bitch. They'll all get you one way or another, honey," she said to Meg. She patted Meg on the arm. Her red polished fingernails were as long as bear claws.

Meg looked at her sisters with wet eyes. "I've learned that I can be okay with all of you because you're like me."

Carmen started singing again, as if to her children. "We are poor little lambs who have gone astray . . ."

"But one thing I know," Meg said. "I'm a gift of all of the life that's in me. I'm not just a plaything on the shelf." She got up, took a clean cup out of the cupboard, and poured herself a fresh cup of coffee. "I have to quit, Belle June."

They could hear the heavy steps of Mabel approaching. "The place is full out there," Mabel said. "I've been serving 'em drinks as long as I can. They're gettin' testy, and most of 'em are drunk."

"Tell 'em we're closed for the night," Belle June said. "Tell 'em to go home to their mothers."

CHAPTER 37

Laramie, Courthouse, 1941

CHRISTOPHER HAMPTON'S MEETINGS with Ben Eckersly to prepare Eckersly's defense took place in the jail, inside a cramped concrete box, a room barren of common amenities except a steel table and two steel chairs.

Eckersly's skin had yellowed and the lines around his mouth had deepened. "I want to tell the truth," Eckersly said.

"Truth is like your hands," Hampton replied. "There's the top of your hands and the bottom. Both sides are true. Depends on which side you're seeing."

Eckersly looked at his palms. "I want to tell the truth," he said. "All except one thing."

"Hold it!" Hampton said. "If you want to lie on the stand about something, I don't want to know it."

Eckersly stared at his lawyer. "Aren't lawyers supposed to hear their clients' stories?"

"If you shot Jaycox and you want to say somebody else shot him, you can say so under oath, even though it would be perjury," Hampton said. "If you want to say it was self-defense, but in fact you shot him in cold blood, you can so testify. Nobody can put a gag on you in the courtroom. But as your lawyer, I can be gagged. If I know you're lying under oath, I can't help you put a lie to the jury. That's an ethic I'm bound by under the law. So be careful what you tell me."

"You're telling me it's okay for me to lie, and its okay for you to argue my lie to the jury so long as you don't know you're telling a lie?"

"It is *not* okay for you to lie, but if you're going to lie, don't tell me," Hampton said.

"Well, I only want to lie about that *one* thing," Eckersly said again. "Sounds like you're protecting yourself instead of me."

"Maybe you need a different lawyer."

"I want to do the right thing," Eckersly said. "My lie is *against* me."

"If you're going to lie *against* yourself, the prosecutor couldn't be happier. It's only when you lie *for* yourself that the law gets upset."

"It's all right, then, for me to tell you the lie that I want to tell if it's *against* me?" Eckersly asked.

Hampton tipped back on his chair and looked at his client for a long time. Was it a lawyer's duty to help the law untangle the law's own entanglements on questions of ethics?

PROSECUTOR RONALD LUCAS marched in aggressive steps toward his witness on the stand. "And what other charges, Sheriff Diggs, were brought against Mr. Eckersly as a result of his arrest?"

"He resisted arrest," the sheriff said.

Hampton was on his feet again, his anger unsheathed. "I move to strike the answer. This witness wasn't present. It's more of that same forbidden hearsay."

"Sustained," the judge ruled.

"I ask the court to instruct Mr. Lucas to desist. He knows better. He's attempting to prejudice this jury with improper evidence."

"Prosecutor Lucas knows how to try a proper case. Mr. Lucas, you will act accordingly." The judge smiled in a way that canceled the tenor of the judge's admonishment.

Lucas walked closer to the sheriff. "Was the defendant, Eckersley, thrown in jail on the charge of resisting arrest?"

"Yeah, and also on a charge of obstructin' justice."

"How long was he in jail on these charges?"

"His lawyer got him out on bail the next mornin'." The sheriff pointed an accusatory nod toward Hampton.

"And where did you next see Chief Deputy Jaycox?"

"At the funeral home. They had him stretched out there on a slab, and his left foot was blowed all to hell—'cuse the French."

"What did you do then?"

"Well, I had to go comfort his wife, Betsy, and their two kids. When I seen her, she was cryin' so hard, she couldn't barely stand up an'—"

"Please, Your Honor," Hampton said, interrupting. "We acknowledge the shock and grief suffered by Mrs. Jaycox and her family. But their grief has nothing to do with whether or not Mr. Eckersly is responsible for it."

"Sustained," the judge said. He offered Mrs. Jaycox a small, sad smile. She was wearing a plain black dress. Her face lacked makeup, and her hair was pulled back and tied in a severe knot.

"Then what did you do?" Lucas asked.

"I went lookin' for Harv's car. I figured it was out by the Eckersly place."

"And did you find the car?"

"Not 'til the next day. We sent a plane to find it, and the pilot radioed in its location. Then me an' a couple of my deputies found the car, and we found where Eckersly had shot Harv's leg off."

"Objection!" Hampton was springing to his feet again. "This is the conclusion of the sheriff. *Who* shot Jaycox, where, and when are crucial issues for the jury and the jury alone to determine."

"Sustained," the judge ruled. "I so instruct you the jurors." The jurors nodded. Several were glancing over at the Jaycox family with conspicuous sympathy.

"So you found the squad car stuck out on the prairies?"

"Yeah, 'bout four miles north of Eckersly's place. An' I'll tell you one thing fer sure. You could see Eckersly's footprints all over the place."

"How do you know they were Mr. Eckersly's prints?" Lucas asked.

"I matched 'em up with his boots. Got 'em right here." The sheriff reached into a brown paper sack sitting on the floor next to the witness chair and pulled out a single battered boot. "And I took a plaster cast of the prints at the scene, and they match."

"May I inquire for the purpose of making an objection?" Hampton asked the judge. The judge nodded his assent.

"Tell me, Sheriff Diggs, were your footprints there?" Hampton began.

"Suppose so."

"Were there footprints of other deputies there?"

"Sure."

"How many deputies were at that scene?"

"Well, off and on . . ." He thought for a moment and counted on his fingers, with his lips moving. "Two of 'em come with me an' four come later."

"Well, Sheriff, could you tell by looking at the footprints of your deputies *why* they'd come there?"

"Course not," the sheriff replied. "Footprints don't tell you that."

"So, we know that Mr. Eckersly was up there. Could you tell by looking at his footprints whether Mr. Eckersly was there to kill Chief Deputy Jaycox or to save him?"

"He had no business bein' up there in the first place," the sheriff said.

"Depends on whether you give the presumption of innocence to Mr. Eckersly, isn't that true?"

"This has gone far enough," prosecutor Lucas objected. "This has nothing to do with the admissibility of the evidence."

"Sustained," Judge Foster ruled.

Then Lucas offered into evidence both Eckersly's boot and the plaster cast of his tracks.

"No objection," Hampton said. "We agree that Mr. Eckersly was there. *Why* he was there, the jurors will decide."

SITTING IN THE witness waiting room, Sarah Eckersly realized how trapped she had felt for most of her marriage.

Life on a sheep ranch out on the interminable prairies was a trap.

How might she escape?

All she could see for eighty miles in any direction were the table-flat plains, and at the far horizon, the mountains rising up as a distant prison wall.

She'd walked out many a morning, Ringo in school, the ranch hands off with the herds, and she'd wanted to scream. But nobody would hear her, and nobody would answer.

That morning, she'd stood outside on the concrete step and screamed—screamed and screamed until she was emptied. The sound of her screaming frightened her. Then her screaming felt good. And after each long scream, she waited, listening.

The wind slapped at her face.

The silence was as empty as old cans.

She screamed once more and a small field mouse scurried out from under the house and ran into the weeds.

Ben Eckersly had promised her peace, but she hadn't bargained for this loneliness, this deep, unbroken boredom. Yes, he was solid as a damnable post—and as predictable. He rose in the morning exactly at five. He built the fire in the kitchen stove, put on the coffeepot, shaved, and then walked out into the dawn to do his chores. When she heard the door shut behind him, she got up, tried to put on a face, and to prepare the same breakfast—pancakes with eggs and bacon.

When he came in with the milk, he handed her the pail. His mouth smiled at her, not at a person, but at an object upon which he deposited the milk pail and the same patient kindness that passed for love. Living with him those years had been as if he'd looked at her once, smiled at her once, made love to her once, because every look and every smile and every movement in and out of the conjugal bed was the same as the first.

Then the baby came, their Little Ben. After he was born, he fit into nature's routine. The cow was freshened with the birth of the calf, and with the birth of Little Ben, she nursed the child on full breasts. There'd been pleasure in that. Then both the calf and the child were weaned. And in the end, there was no escape for either. The calf was fed and slaughtered, and the child was fed and one day he'd be taken from her and be consumed in a world of money, power, and war.

She had no friends.

She worked her small garden during the short summers and got pleasure from that, because the radishes, given water and sheep manure, popped up, and the lettuce grew, not the iceberg lettuce like in the stores, but leaf lettuce that turned limp in the dressing, but it was fresh, and the beans grew on vines around small stakes. The season was too short for corn.

At times, she'd been lifted by the mind's magic and transported to the stage in New York. True, she was only one in a chorus line of two dozen. But she was surrounded by music and people. Men wanted her. She was not a star. But she had talent, and maybe one day she'd become a star if the right man saw her, admired her, and touched her on the shoulder when she was standing in the wings, waiting to go on. Maybe he'd ask her to meet him for a drink at some famous restaurant afterward.

Stardom wasn't necessary. The only necessity was that she would have a real New York address, a job, and a relationship to the world. It was only necessary that she might walk into a store and touch clothes she'd seen only in the magazines. The people who saw her on the street would never know whether she was a chorus girl or a great Broadway star. And the men on the street would turn their heads as she walked by, noticing her long stride and the measured movement of her body. As she stood watering her small garden, she could hear the beat of the music, and her feet began to move with the music on the hard prairie ground.

Then it was time to put out the dinner for the men, the big meal at noon. The lamb roast would be done in the oven, the potatoes already boiled. Her husband walked into the house at exactly twelve, hung his hat and coat on the porch, entered the kitchen, kissed her lightly on the cheek, and said, as he said every noon, "How was your morning?"

"It was fine," she replied, as she always replied. "And how was yours?"

"Had a little problem with the damned posthole digger, and the coupling to the tractor gave out."

"Didn't you have that same problem last year?"

"Yes," he said.

In the winter, she often sat staring at the white ceiling and walls in the kitchen, the white of the snow stuck against the kitchen windows, the endless white of the prairies, the white sheep in the distance, the distant mountains like torn white cardboard, the sky an endless white blanket, and the black-and-white magpies squawking for the white mutton suet she laid out for them.

She thought how it would be to let the director take her, and to become a star. She saw herself lying in his bed under a silk canopy, the sun shining through the stained-glass windows, shedding colored patterns across the room, the Oriental rugs on the floor like the ones she'd seen in the magazines, and the man, renewed by the night, was on her again in the morning. The man took it from her like he had a right to it, spread her legs with strong hands and devoured her as if what she had belonged to him.

An obdurate excitement crept up, the beast wanting her, the beast hot and musky and mad, and she felt the madness envelop her, as if they both would drown in it. At last, she gave it back. It was a sin; she knew that. She'd lain naked and open for the man and before God.

It was rape, the man taking it like that when there was no love. But she couldn't stop him. She could only lie there exposed to his feral thrusting, to devour it in self-defense until it gave up and shriveled up, and she became the victor over rape, the man, soft and quiet now, his insanity released, lying there covered with sweat, his having succumbed to her.

And she hadn't wasted her beauty. After that, the starring role would belong to her, because he said her legs were perfect, and he said her breasts were magnificent—and the star must have perfect legs and powerful breasts. And the star should be blond, because men liked blondes the best, and the director said he liked her natural blondness all over, that it was delectable. That was the word he used, *delectable*.

She'd become resigned to her dreams. Her husband was trapped in the hands of the sheriff, but she was in the trap with him. The state had him, and if the state killed him, it would create another trap, a widow with a child and no place to go except to her parents' home, which would be the trap of all traps.

How could she not love such a deeply decent man, one with all the masculine traits of any woman's dreams? She should feel worshipful of a husband who'd give up his life for their son. But she'd let Ben make the sacrifice. She was a mother first.

At the noon recess, when the two deputies led Eckersly down the long hall from the courtroom in cuffs and chains, she felt a deep, sickening pity. His helplessness. She wanted to run to him and throw her arms around him and protect him as she protected her child. But the law would not allow her even to touch him, not then.

Perhaps never.

THE WITNESS WAITING room offered daylight through a small window that looked out on the frozen landscape. An oak table and armless chairs claimed most of the space.

The state's pathologist sat across from Sarah. He was a dead-looking dandy in a neatly pressed gray silk suit. But for his penciled-in mustache, his face had taken on the look of the cadavers he sliced. He wore a black silk tie and gray kid gloves, which he removed, one finger at a time. The man repulsed her. She tried not to look at him.

"I'm Dr. Peter Lowry." He extended his hand.

She left it extended, a hand that spent most of its time in the bellies of the dead. He retracted his hand. "I did the postmortem on the victim."

"The man who raped me was no victim," Sarah said.

Still smiling the lecher's smile, he asked, "How can you say he was no victim? But for a couple of tendons, the man's foot was shot completely off. I've never seen anything like it, and I've seen plenty of gunshot wounds in my day. He was a victim all right."

She remembered the admonition of Christopher Hampton. It would be better for her husband's case if she remained silent. She turned to stare out the window.

"I know you are cautious about talking to strangers about this case," he said, "but as a man of science, I would find it helpful to know some of the details you might provide as an eyewitness." His teeth were also gray.

"Helpful in convicting my husband, I suppose."

"Quite to the contrary," Lowry said. "I only testify to the facts. How long it took the victim to bleed out is the question."

"Why is that the question?"

"Because if his bleeding was not inhibited by, say, a tourniquet, then nothing could be done to save the man, and if the shooting were an accident, no crime was committed. You see, madam, I don't believe the man was shot where his patrol car was found."

"Why not?" she asked.

He studied his reflection in the room's small window and straightened his tie. "One thing I can say with reasonable medical certainty—that unless a tourniquet were applied to the leg, he would have bled to death in less than half an hour. How long does it take to get from your ranch to the hospital?"

"A couple of hours, if the roads are good."

"Rough roads, I presume?"

"Yes."

"Rough roads would only exacerbate the bleeding," Lowry said.

"It's cold in here."

"I could help," he said, pushing back from his chair.

She turned away, got up, and left him for the ladies' room.

Glancing in the mirror, she saw a woman wearing a plain black dress, her blond hair in accent. She saw the encroaching circles under her eyes. She'd tried to powder them away. They persisted. She would have been too old for the chorus line and too stiffened by her yeoman labors. And she had the child, Ringo. Her love for him choked out such dreams. The child was a touchable dream from the real world, a dream she could feel when she held him to her, one she could hear in his clear boy's voice.

The pathologist's attention sickened her. His staring ripped away her clothes, as if he were cutting the garments from one of his corpses. If he were the last man on this earth, she would never allow him to touch her, not even to shake her hand, not even if he were the director of the show and she would become the star in the morning.

CHAPTER 38

PROSECUTOR RONALD LUCAS in his high, stinging voice directed his next question to the sheriff. "Now, Sheriff Diggs, I take it that you found additional evidence other than footprints in the area of the patrol car up there on the prairies?"

"Why sure. My print man dusted the inside of the car and found Eckersly's fingerprints everyplace. They was on the steerin' wheel—"

"Just a minute," Christopher Hampton objected. "This is the forbidden hearsay again."

"Sustained," the judge ruled.

Of course it was hearsay. Of course the judge sustained the objection. Of course the jury heard the testimony, and of course the jury knew Eckersly's fingerprints were everyplace, even though the judge had sustained Hampton's objection. The defendant would be convicted. The state supreme court would review the record. And the record would be error-free. Hampton knew the drill.

"What else, if anything, did you find at the scene?" Lucas asked.

"We found Harv's shotgun. And I seen where Harv hopped on one leg, fell down into the dirt, and bled."

"What was the deputy's patrol car doing up there in the sagebrush, Sheriff?"

"You'll have to ask Mr. Eckersly that question. I got my own idea."

Hampton was on his feet again. "The sheriff knows better

than that. Mr. Eckersly is presumed innocent and is not required to explain anything. Again I move for a mistrial."

"Well now, calm down," Judge Foster said in his most fatherly way. "We all know he has the right to remain silent. I sustain your objection and instruct the jury to disregard what the sheriff just said. And I admonish you, Sheriff Diggs. You have been around these courtrooms a long time. You know that a defendant is not required to testify. Fifth Amendment. Right, Sheriff?"

"Right."

"So do you withdraw your remark?"

"I do," the sheriff said with a solicitous smile to the judge.

"Thank you, Sheriff," the judge said.

Prosecutor Lucas adjusted his glasses, picked up the short-barreled shotgun that had been lying in a case on the prosecutor's table, and held it out to the sheriff like a person offering something vile. "You recognize this gun?"

"Yeah, that there's the shotgun that Harv carried in his squad car. Found it 'bout twenty feet from where his car was stuck. Gun was layin' on the ground."

"What was the condition of the gun when you found it?"

"Loaded. One shell fired. The empty casing was still in the chamber."

"Did you check the gun for prints?"

"Yeah, but the gun was wiped clean of prints."

"Objection," Hampton said.

"Sustained," the judge said before Hampton could state his grounds. "The sheriff didn't do the work on the fingerprints. We all know that. This is hearsay."

Satisfied he'd cleansed the record, the judge looked down at Lucas with a faint smile of forbearance. "Proceed, Mr. Lucas."

"And do you know why the gun had been taken out of the patrol car?"

"I couldn't say, 'cause I wasn't there when the gun was took out of the car, and Harv is dead and can't talk," Diggs said.

"Were you able to determine where the gun was fired?" Lucas asked.

"Yeah, I can say that fer sure. Anybody could see the hole in the ground. One a them twelve-gauges makes a hell of a blast at point-blank range."

"And where," Lucas asked, "was this hole in the ground in relation to where Deputy Jaycox had been lying and bleeding?"

"Just a few feet away."

"Did you make any measurements?"

"No. Like what difference does it make whether it was twenty-five inches or twenty-nine inches? We try to be practical in my department."

"Did you find any weapons in the vehicle?"

"Yeah. I found Harv's regulation pistol and his knife. He always wore 'em on his belt. His belt with the knife and pistol was layin' on the floor in the front passenger side of the car. Never seen him without it."

"Do you know why his belt with his knife and pistol were lying on the floor of the patrol car?"

"Again, I got my ideas, but I ain't allowed to say, right, Judge?"

"That's right, Sheriff," the judge interposed. "Your ideas, although they may be right, are not evidence."

Hampton was on his feet again. "His ideas may also be wrong."

"Well, yes," the judge admitted. "Let's not quibble, gentlemen. Let's put the evidence before the jury and let them decide what happened. That's the way we do things in this country, isn't it, Mr. Hampton?"

"I would hope so," Hampton replied, retreating slowly to his chair.

Diggs offered, "Well, it was pretty strange that Harv's belt was layin' there on the floor of the car, and he was outside the car, layin' on the ground."

Hampton was on his feet again. "I move that the last volunteered statement be stricken, the jury admonished to disregard it, and the witness instructed to desist this improper and prejudicial conduct. If it happens again, I'm going to renew my motion for a mistrial."

"Well, well, well," the judge said, "we are getting a little far afield here, Sheriff. Your objection is sustained, Mr. Hampton. You are admonished, Sheriff."

As Hampton took his seat, he added, "What's strange is that the sheriff won't follow your rulings."

"You are admonished, too, Mr. Hampton," the judge said, as if to make things equal. He turned to Ronald Lucas. "Proceed, Mr. Lucas, with your next question."

CHAPTER 39

"I WANT TO talk to you about what's good for this family of yours," Christopher Hampton said to Ben Eckersly. "If we tell the jury the truth—that Ringo shot Jaycox because he was raping his mother—the jury might turn you loose. And your boy has a complete defense—saving his mother. Everybody goes home free!"

"What kind of a father hides behind his child?" Eckersly asked. "I have a right and a duty to protect my son. He's been through enough."

"Think about what it's going to be like if you go to prison for the next twenty years—maybe for life—and the boy has to live without a father."

"He lives with at least an honorable one," Eckersly said.

"Good Christ, Ben, the distinction between being honorable and being stupid is pretty damn narrow. We maybe can win this case with the truth. Just put the boy on. Let the truth come out. The jury has a way of knowing the truth."

Eckersly remained unmoved. "I'll tell the truth. I took Jaycox up there and was going to leave him. Then Sarah brought me to my senses, and I went back for him. It's the truth. The jury will believe me. I'm going to tell just that one small lie—that I shot him when Jaycox and I were wrestling for the gun, not Ringo. Besides, he might have died anyway," Eckersly added.

"But they'll put on an expert who'll testify that Jaycox would have lived if he'd been promptly taken to the hospital," Hampton said. "The expert will testify that your jostling him over your shoulder through all that rough country to your pickup was what killed him."

"I killed him trying to save him," Eckersly said. Then he added quietly, as if to himself, "I probably did kill the man. He had it coming. And if that's murder, I have to take what I've got coming. I'm keeping Ringo out of this. A father has a right to save his son."

"We write our own tickets," Hampton said, his words coated in exasperation.

Once more, silence took over.

At last, Eckersly's face softened, his jaws relaxed, and his eyes grew gentle. "Ringo is an artist. He has something I don't have." He was speaking slowly, as if he got satisfaction from his words. "I want Ringo free of this mess. Maybe someday he can paint great pictures. We've saved every one of his drawings. You should see 'em, Christopher. He's got a natural genius for it. Sometimes I wish I could be like him." He looked into the distance. "And in ways, he's already a man. It's a little unusual that a man should hold up his eleven-year-old son as his hero."

BEFORE THE TRIAL began, Ronald Lucas had gathered his principal witnesses for a final "pretrial conference," as he called it. He said he needed to have all of his witnesses on the same page. They were sitting around an oak table in Lucas's small conference room, listening to one another as each told his story.

"I think Eckersly is protecting his kid," Deputy Hullberry said.

"Yeah, I heard that," Deputy Hayward said.

"It's not our problem if Eckersly wants to go down for his kid," Lucas said. "Bedsides, if the kid goes down, he only ends up in the reformatory for a couple of years. And maybe the kid's lying to protect his old man."

"Right," Hullberry said. "It was a beef between Eckersly and Jaycox."

Lucas smiled his approval at Hullberry.

The old jailer, Hank Plowman, was standing up against the wall, trying to dissolve into the plaster. Finally he said, "Well, the kid told me he shot Jaycox because Jaycox was hurting his mother. That's how he put it."

Diggs said, "If I know Jaycox, he was stickin' it to her, and the kid walks in, gets the family shotgun, and shoots him. Then the old man comes along, finds Jaycox there, stuffs him in the patrol car and takes off with him, decides to let him die up there in the sagebrush and tries to make it look like an accident. Then he changes his mind, and Jaycox dies on the way in."

Lucas frowned at Diggs. "If the kid shot Jaycox, but Eckersly comes along and hauls Jaycox out there to die, and he does die, he's guilty of murder. Either way, we got him. But I like my scenario a little better."

To test his argument, and with Diggs and his two deputies as his audience, Lucas began to deliver his proposed final argument to the jury. "This subject, a known hothead—we'll have the guy from the Bureau of Land Management at the trial, the one Eckersly knocked on his ass that time—this Eckersly, had a beef with Jaycox. He pulls a shotgun on him and disarms Jaycox. His pistol and knife, which were found on the floor of his squad car, were always on his belt."

Lucas was pacing the floor. "Eckersly forces Jaycox into the car, gets in the backseat of the squad car, holds the shotgun to Jaycox's head, and makes Jaycox drive the car to the place where the car was later found in the sagebrush. Then he orders Jaycox out of the car and shoots him. Not a nice clean shot through the heart or the head. Instead, he blows his foot off, so that he suffers unbelievable agony as he's slowly bleeding to death. Eckersly watches, his sweet revenge, while Jaycox is helpless and begging for his life."

Lucas stopped long enough to see if his argument was flying with Diggs and his deputies. Satisfied, Lucas continued. "Eckersly drops the shotgun by Jaycox to make it look like an accident. After Jaycox is dead, he picks him up and hauls him down to make it look like he came to his senses and tried to save the man. Then Eckersly comes up with his cock-and-bull story about Jaycox raping his wife. There you have it, gentlemen. Perfect case of first-degree murder."

"How did Eckersly's wife get there?" Diggs asked. "Remember, Jaycox was layin' in her lap when Eckersly drove into the hospital."

"She was probably driving along behind in their vehicle, trying to stop her old man from killing Jaycox."

"What about the kid?" Diggs asked. "The kid keeps claimin' he shot Jaycox."

"Maybe he did. Maybe he didn't. If the kid testifies, I'll argue that he was just a brave little kid trying to protect his father. And I'll dump a fuckin' bucket of scorn on Eckersly for hiding behind his brave little son."

"Sounds good," Diggs said. He turned to the two deputies: "What do you boys think of it?"

They nodded their agreement.

"Well, boys, I'll see you all in court." Lucas slammed his file shut, and leaned back in his chair.

In the hallway, Hank Plowman, stopped Hullberry. "I don't feel quite right about putting the story out that way."

"Why not?" Hullberry asked.

"Well, I don't think it's true."

Hullberry looked down with disdain at the old man. "If we let Eckersly go, the people'll get the idea they can shoot a cop whenever it's fuckin' handy. You're either on the state's team or you're not. What difference does it make if it ain't exactly what happened?"

"Well, if it ain't true, it ain't right," the old man said.

"We'll never know exactly what happened," Hullberry said. "If a man's guilty, it don't make any difference what song and dance we put out, so long as it gets the job done. Now wouldn't you agree?"

"I don't know," the old man said. Then he waddled down the hall, looking straight ahead.

PROSECUTOR LUCAS FLIPPED to the next page in his trial notebook. "As an expert, Sheriff Diggs, state whether or not the evidence establishes that the defendant"—Lucas stabbed a finger in Eckersly's direction—"drove that squad car up there, disarmed the deputy, took him out of the car, and shot him."

"That's improper for a whole raft of reasons," Hampton objected. "First, it's leading. Second, it invades the province of the jury. Third, this is not a matter that calls for an expert opinion. Fourth—"

"Stop!" the judge ordered. "Please stop, Mr. Hampton! As my old grandfather used to say, 'Enough is enough and too much is aplenty.' Your objection is sustained." Most of the jurors laughed.

Lucas began anew. "Well, Sheriff, are these facts consistent with the defendant having forced the deputy from the car and then shot him with his own shotgun?"

Hampton asked to approach the bench, where he whispered fervently to the judge, "Once more, I move for a mistrial. Your instructions to the jury do not unring *this* bell. This jury is now saturated with the idea that Mr. Eckersly hauled the deputy up there at gunpoint, shot him, and left him there to die. I can't dispel that story without putting Mr. Eckersly on the stand. That forces him to give up his Fifth Amendment rights against self-incrimination. You must grant a mistrial."

"I must or I can?" the judge asked Hampton.

"You must."

"I overrule your motion, Mr. Hampton, because the jury could, indeed, come to the very conclusion that Mr. Lucas has offered. Nothing he suggested is outside the inferences that may be properly drawn from this evidence. Although his question is pure argument, I will instruct the jury on the matter. We have an intelligent jury. And the jurors will follow my instructions."

CHAPTER 40

SARAH ECKERSLY, WAITING to testify, returned from the ladies' room, and without acknowledging the presence of Dr. Peter Lowry, the pathologist, she grabbed a paperback novel from her purse and began to read. She saw the words on the page like one sees leaves all at once on the trees.

She looked up, only to see Lowry staring at her, his disgusting message fully displayed. She quickly retreated into the safety of her book. She should leave rather than let the man undress her again with his wolfish eyes. But this was the place where the bailiff had told her to wait until she was called to testify.

Her dress was of proper length and was buttoned to her neck. Lowry, a professional man, should display minimal good manners. But he was an unabated beast. She tried to find her place in her novel. Instead, she saw herself on the kitchen table, Jaycox on her like a crazed animal. She hadn't bitten or scratched him. Her underthings weren't ripped. He'd kissed her, hard. She hadn't kissed him back. She should have severed his detestable tongue with her teeth.

She turned to face the pathologist. "What is it with you?" she asked, her voice laden with disgust. "Don't you understand what's happening to my family? My husband is in there. He needs me, but the judge won't let me be in the same room while they butcher him." She shouldn't have spoken to him.

"I'm sorry." His voice revealed a certain calculated compassion.

"You keep staring at me. Don't you understand how uncomfortable that makes a woman?"

"It's the price you must pay for your beauty." His thin mustache widened with his smile. "You prove that God hates men," he said, "because if he loved us, he'd make all women as beautiful as you."

She didn't answer.

"But beauty can be deceiving."

"I've never deceived anyone."

His eyes began their sweeping again. He sat down on the tabletop above her. She could smell his musky cologne. She saw the sharp crease of his pants against his thin legs, his white hands resting on the oaken tabletop, his nails honed and polished and as clean as the dissecting table.

"You have no business sitting there. I don't even know you." She returned to her book.

"You know me all right." His mustache spread into that lurid smile. "I have your husband's life in my hands," he said. "I should think you'd give that some passing consideration."

She looked up from her book.

"The fact I must remember—or forget—is the length of time it would have taken for the deputy to bleed to death had he been left undisturbed after—what shall we call it—the incident. That fact will dictate the result in your husband's case."

Slowly, he lowered his head toward her. At that moment, the door to the witness room opened. It was old Hank, the jailer.

"Oh, excuse me," Hank said. Puzzlement struggled across the old man's face. "The court's in recess until tomorrow morning at nine sharp. You should be on time."

With the same wolfish smile, Dr. Peter Lowry offered Sarah Eckersly a sweep of his hand toward the door. She walked out in front of him with quick steps. Lowry followed her down the hall, and when she stopped to open the door, he touched her shoulder. She turned slightly to hear what he was saying. Then she walked on out, Lowry following her into the Laramie wind of early winter.

CHAPTER 41

CHRISTOPHER HAMPTON WALKED in determined steps to the lectern to cross-examine Sheriff Bill Diggs. The sheriff was a dangerous witness, but Hampton was prepared. He surveyed the jury he'd helped select. The ones he felt more comfortable with, the rebel types, the younger ones with their long hair and jivey ways who dared expose a sneer at the establishment, had all been removed by the prosecutor with his eight challenges.

Hampton, with an equal number of challenges, had taken off the banker and a preacher. Preachers were the worst. He took off a couple of business types. One ran the local hardware store, the other a men's clothing store. The business types would hang their own grandmothers for shoplifting a Tootsie Roll, and then cheat some workingman out of twenty-seven cents at the cash register. Hampton also challenged an insurance salesman, a used-car salesman, and a shoe salesman. *Salesman* was a euphemism for "smiling liar."

Hampton looked at each of the seated jurors.

From left to right in the back row sat a pleasant-appearing grade school teacher, her hands folded firmly over her lap as if to protect herself from any invasion; a vacant-eyed postal employee in a white shirt, blue necktie, and red sweater, whose ears stuck out like the handles on a tin cup; two red-faced, white-foreheaded, squinting ranchers in blue-jean jackets; a retired, rotund railroad clerk in his black wedding suit, which still nearly fit; and a lumberyard clerk in his navy blue Sunday best.

In the front row were seated a soft-jowled, red-faced professor of Latin Studies with small brown eyes like an inquiring rat's; a taxidermist in a brown World War I flier's jacket, whose eyes called to mind the glass eyes he inserted in his stuffed animals; a pleasant-faced, barrel-bellied plumber in starched, pressed bib overalls; a pretty secretary from the university in a plain black dress, who sat prim as a Pilgrim, her legs duly crossed; a bespectacled librarian blinking and blinking in this direction and that, her legs also duly crossed; and finally a housewife, an older woman who sat with her knees knotted tightly together, thereby forming an impenetrable barricade of matronly flesh. Hampton wished he had a dozen more challenges.

He squinted at the sheriff for a long time, as if struggling to form his first question. Finally he said, "Sheriff Diggs, I take it your purpose here is to convince this jury that Mr. Eckersly shot Deputy Jaycox without just cause."

"I'm here to tell the facts, and there weren't no reason at all to kill the man."

"Would Deputy Jaycox's rape of Mr. Eckersly's wife be good cause?"

"I knew Harv Jaycox like my own brother, and he'd never rape nobody. An' Eckersly ain't got no business takin' the law into his own hands. That's what we got a Sheriff's Department for."

"And if the shooting were done to save his wife from an *ongoing* rape, one happening before his eyes?" Hampton looked over at the matronly woman in the front row.

She crossed her arms.

"I never heard of a man, especially in a rape, who'd keep at it in front of somebody. So don't gimme that," Diggs said.

"Would you make room for the possibility that somebody raping somebody isn't paying attention to *anything* except his perverted sexual urges as he forces them on his victim?"

"I wouldn't know."

"The sounds where the rape was taking place would likely include intense screaming, heavy breathing, the rapist cursing, the table on which the act was occurring creaking under the force of the rapist—can you hear those sounds in your mind's ears?"

"Probably nobody was singin' 'The Star-Spangled Banner,'" the sheriff snorted.

"Do you agree that a rapist, intent on his evil act, might not be immediately aware of another person entering the room?"

"If you say so."

"And if you walked into a room where someone was raping your wife, might you not shoot the man to save your wife?"

"A man might do that, but that ain't what happened here, and you know it. My chief deputy was shot up there where that man"—he shook his finger at Eckersly—"took him and shot him. There was bad blood between 'em."

"Did you inspect the kitchen of the Eckersly's house for evidence of shotgun blasts?"

"No."

"Did you look under the rag rug on the floor in the kitchen?"

"No. And if there was some holes there, they coulda been put there after this murder."

Hampton turned quickly to the judge. "I move that his answer be stricken. He has no right to call this a murder."

"It will be stricken," the judge ruled on the edge of a mumble, "and the jury is admonished to disregard the sheriff's conclusion."

"One thing we can agree upon: You don't know why Mr. Eckersly was driving the squad car up there, isn't that true?"

"I got my ideas."

"You don't *know*."

"He never told me. Eckersly wouldn't talk to me."

Hampton objected: "Mr. Eckersly had no duty to speak to the sheriff, and he has the right to remain silent. Once more, I move for a mistrial."

"Overruled," the judge said. "I admonish the jury that the defendant has the right to remain silent, and nothing should be taken for his exercise of that right."

"You don't know *why* Mr. Eckersly drove up there on that hill, isn't that true?"

"In a way I do."

"Can't you admit that what you *think* you know are only your conclusions?"

"I been around awhile," Diggs said.

"Have you been around long enough to learn that your conclusions may be wrong?"

"That's pure argument," Lucas said.

"Sustained," the judge ruled. "Move along, Mr. Hampton."

"Your conclusions presume a crime, isn't that true?"

"You could say that."

"But aren't you supposed to presume Mr. Eckersly innocent instead of guilty?"

"That's pure argument," Lucas snorted.

"Sustained," the judge ruled. "Perhaps we could get to some facts here."

Hampton turned back to Diggs. "You, of course, recovered bits and pieces of the deputy's foot out there on the prairie by the squad car, where you claim the deputy was shot?"

"No."

"No?" Hampton paused, astounded. "No? Are you saying you didn't find numerous pieces of bone where you claim this shooting took place?"

"No."

Hampton raised his eyebrows and waited for the jury to consider Diggs's answer. "You claim there was bad blood between Mr. Eckersly and Mr. Jaycox?"

"Yeah."

"Could you make room for the possibility that it wasn't bad blood, that it was a father trying to protect a small boy from bulling by you and your deputies?"

"That there's a lie, and you know it." Diggs threw his head back in defiance, so that his great beak created a long shadow across his cheek. "I always did think it was too bad that that boy—nice boy, too—learned of violence from his father."

The judge interposed his own objection. "That was uncalled for, Sheriff Diggs. Any more volunteering like that and we'll have a serious problem. Do you understand?"

The sheriff nodded, and with that Hampton sat down. He thought he should stop while he was marginally ahead.

Lucas stomped to the lectern. "You say you didn't find any pieces of flesh or bone out there by the squad car. Did you find that unusual?"

"No. The prairie's loaded with varmints—coyotes, hawks, rats, and critters like that. All that stuff was probably eaten or carried away."

"Thank you," Lucas said, with a small gesture of his head proclaiming he'd won the fight.

CHAPTER 42

Laramie, Conrad Hotel, 1947

ON A SLEEPY Sunday night at the hotel, the night clerk, working a double shift, sat dozing in his chair. His mouth gaped open. His upper plate had slipped from his gums and hung precariously on his lower lip, where it rose and fell with his heavy breathing. Ringo was stretched out on the lobby couch at the end of his weekend double shift.

The phone at the front desk rang.

The old clerk popped his teeth in and, holding on to the reception desk with both hands, struggled on shaky legs to his feet and grabbed the phone.

The clerk listened for a moment and then said, "Not really our problem. Okay, okay, Belle June, I'll send the boy over to fetch him."

The clerk cradled the phone and yelled, "Boy!"

Ringo shook himself awake.

"Go over to Belle June's place and bring back four thirty-seven. They're closing and he's passed out."

Ringo leaped up from the couch. "He was loaded when he checked in, smelled like a brewery. I can't carry him back."

"Drag him if you have to. It's raining. He'll slide easy."

Ringo went out to the cold, wet street, grumbling to himself. He didn't have any sympathy for the room 437 guest. The man had asked where he could get a load off and had tipped him only a quarter when Ringo told him Belle June's place at 213 Front Street had the best reputation.

Ringo liked to recommend Belle June because the madam was known to contribute some of her hard-earned money to programs at the university.

The house of pleasure was up fifteen steps. Ringo rang the doorbell when he reached the landing.

The door opened and Mabel, the maid, her hands on her hefty hips, gauged Ringo. "We're closed, boy."

Blue cigarette smoke drifted through the doorway from behind Mabel.

"I came for the hotel guest."

"He'll be a handful. He's in the kitchen, drunker than a skunk."

The waiting room was empty and the lights dimmed. As Ringo stepped in, he heard 437's complaining, drunken voice coming through the open door to the kitchen.

Then Ringo saw her.

CHAPTER 43

Laramie, Courthouse, 1941

DEPUTY DARWIN HULLBERRY took the stand like a reluctant but dutiful public servant. The slope of his shoulders suggested he'd worked too hard as a boy, and he spoke in the easy way of one with nothing to hide.

"And what happened when you stopped Eckersly on the highway that night?" Prosecutor Lucas asked.

"Well, sir, he cussed us with words I wouldn't use in polite society."

"What, exactly, did he say?"

"Exactly?"

"Yes, exactly."

"He said, 'You motherfuckers, I'll get you. You don't fuck with me.'"

"What did you do then?"

"I told him he was under arrest for obstructin' justice, and he started for me. I pulled my weapon, and he grabbed the kid and started screamin', 'Don't shoot me. Don't shoot me. You'll hit the kid,' and he was all hunkered down behind the kid, shivering like a cornered rat."

"And then?"

"Well, Chief Deputy Jaycox come up from behind him and put a choke on him. We cuffed him, and he started cryin'." Hullberry's plain, pockmarked face lent a sense of rugged authenticity to his story.

Eckersly leaned over to Christopher Hampton and whispered, "That's a filthy damn lie."

The jurors watched.

"And what did you do after you cuffed him?" Lucas asked.

"We brought him in. He cussed us all the way—especially at Harv Jaycox for using that chokehold on him. Kept sayin' to Harv, 'I'll get you, you motherfucker.'"

Christopher Hampton could feel Eckersly tensing as if to jump up. Hampton whispered, "Don't react. You'll only prove to the jurors that what he's saying is true."

"Your witness," Lucas said to Hampton.

Hampton started slowly, easily, like a boxer feeling out his opponent in the first round. "One thing we can agree on, Deputy Hullberry: It's your word against Mr. Eckersly's, isn't that true?"

Lucas objected: "That's argument, pure and simple."

"Sustained," the judge ruled.

"And the only way that Mr. Eckersly can refute what you've just said is for him to testify and thereby forfeit his Fifth Amendment privilege, which guarantees he need not testify, isn't that true?"

"Argument," Lucas objected.

"Sustained," the judge ruled.

"Mr. Eckersly, like our jurors, has had no training in the courtroom. Do you think it would be a fair contest to put Mr. Eckersly up against a highly trained courtroom lawyer like Mr. Lucas?"

"That's pure unadulterated argument," Lucas objected.

"Sustained," the judge ruled.

"That would be like pitting any one of these jurors against a professional boxer in a boxing match, and that's why Mr. Lucas is attempting to force Mr. Eckersly to take the stand. Do you think that would be a fair fight?"

"This is pure argument," Lucas objected, "and nothing but an argument."

"It may be argument, but it's the truth," Hampton replied before the court could rule.

"Save your argument for the jury," the judge said. "Let's see if you can proceed by simply asking a question, Mr. Hampton. If you can't, you may sit down."

Hampton leafed through his notes. Finally he said, "You know that Mr. Eckersly got into the squad car peacefully, without incident, don't you?"

"That ain't so."

"And who is to contradict you?"

"He can if he wants to." Hullberry pointed at Eckersly.

"Yes, of course." Suddenly, Hampton changed course. "Mr. Eckersly was there with his small boy, true?"

"Yes."

"A father not only has the right but the duty to protect his son, doesn't he?"

"We never touched the boy."

"Were you present when this child was interrogated by the sheriff and Harvey Jaycox?"

"No, I wasn't."

"But you know this boy was being interrogated by the sheriff about a murder of the boy's teacher that the boy couldn't have committed because the teacher was alive when the boy got on the bus to go home."

"I heard it."

"You also know another lad has been charged with this crime, and that the charges against Ringo Eckersly have been dropped."

"I heard it."

"Do you have an explanation as to why this child was harassed about a murder that he didn't commit?"

"I wasn't there."

Hampton fingered through his file and extracted a copy of Ringo's confession. "You've seen the sheriff interrogate witnesses before, haven't you?"

"Yeah."

"You know his methods."

"What methods?"

"His use of profanity, threats, and fear."

"I've never known the sheriff to do that," Hullberry said.

"So the sheriff is always a gentleman when he interrogates kids from whom he's attempting to force a confession?"

"I've seen him get a little impatient."

"You know that this boy had a right not to be interrogated in absence of a parent. And his father had the right and the duty to protect his child from harassment. Isn't all of that true?"

"If you say so," Hullberry said.

"But for some reason, there was an attempt to get the boy to confess to a killing some other boy is now charged with. Could you help us understand how that could happen?"

"You'd have to ask the sheriff."

"You know that Mr. Eckersly brought his son into the sheriff's office voluntarily."

"Yeah."

"Mr. Eckersly didn't have to take his son in to see the sheriff. There was no warrant for his arrest, isn't that true?"

"You'll have to ask the sheriff."

"You pulled Mr. Eckersly over with lights and a siren as he and his boy were driving home, and you told him he was charged with obstructing justice, isn't that true?"

"Yes."

"That was a false arrest, wasn't it?"

"No."

"Protecting the rights of a small boy is hardly obstructing justice, is it, Deputy Hullberry?"

Lucas objected. "That's argument."

"It may be," the judge said. "I'll let him answer."

"I'm not a lawyer. I was told to bring him in."

"So what we have here is a father whose only crime was his attempt to protect his child from this sheriff, isn't that true?"

Lucas: "Objection. Argumentative."

The judge: "Sustained."

"You claim Mr. Eckersly resisted you when you tried to arrest him?"

"He sure as hell did."

"Mr. Eckersly stopped his pickup when you put your flashers on, and he got out of his pickup voluntarily?"

"Yeah."

"You pushed him up against his pickup truck and patted him down, looking for weapons, and he let you do that, isn't that true?"

"To a point."

"And the rest of your testimony in that regard is totally false, isn't it?"

"No, it isn't," Hullberry said.

"Didn't you and Prosecutor Lucas plan this strategy in an attempt to force Mr. Eckersly to give up his Fifth Amendment rights?"

"We never did any such thing," Hullberry said.

"Of course not," Hampton said. "I have no further questions of this witness."

HANK PLOWMAN, THE old jailer, plodded to the stand. He said he didn't know Mr. Eckersly but that he played poker with Mr. Hampton once in a while down at the card room.

"I see," Lucas said, as if conceding colossal misconduct of his witness. "Did you see Mr. Eckersly the night he was incarcerated in our jail?"

"Yes."

"Did you overhear him make any threats that night?"

The old man didn't answer.

"Well, did you?"

The old man was talking into his hands. "I heard him tell his lawyer he better not get him out of jail that night, because he was liable to kill somebody."

"Did he say who he might kill?"

"No."

"That's all the questions I have of this witness," Lucas said with a victorious flourish.

As usual, Christopher Hampton began his cross-examination slowly and in a friendly tone. "Part of playing poker is that you have to lay your whole hand down if someone calls your bet, right? Have you laid your whole hand down?"

"What do you mean?"

"Objected to, Your Honor," Lucas said. "This is nothing but a fishing expedition and falls outside the scope of my direct examination."

"Sustained," the judge ruled. "If you have a specific question, ask it, Mr. Hampton."

Hampton turned to Plowman. "You met with the prosecutor, Mr. Lucas, before you took the stand, didn't you?"

"Yes."

"And you told prosecutor Lucas something you haven't told this jury, isn't that true?" Pure guess.

The old man looked over at Lucas. Seeing the prosecutor's glare, he turned back, looked at his feet, and said, "I can't remember."

"What was the subject of your conversation?"

"I can't remember."

"When did this conversation take place?"

"I can't remember."

"Where did it take place?"

"I can't remember."

"You told Mr. Lucas you thought Mr. Eckersly was innocent, didn't you?"

"I can't remember."

"And Mr. Lucas told you that if you got into trouble up here on the witness stand, just to say 'I can't remember,' isn't that true?"

"I can't remember."

"Are you more honest in playing poker than you are testifying on this witness stand—that is, when I called you, did you lay your whole hand down?"

"That's ridiculous!" Lucas said. "I object."

"Sustained," the judge said.

Hampton turned to Eckersly and whispered, "I think I can get this old boy to admit that Ringo told him *he* shot Jaycox. If I can get him to admit it, we won't have to call Ringo to the stand. This may be our last and only chance."

"I don't want Ringo involved in any way. He's gone through enough already."

"You write your own history, and unfortunately, you write Ringo's, as well." Hampton turned to the judge. "I have no further questions of this witness."

CHAPTER 44

THE PATHOLOGIST, DR. Peter Lowry, his penciled mustache in place, a smile welded on his face, was duly sworn and his qualifications laid out in painful detail by prosecutor Lucas—his residency in pathology, his decades of experience, the numerous articles he'd published, the various professional honors bestowed on him, and on and on, so it appeared the man knew everything, past, present, and in the world to come, concerning the human organism and its fleeting trek on this planet. Moreover, he was a professor at the University of Wyoming.

"And do you have an opinion, Dr. Lowry, based on reasonable medical certainty, as to the cause of Deputy Jaycox's death?"

"Yes, simply put, he bled to death, with an onset of shock secondary to a gunshot wound to the foot." He flicked a speck off the sleeve of his gray suit coat.

"Now, Doctor, do you have an opinion as to how long it took for Chief Deputy Jaycox to die?"

"Yes, I do. It depends on whether anyone was successful in stopping the bleeding between the time he was shot and the time he arrived at the hospital. Any such success would, of course, have extended his life."

"I see," Lucas said. "And so do you have an opinion as to a range of time during which the deceased bled to death?"

"Yes, I believe under the circumstances of this case it took

Chief Deputy Jaycox between two and three hours to bleed out and die from lack of blood and from secondary shock."

"So had the defendant"—Lucas was jabbing his finger at Eckersly—"taken the victim directly to the hospital, his life could have been saved?"

"Given prompt and proper treatment on arrival at the hospital, that is a likelihood."

"Thank you," Lucas said. He turned to Christopher Hampton with a budding snarl. "Your witness, counsel."

Hampton stood, taking in the smiling pathologist.

Finally the judge, as if to awaken Hampton, prompted, "Mr. Hampton?"

"I was just thinking, Your Honor."

"That's a dangerous undertaking, Mr. Hampton," the judge quipped.

Hampton turned to Dr. Lowry. "You gave the time required to bleed out, 'under the circumstances of this case,' as from two to three hours. *What* circumstances?"

"I was wondering when someone was going to ask me that," Dr. Lowry said. "I believe this man was treated with a tourniquet. Without a tourniquet, he would likely have died within half an hour, maybe less, considering the extent of the unattended blood loss and the accompanying shock."

"Would you have told us that if I hadn't asked you the question?"

"I don't know."

"Did you tell Mr. Lucas that before you took the stand?"

"Yes."

"So he knew all along that Deputy Jaycox likely would have bled to death after being shot but for the application of a tourniquet, isn't that true?"

"I told Mr. Lucas."

"Did you inquire as to who might have applied this tourniquet?"

"Yes, I did. I inquired of Mrs. Eckersly."

"And where did this discussion take place?"

"In our offices."

"Your offices?" Hampton asked in surprise. "When did this occur?"

"Yesterday," he said.

"And did you learn from Mrs. Eckersly that a tourniquet had been applied to Deputy Jaycox?"

"That's hearsay," Lucas objected.

"This man is an expert," the judge ruled. "Under the rules, he may answer."

"Yes," Dr. Lowry said. "From my conversations with Mrs. Eckersly, I concluded that the victim was provided a tourniquet shortly after his injury, and the nurse in attendance at the hospital confirmed that the tourniquet was in place when the body was received at the hospital."

"As a forensic pathologist, you are somewhat acquainted with the law?"

"Yes."

"Do you contend that Mr. Eckersly had a duty to save the life of Deputy Jaycox if he shot Jaycox to stop his rape of Mrs. Eckersly?"

"Objection," Lucas said. "The question is argumentative."

"Your Honor," Hampton retorted quickly, "if Deputy Jaycox was shot in an attempt to stop an ongoing rape, Mr. Eckersley had no duty to save the man's life."

Lucas rose from his table and, gesturing with both hands as if beseeching reason, cried, "There isn't the slightest evidence that this shooting was justified. The evidence is that the gunshot amputation of Chief Deputy Jaycox's leg was vicious and malicious and born of bad blood between the victim and the defendant. The evidence is that the defendant intended—and I repeat, *intended*—that his victim die slowly and painfully, and he took pains to make the shooting appear as an accident until, for reasons we have yet to determine, he had a change of heart."

Lucas stepped closer to the bench. "But even if the shooting were lawful, and even if Eckersly tried to stop the bleeding, once he took the life of Chief Deputy Jaycox in his hands and decided to abandon him on the prairie to die, he became criminally responsible for his death. That he changed his mind does not—I repeat, *does not*—relieve him of that crime."

The prosecutor sauntered confidently past the jurors, taking them in as he passed. "If a person attempted to save an occupant in a car wreck by giving him aid but then decided to drive the bleeding victim out someplace where, for his own malicious reasons, he abandoned him and let him bleed to death, slowly, painfully, intentionally, that citizen would be guilty of murder!"

Hampton jumped up. "But if the accident victim would have died no matter what aid was given or withheld, how could that person be guilty of a crime? Tell me that."

"I'll tell you how," Lucas said. "If he deprived the victim of one minute of life, he's guilty of murder. Moreover—"

Judge Foster interrupted. "Well, gentlemen, I've given you both the opportunity to state your respective cases. The jury will have an opportunity to decide this under a proper instruction on the law. Mr. Lucas's objection is sustained. Proceed, Mr. Hampton."

Eckersly whispered to Hampton, "Ringo put the tourniquet on Jaycox. It was on him when I got there."

Hampton turned back to the witness. "So, Dr. Lowry, if someone hadn't made a conscious effort to save Deputy Jaycox, he would have died long before he could have reached the hospital under the best of scenarios, isn't that true?"

"That's my opinion."

"Thank you," Hampton said, and sat down.

But Lucas had more questions. "Once the tourniquet was placed on Deputy Jaycox's leg and the bleeding stopped, he could have lived two, maybe three hours, isn't that also true?"

"Presumably," Dr. Lowry replied.

"Did you discover from your conversation with Mrs. Eckersly, who, I'm told, was holding the deputy's head in her lap on the way to the hospital, *when* the deputy took his last breath?"

"I neglected to inquire," the pathologist said.

Hampton, too, was on his feet: "If the time of Jaycox's death can't be established, then Eckersly's detour with Jaycox can't be proven as the cause of his death, isn't that true?"

"That's right, counsel," Dr. Lowry said.

Prosecutor Lucas pondered for a moment. "You say that you had this conversation with Mrs. Eckersly in your offices?"

"Yes."

"And where in your offices?"

"In the adjoining examining room belonging to my associate, Dr. Jameson."

"And why did you have this conversation in an examining room?"

"For privacy." Dr. Lowry said, his indelible smile still challenging the prosecutor. "My laboratory is hardly a place to interview anyone. Had I been interviewing you, I would have taken you into the privacy of an examining room."

"I see," Lucas said. "Yes, I see it all quite plainly. I have no further questions of this witness."

Dr. Lowry got up from the witness stand and was taking his first steps toward the exit when Lucas, who had been returning to counsel table, stopped and, facing the departing Lowry, asked, "Isn't Dr. Jameson a gynecologist?"

Dr. Lowry stopped. "Yes."

"My understanding is that there are two furnishings in a gynecologist's examining room: one a chair, and the other the examining table with stirrups.When you had your private conversation with Mrs. Eckersly, which did she occupy?"

The smile slowly faded from Lowry's face. Finally he said, "You are an impudent son of a bitch," and with that he stomped out of the courtroom to the sound of the judge's gavel slamming and slamming again and again.

CHAPTER 45

Sheriff's Office, 1940

SHERIFF DIGGS STUCK his pesky, protrudent nose like an accusing finger into Ham Swanker's face. "So where the fuck's the knife you say you stabbed your teacher with?"

"I don't know, sir," Ham said. "It must have had legs and walked off."

Diggs started to smack the boy, but thinking the soft approach might be better with a smart kid like Ham, he said, "You probably got it hid someplace. So how did this here murder happen, son?"

"It was an accident. I was struggling with our teacher for my knife, and I was backing up, and I must have tripped and fell, and she fell on top of me."

"Right, kid. Tell me another."

"I was innocently trying to retrieve my knife."

"That's bullshit," Diggs hollered. "I'm gonna send you to the pen, and they're gonna make you eat shit for the rest of your fuckin' life."

"Hardly," Ham countered. "Your threats notwithstanding, I'm but fourteen years of age, and I'm still a juvenile under the law. Therefore, the most egregious penalty that can be foisted on me is the reformatory at Rawlins. I will suffer there until the state's only option will be to free me."

"You're a smart little bastard, even if you can't speak the fuckin' English language."

"Moreover, any outcome in this case will be far more acceptable to me than sending me home. If you send me home, my father will likely beat me to death."

Half an hour later, Diggs returned and shoved a written confession in front of Ham. "You sign this, or I'll send you home to your old man."

Without reading the confession, Ham signed it. Then he looked up at the sheriff and smiled.

Later, Sheriff Diggs said to Deputy Hullberry, "Maybe he didn't intend to kill the teacher. But it's the phoniest excuse I ever heard."

"Those Swankers got a lotta money, but they're a lyin' bunch of lowlifes," Hullberry said.

"How do you think they got all their money—tellin' the fuckin' gospel truth and singin' in the church choir?" Sheriff Diggs replied. "What we got here is a fourteen-year-old. I can probably get him prosecuted as an adult, but the jury might just buy his bullshit. Maybe it *was* just an accident."

"You're getting' soft in your old age," Hullberry said. "They oughta send the murderin' little bastard to the gas chamber."

"But remember, he's got somethin' he can give us," Diggs said.

After Ham signed the confession—admitting that he outright stabbed his teacher in the chest because she was going to report him to his father, and he was afraid his father would beat him to death—Diggs continued with his interrogation of Ham. "You know who shot my chief deputy, Harv Jaycox, don't you?" The sheriff's eyes were on the boy like those of a hawk with its talons sunk in deep.

"I wasn't an eyewitness to the event," Ham said.

"Of course you never seen it," Diggs said. "I suppose your gonna tell me that your buddy Ringo had nothin' to do with it."

"He's my brother," Ham said.

"Oh, Christ on a crutch!" Diggs moaned. "That's a bunch of bullshit. Anyways, if you wanna save your brother, you better tell me how that Eckersly bastard admitted that night that he killed my chief deputy, Harv."

"He actually did admit it," Ham said. "He told Ringo and me that he was responsible for the death of Deputy Jaycox—not Ringo."

"How the fuck did that come up?"

"Ringo was attempting to convince his father that he killed Jaycox, but his father said no, that he was responsible for the deputy's death. Ringo would never kill anyone, much less a deputy sheriff."

Having pled guilty to murder, Ham ended up at the state's reformatory for boys at Worland.

FOR ECKERSLY'S TRIAL, Diggs got Ham all dressed up in a new blue suit, a white shirt, and a new pair of black lace-up, low-cut street shoes. He wore a red-checkered necktie, not too flashy, and his hair was freshly cut and slicked back with hair oil, so that he looked as honest and handsome as any young Mormon missionary about to knock on the door of some unsuspecting Baptist householder.

Prosecutor Lucas and Sheriff Diggs argued about calling Ham as a state's witness. Lucas said, "This kid, as smart as he is, will never stand up to cross-examination. Remember, he's just fourteen years old. And he's a confessed murderer doing time at the state's reform school. Am I supposed to put a murderer on the stand to convict Eckersly of murder? I already got him convicted."

"You ain't quite got him yet," Diggs said. "I was talkin' to Suzy Layman last night. You know Suzy. She comes to all our trials, and she ain't hardly ever wrong. She says she can't believe a nice-lookin' man like Eckersly woulda done that. An' she says even if he done it, he probably had good reason. She says that if she was on the jury, she'd be askin' a lot of questions—like how come there weren't the first sign of Harv's foot out there? Hawks and mice don't eat the bone and boot pieces that would've been there."

Lucas was thumbing through his file while Diggs was talking.

"But the big thing, Suzy says, is that Jaycox probably would've bled to death no matter what Eckersly done, and she ain't all that sure he done anythin'. It's the way he sits there in the courtroom lookin' handsome and innocent as hell. And she likes his lawyer. She thinks you're a mean little punk. Course she's wrong about that." Diggs laughed.

"She's a gossipy old whinny," Lucas said.

"Yeah, but she usually hangs in about where the jury is. Woman's intuition, she says."

"Women don't have intuition," Lucas said. "Women have suspicious minds and big imaginations. Sometimes they get lucky and call it intuition."

"I been watchin' this jury. You might just be losin' this one, Ron."

"Don't see how. Hampton hasn't laid a fucking finger on me."

"Well, we got this Swanker kid all dressed up and ready to go, and he'll say Eckersly admitted killin' Harv Jaycox. Up to you if you wanna call him."

Lucas thought that if he didn't call the Swanker kid, and he lost the case, Diggs would claim it was because he wouldn't take his advice and put the kid on the stand. So Lucas called Ham Swanker to testify.

Lucas took meticulous pains to lay Ham's whole story out to the jury so that there'd be no backfire when Hampton cross-examined.

"So, Ham, you reside at the Boys' School at Worland? Why?"

"I am guilty of nothing. You are looking at an innocent victim of the system. I was charged with murder, and I pled guilty."

Since his detention at the Boys' School, Ham had developed an aggressive overtone. "I signed a confession because Sheriff Diggs said if I didn't, he'd send me home, and—I hope my father hears this—I'd rather be confined as a juvenile offender, indeed, as a murderer, than pass over the threshold of my home again. My father would have beaten me to death. He beat me as a matter of habit. Would the jurors care to see the scars?" He started to take off his coat.

"That won't be necessary," Lucas said. "So you ran away after your schoolteacher was killed and hid out. But a few days later, Mr. Eckersly discovered where you'd been hiding?"

"Yes. Ringo and me."

"And how do you know that Mr. Eckersly killed Deputy Jaycox?"

Christopher Hampton jumped to his feet as if he were spring-loaded. "Objection! This boy's testimony is gross hearsay."

Before the judge could rule, Ham said, "Ringo said he killed Deputy Jaycox, but his father said, no, *he* killed the deputy."

Lucas turned to Hampton. "You may examine."

Hampton leaned over and whispered to Eckersly. "Maybe I can get this kid to admit he wanted to protect his so-called brother, Ringo, from a charge of murder."

"Stay out of that," Eckersly said. "You know how I feel about putting any focus on Ringo."

Hampton rose slowly, shuffled through the papers, and in a friendly voice said, "You look nice, Ham. Sheriff got you all dressed up?"

Ham nodded.

"New suit?"

Ham nodded.

"Haircut?"

Ham nodded.

"How do you like it at the Boys' School?"

"It's tolerable, but barely. We are treated as vicious incarcerated animals, as it were."

"The sheriff has been good to you?"

"I am grateful. He kept my father at bay, so to speak. Never let him get near me."

"And if you don't say what Sheriff Diggs wants you to say, he threatens to send you home to your father, isn't that true?"

Ham nodded in the affirmative.

"Is that a 'yes'?"

"Yes," Ham said.

Hampton offered Ham a kindly father smile and sat down.

During the recess, Lucas and Diggs were at the water fountain. "I told you we shouldn't call that smart-ass kid," Lucas said. "I talked to Suzy Layman myself. She told me she thought you threatened the kid. She said, 'That boy, Ham, couldn't have killed his teacher.' She said, 'I know Sheriff Diggs. He can be pretty tough, and the kid may be fourteen, but he's just a child. Diggs has him like a dog on a leash,' and she was pretty upset."

"So what you gonna do 'bout that?" Diggs asked Lucas.

"Eckersly is protecting his kid, right? Let's see how much he wants to protect him. Get a subpoena out for Eckersly's kid," Lucas said.

"Jesus H. Christ!" Diggs exclaimed.

"More than one can play this game. I'm going to rest my case. We'll see what kind of a defense Eckersly lets Hampton put on when he finds out I got his kid subpoenaed to testify as my rebuttal witness against his *own* father. Then things are going to start falling apart." Lucas sauntered down the hall in long steps, his feet slapping angrily on the marble tile.

Diggs hollered after him, "I don't think you wanna call that Eckersly boy to testify," but Diggs didn't know whether Lucas had heard him.

CHAPTER 46

SARAH ECKERSLY SLIPPED up to prosecutor Ronald Lucas as he got to his car.

She spoke his name softly, and when he stopped and turned, she stepped up to him with a smile on her face, suddenly withdrew her husband's razor-sharp hunting knife from under her coat, and stabbed him in the chest like the teacher had been stabbed.

She knew her fantasies were but her hate-filled offerings to her demons, and that in the light of day they'd slink slowly away. She pulled the covers tightly around her shoulders and reached over to where her husband would have slept.

The bed was cold in the small motel where Hampton had deposited her for the trial. She'd kept Eckersly's side of the bed untouched, as if to sleep there was to admit he'd never come home again. The sound of his heavy breathing had been a comfort to her, the warmth of his body warming hers. She thought of the lies she'd tell on the witness stand to save him. Of course she'd lie.

But other visions kept breaking through. She saw the skinny, white-bodied Dr. Lowry, his arms like a girl's arms. She saw the small sprinkling of hair on his spindly chest. She retched. She tried to drive the memory from her mind, but the feel of him kept flooding in, and the feeling froze the fluids of her heart.

She tried to lead her mind to other times. She thought of the night she and Eckersly had gone to the dance at the Honikers' wedding. Maybe they'd had too much to drink. She'd always rationed her passion as if it were a fund that could never be replenished. That night in Eckersly's animal urgency, his powerful body taking from her what he wanted, he'd plunged her into a forgotten place she'd only felt before with Jim Skaggs.

The following morning, she'd seen Eckersly's shame. His eyes, which usually took their morning feast of her, were locked on his breakfast plate. It was as if he'd raped her. But Sarah, surprised and silent, in some strange way, felt satisfied.

Lowry's body had felt like a dead frog, his mascaraed mustache smeared on her mouth. When it was over, she'd scrubbed at her face to wash the awful black away. She hadn't fought him. She'd given him nothing. The price for his testimony to save Eckersly was no price. How could it be anything if it were extorted from her and not given?

But in the darkness of her bed, she saw where she'd been—in the stirrups of a gynecologist's examining room, Lowry's hands in rubber gloves, so that he'd seemed encased in a condom. There being no one to hear her, she had let her sobs escape untethered into the listening night.

WHEN THE JUDGE CALLED the court to order that morning, prosecutor Lucas rested the state's case. Christopher Hampton requested a short recess.

"No," Judge Emery Foster ordered. "We're going to get this case over with. Call your first witness, Mr. Hampton."

Hampton retrieved Sarah Eckersly from the witness room and escorted her down the long aisle through the spectators' gallery. They walked past where her husband sat, and without looking in his direction, she proceeded toward the witness stand.

Each of her steps was taken with caution, as if she were on the edge of collapse. At once, Eckersly experienced a visceral rush. He wanted to jump up and save her from what he knew was about to happen and that would burn irreparable scars on their lives. He watched her settle into the witness chair. He could have stopped it—a word whispered to Hampton. But his case belonged to her, as well. And he had no right to deprive her of saying what she wanted to say—words she'd never shared with him.

Her black dress, a widow's dress, extended to her crossed ankles. She wore low-heeled black shoes. Her long blond hair had been shortened to accommodate the working cap she wore at the ranch. Resigned to her fate, she turned to Hampton, awaiting his first question.

"You are Sarah Eckersly, the wife of Ben Eckersly, who sits here at counsel table?"

"Yes," she said in a distant voice.

"Under the law, husbands and wives are granted what the law calls 'privilege.' Neither husband nor wife can be required to testify for or against the other. Do you understand?"

"Yes."

"You are testifying voluntarily?"

"Yes."

At once, Hampton traveled to the core of her testimony. She told the jurors in an unsteady voice how Harvey Jaycox had returned their son the night her husband had been arrested. She was frightened when the boy came home "in his condition," as she called it, and without his father.

"What do you mean, 'in his condition'?" Hampton asked.

"My son was naked from the waist down."

"What did Chief Deputy Jaycox have to say about that?"

"He said they saved his pants for evidence, and he said he'd saved Ringo. He made a vulgar reference to the fact that otherwise he would have been raped by the other inmates. He said if I would cooperate with him, he'd keep my son out of jail."

"What did you say?"

"I said nothing."

"What did you take him to mean by 'cooperate'?"

Sarah's clutched her fingers together. "He had his feet up on my antique kitchen table and was leering at me in a very vulgar way."

She told how Jaycox came back the next day.

"What happened then?" Hampton asked.

Sarah looked into the audience and saw Betsy Jaycox with her young son on one side and her daughter on the other. How Sarah had dreaded this moment. She knew her testimony would add to the woman's pain, her husband's life smeared with the infamy of rape. What difference if she said they were just making love on the table, and that they were caught in the act? But why should she lie about it? It was the same as rape.

She looked away from the woman. "He forced me to have sex with him."

"Are you saying that he raped you?" Hampton asked.

"Yes."

Betsy Jaycox jumped up from her seat in the courtroom. "That's a horrible lie," she shouted. "My husband would never do that."

The judge pounded his gavel.

Seven times he pounded. Seven.

"Remove that woman from this courtroom," the judge ordered.

Deputy Hullberry, standing by the courtroom door, ran to where Betsy Jaycox had collapsed in her chair. "Come on, Betsy," he whispered, "let's get out of here. You don't have to listen to that bitch's lies." She struggled to her feet. The deputy led her by the arm like an usher at a funeral helping the widow from her seat.

"Proceed, Mr. Hampton," Judge Foster ordered.

"May we have a recess, Your Honor?" Hampton asked in a quiet voice.

"I said to proceed, counsel!" Judge Foster ordered.

Hampton turned to Sarah Eckersly. She was pale, and her lower lip was quivering. He waited as long as he dared before he asked, "Did you struggle?"

"Yes, of course," she said.

Hampton reached into the duffel bag. He handed her the dress, the one with the top buttons pulled off. Sarah said Jaycox had ripped them off. Hampton showed her the pieces of broken cup. Yes, he'd knocked the cup off the table, her husband's favorite cup.

"And then what happened?"

Sarah's testimony had reached the crossroads. Which road would she choose—the one that might lead to her son's safety or the one to her husband's freedom?

If she told the jurors the truth, that Ringo had shot Jaycox, and that her child was very brave, a hero, perhaps the truth might save them both. Still, she would be risking the child. The Children's Services workers would begin asking questions. The sheriff would want revenge, and the prosecutor, that dried-up sliver of evil, would search for other charges to bring against Eckersly. Ringo would be questioned. He was sensitive, and he wasn't clever. He'd likely disintegrate under cross-examination, and then both he and his father would be in jeopardy. She felt weak and brittle. Mothers cannot argue. Mothers are stricken with the disease of motherhood, for which there is no cure. A marriage is different. A wife's path and a husband's path—two independent paths—are joined, and as they are joined, so, too, they can be separated. But a mother and a child are a matter of blood.

"And then what happened?" Hampton repeated.

Sarah Eckersly stared into her hands.

CHAPTER 47

SHE'D DREADED THIS moment. "And then what happened?" Christopher Hampton had asked.

Sarah Eckersly stared into her hands.

"Who shot Deputy Jaycox?" Hampton asked.

In her mind's eye, Sarah saw Ringo standing in the doorway of the kitchen with the shotgun, the boy's innocence spread across his face, his eyes like his father's, brave and unyielding. How could she deny her son? "My son, Ringo, shot the man."

Eckersly jumped to his feet. The jurors were watching. Gathering his senses, he sank slowly down into his chair.

"The man was on top of me. Ringo made him get off. Then the deputy tried to grab the gun from Ringo, and the gun went off and shot off his foot." She was afraid to look at the jurors.

"Then what happened?"

"Ringo put a tourniquet around the deputy's leg, and then he left."

In a faltering voice, Sarah told how Eckersly came home, carried the deputy to the police car, and started into town with him, and how she was following in their pickup. "But when he came to the crossroads, my husband must have gotten confused. He was very distraught." Her words were coming fast. "And when he realized he'd taken the wrong road, he tried to cut across to get back on the right road. Then the police car got stuck. He put the deputy over his shoulder and hauled him back down to our pickup, where

I was waiting, and we hauled him into town. I held the man in my lap. He died on the way in." Her eyes were dry, her voice flat as lumber.

Hampton turned to prosecutor Lucas. "You may examine the witness."

Lucas rushed to the podium, dragging his yellow lawyer's pad with him.

In loud, jarring words, he began his cross-examination. "You remember when we wanted to talk to you and you refused to talk?"

"Objection! She has an absolute right not to talk to Mr. Lucas. It's called husband-wife privilege. Every lawyer knows that."

"Sustained," the judge ruled.

"You claim you were raped? Did you see a doctor?"

"No."

"Did he ejaculate in you?"

"Objection!" Hampton cried. "Is there not the simplest human respect for the victim? Must Mrs. Eckersly be raped again by this prosecutor?"

The judge spoke in a quiet voice. "He has a right, Mr. Hampton. This is cross-examination."

Lucas took several steps toward the witness. "Mrs. Eckersly, will you answer my question?"

"My son, Ringo, came into the kitchen before he reached that point."

"And where was this taking place in the kitchen, pray tell?"

"On the kitchen table."

"You don't mean to say!" Lucas chortled, "On the table?"

"Yes. He was standing on the floor. He had me pushed down on the table."

"His pants were off?"

"They were around his ankles."

"Were you wearing panties?"

"Yes."

"Oh, now I see," Lucas said. "He was kissing you, ripping at your dress, taking his pants down, taking your panties off, and all the while holding you down on the table!" He turned his back to Sarah like a matador to a mortally wounded bull.

"It didn't happen that way," she said.

"Well, pray tell how this alleged rape *did* happen."

"I don't know," Sarah said in a far-off whisper.

"You don't know how your panties got off? Surely they didn't just walk away. And by the way, where are your panties?"

"At home."

"You didn't bring them because they weren't torn, were they?"

"No."

"Actually, Chief Deputy Jaycox didn't touch you at all. That's true, isn't it?"

"No."

"What really happened was that your husband shot him, isn't that true?"

Sarah began searching the audience as if to find support.

"And with your own eyes you saw your husband shoot the chief deputy."

"No," she said. "My son shot him. He was raping me."

"I remind you, you're under oath. Chief Deputy Jaycox didn't rape you, did he?"

The room waited.

She stared into space. Finally she whispered, "No. I gave him what he wanted to save my child."

"Then your husband forced Chief Deputy Jaycox at gunpoint into the squad car and drove off with him. That's true, too, isn't it?"

"No, my husband carried the man to the car. He was already shot. My husband wanted to take him to the hospital."

"Yes, of course," Lucas said. "That's why your husband drove the deputy *away* from the hospital."

"No," she said.

"You want the jury to understand that you were not a party to any conspiracy to murder Chief Deputy Jaycox, is that true?"

"Yes."

"And the truth is, your husband shot Chief Deputy Harvey Jaycox because he had a *beef* with the man."

"No."

"Your husband was angry about how Chief Deputy Jaycox had arrested him earlier, isn't that true?"

Her silence filled the room.

Lucas waited.

Then Lucas said, "I have no further questions of this witness."

The judge ordered a short recess.

Hampton turned to Eckersly. "I'm not permitted by court rules to go talk to Sarah in order to get her testimony straightened out, and I can't lead her on the stand with my questions. Lord only knows what she'll say and how she'll say it."

Eckersly's face was a mask of misery.

"Either I try to repair Sarah's testimony, and it may just get worse, or I put you on the stand. If we don't do something, you're going to go down for first-degree murder."

"I'm not going to lie except for that one thing: I'm keeping Ringo out of this."

"You're going to lie yourself into a conviction." If Eckersly told the truth, that Ringo shot Jaycox, the jury would turn against him for trying to put the murder of Jaycox on a small boy. "The jury believes you shot Jaycox. And the jury believes Sarah lied about Ringo to save you."

"How do you know what the jurors believe? You've told me more than once that you can never predict what jurors believe."

Then Hampton saw Lucas swaggering to their table. "Maybe we ought to talk," Lucas said. Without invitation, he plopped down next to Hampton. Absently, he took Hampton's pen from the table and began tapping it. "You want to settle this case?"

Hampton saw the prosecutor's chilling smile.

"You plead Mr. Eckersly to second-degree murder, and I'll leave it to the judge to sentence him. Think about it," and before Hampton could respond, Lucas got up and walked away.

"What's he talking about?" Eckersly asked.

"Second-degree murder carries twenty to life. You could be out in eight or ten years with good behavior. What do you want to do?"

"What should I do?"

"I think Lucas has the jury believing you had a beef with Jaycox, that you took him out under gunpoint, shot him, and left him there to die. He'll argue that even if you changed your mind and took him to the hospital, that doesn't erase the original crime."

Hampton picked up the pen Lucas had toyed with. "On the other hand, the jury might believe you went home, found the guy doing Sarah, and that you shot him. A couple of those old boys on the jury might understand that. And if they did, and if they like you when you testify, they could turn you loose. Lucas sees that possibility, too."

"A man shouldn't have to gamble with his life," Eckersly said.

"We all gamble on the decisions we make, or we gamble if we don't make them."

Then Lucas ambled back and handed Hampton a paper. "Thought you might like to see a copy of this." It was a subpoena for Ringo. "The kid's going to be my first rebuttal witness." Lucas raised his eyebrows at Hampton, then gave a slow, mocking bow and walked away.

"Can he call Ringo to testify against me?" Eckersly asked.

"The son of a bitch is trying to force you to plead guilty by threatening to bring in Ringo to testify. Lord knows how he can manipulate a scared kid in front of a jury. Maybe I can stop it. Ringo has Fifth Amendment rights, too, you know."

Eckersly tried to think it through. What would his life be like the next ten years behind bars? He was a man of the open spaces, like the coyotes that wandered over the desert and lived off the sheep. What would become of Sarah? She was still young and beautiful. Yes, she'd wait for him and wither from loneliness and grow old and bitter. And Ringo? He was at an age when he needed a father the most.

Eckersly studied Hampton. He looked like a battered boxer at the end of fifteen rounds. After Ringo shot Jaycox, if Eckersly had let Jaycox bleed to death in the kitchen, he'd have been guilty of nothing under the law. He had no legal duty to save him. But Sarah's testimony set the trap for his conviction. Sarah's decision to save Ringo by giving Jaycox what he wanted had ended up killing Jaycox. Something dark followed her.

"If I testify, will they call Ringo for sure?" Eckersly asked Hampton.

"Lucas says he will. But he's a game-playing bastard."

"It would be their mistake to call Ringo. He won't lie."

"Right, but Lucas can make it look like the boy is taking the blame to save you."

"If I don't testify, they won't call Ringo?"

"Who knows? Maybe not."

"Then for sure I won't testify," Eckersly said. To stubbornly stay the course, to keep his neck bowed, his eyes straight ahead, and to let nothing intervene was one way to make a decision. He'd usually made his decisions that way.

"Think what it'll do to Ringo for the rest of his life if he knows his father went to the pen to save him," Hampton said.

"A man should set a good example for his child," Eckersly said, his jaw set.

"Then I won't ask Sarah anything more?" Hampton asked.

"Right."

"If they convict you, what will happen to Sarah?"

"Don't know."

"Do you care?"

The jurors walked in and took their seats.

"Yes, I care."

"Don't you think you should testify to try to save both Sarah and Ringo? When you go down, they both go down with you."

Eckersly stared straight ahead.

The judge took the bench and called the court to order. "Do you wish to examine Mrs. Eckersly further, Mr. Hampton?" Judge Foster asked.

"I have no further questions," Hampton said.

Sarah rose from where she was sitting. She walked in slow, straight steps down the aisle, through the low swinging gate of the bar, and up to the counsel table, where Eckersly sat with Hampton. As the jurors watched, she leaned down and kissed Eckersly lightly on the cheek. Then she looked into his eyes. "I hope you can still love me," she said. "I did it for our son."

"I know," he said.

"Can we go on from here?"

He didn't answer.

Then she walked back up the aisle and out the courtroom door.

CHAPTER 48

AFTER JUDGE EMERY Foster recessed court for the day, Eckersly lay in his cell, resigned to his fate. He'd be convicted of murder and perhaps sentenced to death.

He tried to think things through. If life had any purpose, it was to protect one's young—to hope that each succeeding generation bettered the human condition, even if the change in a single lifetime was no more measurable than the lapping of a single wave on the shores of the ocean.

In the end, what value did his life have except to protect his child? To make a sacrifice for someone a man loved was not a bad bargain.

His love for Sarah was different. It was a selfish love. He needed her for himself. Yet he couldn't capture her, not in her secret places. True, she gave herself to him in the same way she made his breakfast, washed his clothes, and mended his socks. She provided him what she thought he needed, what he was entitled to—a good and dutiful wife. But she didn't open her secret vault to him.

In his cell at night, when reason was muted, when he was the most vulnerable, he found himself wondering whether she'd given—yes, *given*—it to Jaycox? He tried to cast the question out. To hold on to it hurled him into endless torment. Insanity came to men who were hopelessly lost. But he still wielded power over himself.

Yet there'd been that time after Sam and Heide Honikers'

wedding when he thought Sarah wanted him to release his beast. There'd been a big party, a shivaree, in their barn, and he and Sarah drank maybe a few too many, and toward midnight they danced the slow ones, and she danced close to him.

When they got home, they were still feeling good, and he'd felt a certain abandon, something without tenderness, without concern except for the release of his long-caged libidinous powers. Deep into it, Sarah became wild and wet, and she was panting as if she were in pain. But she said nothing in the afterglow, and he asked no questions.

The next morning, she made his breakfast as usual. She put the pancakes and eggs in front of him without words. But the yolk of one egg was broken. She'd never served him a broken egg. He said nothing about such a triviality.

He shifted his position on the hard cotton jail mattress in his cell. It seemed more hostile than usual. He longed to lie on the bare earth. Night and day, the light down the hall glared into his cell. He slept with his back to it. His shoulder began to ache. He heard the moaning, the snoring, and songs of the drunks. He stared at the bottom of the empty bunk above him. In an endless war, the self raged against the self. And the self finally surrendered. In the morning, he'd tell Hampton he'd testify.

BEN ECKERSLY WALKED to the witness stand, straight as innocence, as dark and tall as handsomeness. He was a brave man. Everyone said so. He'd never made a concession to fear except for Ringo. If the jury believed him, he'd save Ringo.

Perhaps he'd save himself.

Hampton had him dressed in the only suit he owned, a dark navy blue one with out-of-fashion wide lapels. It hung slightly at the shoulders, in protest of his severe loss of weight. He answered Hampton's questions in a quiet, steady voice, the solid sound of a good man. Hampton took him to that part of his testimony when he'd been stopped by Jaycox, arrested, and charged with resisting arrest. Then Hampton asked, "As a result of that false arrest, did you have a beef with Jaycox?"

"Objection!" Lucas hollered. "There's *no* evidence there was a false arrest."

"Overruled," the judge said. "He has a right to his theory of the case."

"Yes," Eckersly replied. "I had a beef with the man. He had no business claiming I resisted arrest. He made that up. He lied."

"Did you threaten to kill him?"

"No."

"You heard what the jailer said—that you told him he'd better not let you out that night because you were liable to kill somebody. Did the jailer tell the truth?"

"Yes. I said that."

"Why did you say it?"

"I was angry. They arrested me without cause, and they'd separated me from my son, and abused him and frightened him with a false accusation that he killed his teacher. All I'd done was take my son home. The sheriff had no right to question a child that way, especially without a parent present."

He testified how Hansen and Longley—his absentee bosses—had put up his bond. And when he got back to the ranch, he saw the sheriff's patrol car parked in front.

"When you went in the door, what did you see?"

The jurors were leaning forward, listening intently.

"I saw Jaycox on the floor of the kitchen. His foot was hanging by a single tendon."

"What else did you see?"

"I saw my wife, Sarah. She was in shock. Jaycox was screaming and cursing. There were two holes into the floor, obviously from shotgun blasts, and there was blood everywhere." Eckersly told how he'd carried Jaycox to the squad car, put him in the backseat, told Sarah to follow him, and how he'd driven toward town and the hospital.

"When you got to the forks, you took the wrong fork. Why?"

"He was begging me not to kill him. The more he begged, the more I thought I *should*. He'd raped my wife. I left him out there to die."

"You changed your mind?"

"Yes. The squad car was stuck. Sarah insisted I go back for him. He was still alive. I carried him over my shoulder to our pickup. Sarah sat in the truck bed and held his head. I drove him to the hospital. By the time we got there, he was dead."

Hampton hesitated. Then he asked, "Are you sorry for what happened?" For the love of God, Hampton thought, I shouldn't have asked that.

"I wish it hadn't happened. I'm sorry the man died."

Hampton decided not to risk another question.

Lucas rushed to the lectern for his cross-examination. His eyes were locked on Eckersly. He began in his piercing, accusatory voice. "So, sir, you want to blame your son for shooting Deputy Jaycox? That seems very brave of you."

"I've been sworn to tell the truth."

"Yes indeed. Let us see if you can tell us the truth. How did your boy know where the shotgun was?"

"He knew where we kept it in the closet in our bedroom. He'd seen me put it there many times. He knew how to shoot it. We'd gone rabbit hunting together."

"Of course," Lucas said in a taunting voice. "Now I suppose this eleven-year-old boy also knew how to place a tourniquet on the deputy?"

"Yes. He'd seen me stop the bleeding on wounded sheep."

"No doubt," the prosecutor mocked. "And what became of the parts of his foot, the bone and flesh? I suppose your boy cleaned that up, as well."

"No, Sarah did. If you go to our house today, you'll see the holes in the floor from the shotgun blasts."

"But you never called Sheriff Diggs, did you?"

"No."

"Now let's get to the facts. You claim you put the wounded deputy in the squad car?"

"Yes."

"And you're trying to make this jury believe he was already shot when you put him in the squad car?"

"That's argumentative and improper," Hampton objected. "He's testifying under oath."

"Sustained," the judge ruled.

"If you look in the squad car, you'll see his blood in the back-seat."

"And you admit, actually admit, that you intended to let the man die?"

"Yes, until Sarah insisted that we take him into the hospital."

"And you admit, then, that you intended to kill Chief Deputy Jaycox?"

"No. Not to kill him, but not to give him any help."

"What an interesting distinction!" Lucas chortled. "Then, realizing you'd taken steps to commit the crime of murder, you tried to undo it by hauling him into town. Isn't that what you're telling us?"

"I went back for the man and got him to the hospital. He died on the way. I wish it had been otherwise."

"Yes, of course," Lucas said. "Many regret their criminal acts after it is too late."

"I move that the prosecutor's last remark be stricken and that the jury be admonished to disregard it," Hampton objected.

"Sustained. So ordered," the judge said.

Lucas walked toward Eckersly on the witness stand. "You hated Chief Deputy Jaycox, didn't you, and you intended to wreak vengeance upon him?"

"He raped my wife." Eckersly's voice was steady. "He lied to the sheriff about me. He abused my son, and he said I committed a crime that I didn't commit. He was a liar, a rapist, and a child abuser. I should think he was deserving of some hostility from me."

"Well, if you don't sound like a lawyer!" Lucas taunted. "Did your lawyer tell you to give that answer?"

"My lawyer told me to tell the truth."

"Did your lawyer have to tell you to tell the truth?"

"No."

"So what we have here is someone, namely *you*, who despised his helpless victim and who took his victim out on the prairie and left him there to die. You admit that, don't you?"

"I did leave him out there to die."

"But you refuse to admit that you took him out there at gunpoint and shot him—that *you*, not your little son, shot him."

"Yes, I refuse to admit that, because it's not true." Tinges of anger began to fringe Eckersly's testimony.

Waving his finger at Eckersly, Lucas hollered, "You refuse to admit it because if you did, the jury would have no choice but to find you guilty of murder, isn't that true?"

"No. I refuse to admit what's not true." Eckersly's anger began to mount.

"Yes, of course. The jury will decide," Lucas chided. "I have no further questions of this defendant." He strutted back to his table, looked over at the jury, tipped his head back, and took in the entire jury panel, one juror at a time.

Hampton leaned over and whispered to Eckersly, "I think we're going to need some help, Ben. This jury may think you're nothing but a coward, trying to dump the blame for this shooting on an innocent child. Ringo is all we've got now."

The jurors were watching and waiting.

Eckersly whispered in reply, "I'd decided to lay it all down to save an innocent boy. Now it seems I have to turn to that boy to save me."

"Lucas thinks he has us checkmated—got us for twenty years to life if you plead to second-degree murder, and he may get us for murder if we go to the jury. What do you want to do, Ben?"

Hampton had intended to rest his case after Eckersly's testimony. But Eckersly, too, had fallen short. If Hampton rested his case now, Lucas would likely rest his. The jury would never hear Ringo's testimony. And Eckersly's conviction would probably follow.

"Call your next witness," the judge intoned with growing impatience.

"I've been thinking about what you told me earlier," Eckersly whispered to Hampton, "—how I'd feel if I were Ringo, and my father went to prison, and I was never given a chance to tell the truth. Might not get over it."

"I have to advise you, Ben. There's risk there, too. Lucas will make it look like Ringo is lying to save his father, and that we put the boy up to it."

Hampton knew that as a matter of strategy it would be better to let Lucas call Ringo, as he'd threatened to do. Then Hampton would have the advantage of cross-examining the boy with leading questions. But if Hampton called Ringo, the advantage would be reversed and Lucas would lead the boy in ways to make the jurors believe that he was lying to save his father.

Was Lucas bluffing when he threatened to call Ringo as his witness? Hampton walked to Lucas's table to test him. "Are you going to call the boy to the stand?" Hampton whispered.

Lucas whispered, "I'm sure you'd like to know that. I have the kid subpoenaed. Why wouldn't I call him? You should consider my offer of a plea to second-degree murder. Then I won't have to call Eckersly's kid to testify against him."

The judge began to rattle his papers impatiently.

"If you don't take my offer, you'll just have to wait and see whether I call his kid or not," Lucas said. "I likely will. But then, I'm a man known for a sudden change of mind."

Hampton turned to the judge. "The defense calls Ringo Eckersly."

Lucas jumped to his feet, realizing his bluff had been called. "You son of a bitch," he whispered to Hampton in a high hiss, "you've double-crossed me, and nobody double-crosses Ronald Lucas and doesn't pay the price."

CHAPTER 49

RINGO, JUST PAST eleven years, walked down the courtroom aisle toward the witness stand, accompanied by one of the courtroom deputies. Fear walked with the boy. The jurors watched him, and the judge, dour, forbidding, and appearing pissed-off, peered down at him. The onlookers filling the courtroom were fixed on him, some whispering excitedly to one another. Sheriff Diggs squinted mean eyes at him, while prosecutor Lucas stared at him like a rifleman taking aim in a firing squad.

Christopher Hampton rose from counsel table to meet Ringo. "Hello, Ringo, do you know what an oath is?" he asked like a kindly grandfather.

Ringo's high, clear voice pierced the muffled sounds in the courtroom. "Yes. It means to tell the truth no matter what."

Hampton nodded to the clerk, and the clerk administered the oath: "Do you promise to tell the truth, the whole truth, and nothing but the truth?"

"Yes, sir."

"Do you know who I am?"

Yes, sir. You're my father's lawyer."

"Did you tell Mr. Lucas how Deputy Jaycox got shot?"

"He made me tell him." Ringo glanced quickly at the glaring Lucas. "He had me at his place."

"Did you tell him what you're about to tell us here today?"

"Yes, sir. He said I was lying."

"Are you afraid?"

He wanted to be brave like his father. But he wasn't brave.

Hampton asked again, "Are you afraid?"

"Yes, sir."

"And what are you afraid of, Ringo?"

"Him," Ringo said, pointing at Lucas. The high, desperate sound from the voice of the child chilled the courtroom. "My daddy didn't shoot him. I did."

"Why did you shoot the man, Ringo?"

"He was hurting my mother." He grabbed the witness chair's hard oak arms, his knuckles white.

"Where were the man and your mother?"

"He had my mother pushed down on our table. And they didn't know I was there."

"What do you mean?"

"I came in our front door." Ringo looked to his father, and when he saw his father's face, he started to cry. He felt shame, as when he'd been afraid to ride the old ewe. But he would never cry again. Not now that his name was Ringo.

"Will you tell the ladies and gentlemen of the jury what you did when you saw the man hurting your mother on the table?"

"I went to the closet for our shotgun."

"What did you do then?"

"I told him to get off of my mother. Mama said he was hurting her."

"Did he get off?"

"Yes, sir."

"What happened then?"

"He told me to give him the gun, and I wouldn't give it to him."

"Why not?"

"Because he was hurting my mother."

"Then what happened?"

"He tried to take the gun, and it went off, and it shot his foot off." There being nothing more to tell, he started to get down from the witness chair.

"Just a minute, Ringo," Hampton said. "What was your mother doing?"

"She was screaming."

"Was the man bleeding?"

"Yes, sir."

"What did you do?"

"I tore off a piece of our dish towel and tied it tight around his leg. Then I left."

"Where did you go?"

"I went out on the prairie."

"Why did you leave?"

He looked down, shame invading his face. "I was scared."

Hampton turned to Lucas. "Do you have any questions?"

Lucas jumped to his feet like an attack dog at the gate. He stomped up within a couple of feet of Ringo and glowered down at him.

Hampton turned to the judge. "Would the court direct Mr. Lucas to stand back from the boy? He needn't frighten him more."

"Step back, Mr. Lucas," the judge ordered. "You may question from the lectern."

Lucas turned to Ringo. "That's quite a story you've told us." Then, realizing that the jury was likely sympathetic to the child, he peeled off his hostility, smiled at Ringo, and said, "Don't worry, son, nobody's going to hurt you in here." He gave him a moment. Then he asked, "You love your father?"

"Yes, sir."

"You know your father is charged with murder?"

"Yes, sir."

"Do you know what could happen to your father if this jury finds your father guilty?"

"Yes, sir. He could go to the gas chamber."

"Who told you that?"

"That deputy guy."

"And if your father were sent to the gas chamber, that would hurt you a lot, wouldn't it?"

"Yes, sir."

"You'd do anything to save your father, wouldn't you?"

"Yes, sir."

"Would you lie to this jury to save him?"

"Yes, sir."

"You would *lie*?" Lucas cried, his voice rising a full octave.

"Yes, sir."

"Even though you took the oath to tell the truth?"

"Yes, sir."

"Well then, there's nothing you can say that we'd be entitled to believe. That's true, isn't it?"

"Yes, sir."

"And you want us to believe that *you* shot Chief Deputy Jaycox and not your father, is that right?"

"Yes, sir."

"And you don't want to tell this jury that your father shot Deputy Jaycox, isn't that true?"

"Yes, sir."

Lucas smiled at Ringo. "Thank you, son." In a near lope, Lucas returned to his table. "That's all the questions I have."

Hampton asked his first question on redirect examination as he was walking to the lectern. "Ringo, why don't you want to tell this jury that your father shot Deputy Jaycox?"

"'Cause he didn't," Ringo said.

"I have no further questions," Hampton said.

"I have no further questions," Lucas said.

Ringo climbed down from the witness chair. He walked past his father without looking at him. He walked as straight as an Indian chief out the courtroom door, where Mrs. Cynthia Foley, his foster parent, had been waiting for him.

CHAPTER 50

Laramie, 1947

Ringo ran down the fifteen steps and headed in fast, determined strides for his pickup. Meg ran to keep up.

Before he could get his old wreck started, Meg jumped in beside him. He locked his eyes straight ahead.

The streets were empty. A sallow moon was setting. They drove up the street in steely silence. She searched for words. She felt sick. She reached over to touch his hand, but then, afraid, she pulled it back.

He couldn't look at her.

He stopped the truck in front of her apartment.

"You have to get your painting things," she said.

He followed her up the stairs and stood against the wall, facing her.

"I quit tonight," she said.

When she moved closer, he felt his hands pushing against the cold plaster. His head was thrown back, a man holding on at the precipice.

"You hate me, don't you?" Her voice was flat and frozen. "Please tell me you hate me. I couldn't bear it if you loved me."

"I loved you," he said, as if addressing the dead.

"It was my work. I was only working my way through school. It meant nothing."

"You're a whore. I loved a whore." He pushed Meg's chin up with the heel of an angry palm. Then he pulled his hand away and walked to the window. The timid gray of dawn began showing itself.

"I never made you any promises," she said to his back. "I'm still the same woman you claimed you loved."

"I could never love a whore."

"You would have fucked a whore up in the house if you'd had the courage to climb those stairs. Or have you forgotten?" She laughed a hollow laugh. "You told me."

He spun around to face her. His pain gave birth to anger.

"Are you going to kill me?"

He stared at her.

She took a bottle of whiskey and a couple of glasses from the cabinet and poured a shot into each glass and handed a glass to Ringo. "Here's to us," she said, lifting her glass.

He lifted his glass. "Here's to a whore." The taste of the whiskey twisted his face.

She reached for the bottle and poured another. "When you become a lawyer, you'll either sell yourself to criminals and help them lie about their crimes or you'll sell yourself to corporations that'll use your skill to fuck the people over. You'll sell your *whole* fucking self for money. I only sold my ass."

She walked wearily to the couch, set the bottle on the coffee table beside the book of Monet's paintings, and sat down. "Beauty is the only morality."

"You have morals?"

"Yes, I have morals," she said. "I sold my ass and made men happy. I never sold myself. I *gave* myself to you."

He stood stiff and mute.

She emptied her glass. "You men and your morals. You tell the women you want to fuck that you love 'em, and all you want is their pussy. You call that moral?"

His silence was noisy.

"You told me you loved me. Did you love me, or did you just love my pussy?"

His face signaled the danger, but she pushed further.

"I never told any of my johns that I loved them. I never told you I loved you. A whore can't love anybody."

He walked to the small window that overlooked the landlord's backyard. The grass of spring had resurrected to an innocent green that announced new life. The eager buds on the limbs of the cottonwoods were threatening to bud. Another season. But spring made no promises.

"I loved you," he said.

"You loved fucking me."

"I loved you. You made a fool of me."

"If I'd met you up in the house, it would have been better. Neither of us would have been hurt." She struggled to her feet and walked to where he stood peering out the window. "I never married some poor bastard for his money. Could have. Lot of times. Those are the real whores. They fuck for money and lie about it. I never lied about it."

"You lied to me."

"No. I never lied to you. You never asked how I got the money to go to school, and how I could rent this apartment and afford the clothes you liked to see me in. You never asked me where I got the money I forced you to take so you could pay your tuition last quarter. The money came from a whore, honey, a dirty fucking whore."

"I thought you had rich folks, or something. I didn't care about your money."

"You'll never be a lawyer. You're an artist. But so am I. I was born to make people happy. I wanted to hear people laughing. And I wanted to laugh with them."

"We had plenty of laughs," he said. "The last laugh was on me."

Her familiar scent drifted over him. He wanted to run out the door, to run down the steps and then to run and run, to where, he didn't know, but never to stop running.

"The world is populated with whores," she said. "Some preachers are the biggest whores. They promise heaven for money. Then they sneak up to the whorehouse, pay some poor working girl with the money the faithful paid them, and after they fuck, they pass judgment on her like you're passing judgment on me. A working girl is just trying to make an honest dollar by selling her ass. It's all she has to sell."

She was right, he thought. If he hadn't been such a coward, he would have met her in the whorehouse that first night when he came to town, and no one would have been hurt. He felt the cold of the brass doorknob in his hand. He turned it to leave.

Ringo started down the steps of Meg's apartment. "Wait, Ringo." He stopped on the third step. He wouldn't look back. She came rushing out the door with his paint box and dragging his easel behind her. "I won't be needing these," she said. He took the paints and walked on down the stairs, dragging the easel behind him.

CHAPTER 51

PROSECUTOR RONALD LUCAS was delivering his final argument to the jury. He was speaking to the pleasant-looking housewife, the older woman in the front row.

"For the sake of argument, let's assume that the boy, Ringo, did, in fact, shoot Deputy Jaycox. Still, it was Eckersly, not his son, who killed the chief deputy by dumping him out there on the prairie and, after that, hauling him around during those detours that were obviously intended to do him in. We're not demanding that Eckersly be a Good Samaritan. If someone wishes to watch a man bleed to death and not raise a finger in assistance, the law permits that person to do so. But if someone takes possession of a helpless man and *intends* to kill him by depriving him of his chance to live, and the victim dies as a result, he's committed murder." Prosecutor Lucas stayed locked on the first rancher for a beat.

Lucas turned to the second rancher. "The defendant, Eckersly, could have left Chief Deputy Jaycox to die in the kitchen, and he would have been guilty of nothing except a moral lapse that the law does not punish." His voice gathered his held-back rage. "But when he *intentionally* deserted Chief Deputy Jaycox out on the prairie to die, as he's admitted, that became his attempt to kill Chief Deputy Jaycox, and that act is punishable under the law.

We, as citizens of Albany County, can never put our stamp of approval on such conduct."

To the grade school teacher, Lucas said, "I cannot tell you what forces took over this child named Ringo. At best, this whole affair must have been a terrible shock to his tender psyche. We all know how children imagine things. Who knows what nightmares pass through the innocent mind of a child, so that the child cannot distinguish fact from fantasy?"

The grade school teacher nodded her agreement.

Lucas took in the entire jury, one juror at a time.

Then Lucas turned to the gray-faced professor. "Alone with the sheriff, this boy either imagined threats or he dipped into his shallow vessel of experience and conjured up this story in order to protect his father. Rather than condemn the child, we should admire his courage. He had forewarned us. He would lie to save his father." Lucas bowed his head in reverence.

"This is a tragedy. It saddens me. You'll remember that I did not call this child as a witness. What prosecutor with a semblance of a soul would use a boy to convict his own father? This child was called by the defense to endure this nightmare. I shall say no more about that heartless decision. History will record its disapproval of that cowardly act, as will doubtless be reflected in your verdict."

Lucas turned to the blinking, bespectacled librarian, her legs still duly crossed. "I wish the table in the kitchen could speak to us. If the table could speak, it would tell us the truth. I can hear it now: 'I've been serving this family for many years, and many others before them. I was sitting in the center of the kitchen, as usual. Then Chief Deputy Jaycox came in to arrest Mr. Eckersly. Mr. Eckersly burst through the kitchen door, carrying a twelve-gauge shotgun. It was a frightening scene, the worst I've ever witnessed, and I'm an antique table that's been around a long time. When Mr. Eckersly saw the chief deputy sitting there, he hollered a profanity at him, and shot him. The shot blew his foot away. It was horrible. Then he carried the bleeding deputy out of the kitchen, and that is the last I saw of him.'"

Satisfied that the jury had the scene in mind. Lucas said, "Whatever the facts were in the kitchen, even assuming the boy told us the truth, must we argue whether the defendant did, in fact, commit a crime when he drove the deputy off and abandoned him in the sagebrush to die? That man"—he pointed at Eckersly—"knew he had committed a crime. He knew it and attempted to cover up his crime. That is the lurking evilness here!"

Lucas marched back and forth in front of the jury, anger welling in his voice. "Justice demands your verdict of guilty! There sits a murderer!" he shouted. "Let your verdict show *your* courage. If there's been no truth in this courtroom, let your verdict finally tell the truth!"

With that, Lucas sat down, flipped the pages of his notebook to see if he'd forgotten anything. Then he leaned back in his chair and waited to see how Christopher Hampton could possibly overcome the power of his argument.

CHAPTER 52

CHRISTOPHER HAMPTON STOOD peering down at his boots, the jury watching, waiting. Finally he looked up. "I wish I weren't so afraid," he said softly. "I keep asking, What if I'm unable to show you how Mr. Lucas has failed in his case? As His Honor will instruct you, it is Mr. Lucas's duty to prove his case to each of you—not to some of you, but to *each* of you—that Ben Eckersly is guilty of the crimes charged and to prove those charges beyond a reasonable doubt. And Mr. Lucas *has* failed in his case. After rotting in jail for these long months of horror, it's time for Ben Eckersly, this man of the great open spaces, to go home to his family."

Hampton stopped and stared at his boots again. When he looked up, he said, "I have this picture in my mind: It's of Ben Eckersly walking out the front door of this courthouse into the sunshine with his wife, Sarah, with his son, Ringo, and with you. I see their faces and yours beaming with joy. He's free. Ringo is with his beloved father. Sarah has survived this hell for her man and her child. They're together at last, this small family." Hampton stopped and looked from one juror to another. "But what if I fail, and instead this man is dragged back in chains to rot in a filthy prison cell, and Ringo and Sarah trudge back without a father or a husband?"

Once more, Hampton looked down at his boots. "I'll try to tell you the whole truth. I believe that each of you knows when the whole truth is concealed behind a fraudulent mask. I say a fraudlent mask, because half-truths, parts and pieces of the whole truth, are as fraudulent as whole lies."

Then Hampton spoke to the plumber. "This is the story of a man much like most of us. He loves his family. If his life has meaning, it rests in the sanctity of his marriage and the safety of his wife and child. He is their protector." Hampton spoke to the housewife in the flowered dress that caressed her ankles. "In the same way that a woman nurtures and protects her child, so, too, the husband is charged with protecting them both."

He turned to the taxidermist in his flier's jacket. "This tragic story began when Sheriff Diggs accused an innocent child by means that can only be described as a vile rape of justice. And that rape gave birth to yet another rape of justice when Chief Deputy Jaycox, exploiting a mother's fear for her child, forced himself on Sarah Eckersly to satisfy his bestial, sexual demands like a snotted bull in the breeding pasture."

Hampton addressed the plumber, whose arms were now un-crossed, his spacious body open and unprotected. "Yet Ben Eckersly's final effort was to save Deputy Jaycox's life. Even after Ben Eckersly had succumbed to darker instincts, instincts that exist in any man whose wife has been defiled and whose child has been abused, he returned to the right decision with the help of his wife, Sarah, and together they attempted to save the very man who had desecrated their marriage and who'd tortured their child. Now, for that, prosecutor Lucas asks you to declare Mr. Eckersly a murderer."

Hampton looked into the face of each juror for a moment. Then he said to the grade school teacher, "Who can we believe here? This prosecutor attacks this child and claims he's a liar. He attacks the child's father and claims he's a liar. He attacks the child's mother and claims she's a liar. Everyone lies—an innocent child, an honorable father, a loving mother. Everyone lies, everyone except Mr. Lucas's witnesses. And Mr. Lucas himself has changed his theory of this case time after time to match the unfolding testimony." Hampton's voice was calm. The sound of truth was in it.

"Prosecutor Lucas began his argument by claiming that Ben Eckersly took Deputy Jaycox at gunpoint and shot him on the prairie with the deputy's own shotgun. When there was no evidence of bone or boot leather on the prairie, when he was challenged by the truth—that there was blood in the backseat of the deputy's car and holes in the kitchen floor—he changed his theory to claim Ben Eckersly shot the deputy in cold blood in their kitchen, and he supports his argument with the testimony of an antique table. He then asks you to convict a man of murder on the say-so of a table."

Hampton waited, as if he expected a juror to jump up and say, "That's ridiculous." Then he continued: "Once the eyes of this prosecutor are on you, there's nothing you can do, and there's nothing you can say to establish your innocence. Whatever you say and whatever your witnesses say will be smeared with the filthy brush of lies. That, ladies and gentlemen, is the reason that under our law Mr. Eckersly is presumed innocent. And all of the pretty pettifoggery of the prosecution can't wipe away that sacred presumption of innocence that binds each of you as jurors. Each of you."

Hampton turned to the housewife again, who seemed to inhale his every word. "Yes, Sarah Eckersly was raped. Rape comes in many forms. The woman was forced to give to Jaycox what he demanded because she was afraid for her child. What mother wouldn't give whatever was hers to give to save her child? And what husband, when he learned of such a rape, might not leave the fiend to his fate out on the prairie?"

Hampton paused to let his argument settle in. "Prosecutor Lucas argues that once having undertaken to save Deputy Jaycox, Mr. Eckersly had a duty not to abandon him on the prairie. But he forgets the crucial testimony of Dr. Lowry, who said that Deputy Jaycox would have died within a few minutes from loss of blood and shock but for the fact that a tourniquet had been put on the man. We heard nothing about a tourniquet from the prosecutor. Nothing! The prosecutor says the boy, Ringo, is a liar. If Ringo didn't shoot Jaycox, and if he didn't put the tourniquet on the deputy in an attempt to save the deputy's life, then *who* put the tourniquet on him?" Hampton waited for his question to anchor in the jurors' minds.

Then he spoke to the rancher on the right. "Once Deputy Jaycox was shot, he was destined to die. No one has told us how long it takes to drive directly into town from the Eckersly ranch house. On a good day, did it take two hours? Or more likely, two and a half hours?"

Hampton turned to the lumberyard clerk. "Mr. Lucas, who attacks everyone who had the courage to tell the truth, including that small boy, was so busy attacking, so busy calling people liars, that he failed to prove his case. The court's instructions to you make this very clear."

Hampton picked up a copy of the judge's instructions from his table and began to read to the jury:

> *If an accused does not intend to kill, but a person dies from his conduct, he cannot be guilty of murder, because murder requires intent.*
>
> *On the other hand, if a man intends to kill, but his act does not result in the death of the person, in the same way he cannot be guilty of murder.*
>
> *To be guilty of murder, one must both intend to kill and his victim must die because of his intended act.*

Hampton spoke to the plumber. "Mr. Eckersly found the wounded Jaycox in his house, writhing on the floor. This was the man who had raped his wife. What was his legal duty toward Jaycox, if any? He had none. If he offered no assistance and left

Jaycox there to die, he would have violated no law. The undertaker would have come, taken the body, and we wouldn't be here today.

"*When* on the trip to town, did Jaycox die? We were never told. Why didn't Mr. Lucas ask Mrs. Eckersly that simple question?" Hampton waited, and the silence while he waited became very loud. Hampton turned to Lucas and held out his arms to solicit the answer. The silence grew louder.

"This prosecutor assaulted Mrs. Eckersly again by humiliating her in a public courtroom, forcing from her those painful, lurid details about the rapist's ejaculation, but he could not ask her the turnkey question in this case: *When* did Deputy Jaycox die?"

Hampton waited. "Why didn't Mr. Lucas ask her? He didn't ask her because he knew her answer would destroy his case: that Jaycox died almost immediately after they started into town. Mr. Lucas knew that even if Mr. Eckersly had not taken that detour, Jaycox would have died long before they arrived at the hospital— which means but one thing: that Ben Eckersly must be acquitted because"—Hampton stopped and waited for his words to settle— "because no matter what Mr. Eckersly did or failed to do, he did not *cause* the death of Harvey Jaycox."

Hampton spoke to the jurors with his arms and hands, which kept cadence with his argument. "About Mr. Lucas's last hope for any conviction: 'Please,' he says, 'please convict him of something, please. I need a conviction.' Can Mr. Lucas now come in the back door, begging you to at least give him an 'attempt to murder' conviction? What kind of foolishness is this? It's like attempting to beat a dead horse to death."

Hampton again spoke to the plumber. "Deputy Jaycox and Sheriff Diggs brought this tragic matter on themselves. We don't treat people in Albany County as if they exist under a reign of terror, with no more rights than people living under a dictator like Hitler."

Hampton continued in a quiet voice. "Everybody lies in this case except those who support the ambitions of Mr. Lucas. My old mother used to say, 'The truth will out.' Mr. Lucas asks you to end the life of a man and his family based on the speech by a table! I don't recall having ever heard a table talk. A brave mother did what a brave mother had to do. A brave boy told what a brave boy had to tell. A father, suffering a savaged wife and child, finally tried to save the life of the fiend who'd raped his wife. In the end, that was the mark of the man, and it took great courage and it took great character."

Again Hampton spoke to the jurors, one at a time. "The venal attacks against honest ranching people by falsely charging them as liars, and the ever-changing stories of this prosecutor to win a conviction at any cost, must stop. The greater courage will be when each of you gives back to the people of Albany County the just protection of the law.

"Ladies and gentlemen, today, here and now, I see beauty rather than horror.

I see this father, this husband, walking out hand in hand with his family and with you, the jury. I see you walking together down the steps of this courthouse to freedom. I see the joy on their faces and I see the joy on yours." Hampton lingered in front of the jurors for a moment. Then he turned and sat down next to Ben Eckersly. Eckersly reached over and put his hand on top of Hampton's and did not want to take it back.

CHAPTER 53

DURING THE RECESS, Hampton explained to Eckersly that Lucas would be delivering his rebuttal.

"Rebuttal?" Eckersly asked.

"Yeah, under the law, Lucas gets the the last word. He can contradict whatever I said. Is that fair? Hell no, it's not fair. But that's what convicts most of the poor bastards on trial."

When Lucas returned to the courtroom, he was angry. His fists were clenched. He marched to the front of the jury box, grabbed the lapels of his suit coat, and said, "I have a vision, too. My vision is of a murderer walking free, laughing as he goes, and as he walks down the courthouse steps with you, he's amused that he was able to get away with this murder by blaming his little boy. That is a horror to me. That is my vision of it, and the facts of this case support it."

He stomped to one end of the jury box and then to the other. He pointed to Eckersly. "This defendant took possession of the bleeding, dying body of Betsy Jaycox's husband and the father of their two children, all of whom loved him, and he"—Lucas was still pointing at Eckersly—"made sure he'd die by delaying his delivery to the hospital. He is a murderer, plain to say." He bared his teeth like an attack dog held back on the leash.

"But Mr. Hampton does Chief Deputy Jaycox an even greater injustice. He makes a rapist of him by simply charging him with it when there's no proof, except the flimsy word of a woman trying desperately to save herself. It's easy to accuse Chief Deputy Jaycox of rape. He's not here to defend himself. Only you can defend him."

Lucas looked from juror to juror. "You heard Deputy Hullberry tell how Eckersly resisted arrest, swore at the deputies, and called them names I will not repeat. He was properly charged with resisting arrest. He had a beef with Chief Deputy Jaycox. He threatened to kill him, and he did kill him. The case is that simple."

Lucas's hard voice attacked the jurors' ears without mercy. "This garden of tragedy grew as it was cultivated by those sitting over there at the defense table. It began with the senseless murder of Chief Deputy Jaycox. But tragedy grows its own fruit. The victim, Chief Deputy Jaycox—yes, he's the victim—is accused in this courtroom as a rapist! And on what evidence? A broken cup? Two buttons off a dress? He's accused on the bald blame of a woman whose pathetic testimony was given to save herself, to save her breadwinner, and to save her child, who admits he'd lie to save his father. What we have here is not one crime. What we have here are multiple crimes, lies under oath and—perhaps the worst crime of all—converting an innocent child into a perjurer. It sickens."

The prosecutor's voice began to soften. "Yes, I, too, have a vision. My vision is of the widow, Betsy Jaycox, the wife of our fallen servant. My vision is of their children. That nice young boy and his pretty sister are waiting to hear whether you will forever smear their father's good name as a rapist. Will these children walk out of this courthouse with you? Will they walk out proud of their father, proud of justice, and proud of you? Or will they slink out the back door, children whose father has been adjudicated a common rapist by your verdict? You decide. Do you march out with a murderer and his family, or do you proudly march out with a widow and her children? The lives of this good family are in your hands."

Lucas closed his notebook.

After the court's instructions on the law, the jurors left the courtroom to deliberate. As the jurors passed, none stole a parting glance at Eckersly, nor did they look at Lucas. They walked straight ahead without expression, like people passing an open coffin and afraid to glance in.

Then Darwin Hullberry came for Eckersly. He held out his hands for the deputy to cuff him.

"How long are they going to be out, Christopher?" Eckersly asked.

"Could be an hour. Could be days."

"They're going to convict me," Eckersly said. Then he saw Hampton look down. "But I had a damn good lawyer," he quickly added. "Thank you."

CHAPTER 54

IN THE COLD concrete of his cell, Eckersly awaited the jury's verdict in the company of *Fear*, his constant companion. It crept in like an evil virus, clutched at his throat, and left him weak. He worried most about what would become of Sarah and Ringo.

His small son was braver than he. He must have inherited his courage from his mother. Not once did Ringo admit to fear. And with great courage, he'd even threatened Sheriff Diggs. What kind of a child would have shot the foot off of a marauding deputy and then had the presence of mind and the compassion to place a tourniquet on the man? He was a gift, and Eckersly felt he'd failed his child.

Eckersly thought about Sarah. Once in the night, he'd heard himself curse, "You whore." Instantly, he was sorry for his words. Still, if you put a gun into the hands of any raped woman, wouldn't she pull the trigger and watch the son of a bitch fold to the floor with both satisfaction and relief? But she'd wanted him saved. Perhaps she was only acting out of some overriding human compassion that she could even offer her rapist. How would he ever know?

Then the old jailer, Hank Plowman, came with his supper—deer meat and boiled potatoes. He couldn't eat it.

"I believed your boy," Plowman said.

"Thanks," Eckersly replied.

"I heard the jury arguin' in there when I walked by. As long as they're arguin', it's a good sign. It's when they ain't arguin' that a man has to worry." He gave Eckersly a sad smile, and hobbled on down the line.

HAMPTON'S WIFE, MARY, was waiting at his office when Hampton walked in at the end of the day. She'd made a pot of beef stew and brought along fresh homemade rolls.

"How did it go?" she asked. She saw his face. She'd seen it before, the haunted eyes.

"I'm going to lose," he said. "Lucas was too good for me."

"How can you say that?" She took his coat and pulled out his chair from his desk. He fell into it. She handed him the bowl of stew. "You always claimed Lucas was just a snotty kid who needed to be taught a lesson."

"I didn't teach him a lesson today. The jury's gonna convict. Lucas has 'em worried about the Jaycox family. He pulled that out at the last."

"Eat your stew. I made it especially for you. Your favorite recipe."

He nibbled at the end of the spoon. The jury needn't tell a lawyer that he's lost. The lawyer knows. He's suffered a deep soul bruising, a sense of the final blow to a man who's been pummeled to the ground over and over until he can't rise up again. And a lawyer knows by the way the audience in the courtroom looks at him and even shies from him, as if his defeat is communicable.

"I ought to get out of this business," Hampton said. "I can't win the important cases, the ones where my clients are innocent. I'm not good enough to do this work. I should have learned that a long time ago. I should have been a store clerk."

"You're just feeling sorry for yourself," Mary said. She put her hand on top of his. His hands felt cold.

"My witnesses didn't hold up," he said. "They did the best they could, but they didn't hold up."

"There are some people who just can't be defended," Mary said. "Try to remember that."

CHAPTER 55

Bear Creek Ranch, 1941

IT TOOK SARAH Eckersly two hours and seventeen minutes to return to the ranch from town. The ranch yard was empty except for the old dog, Buster, who came bounding up, his tail beating at the thin night air. She stooped to give the dog a passing pat on the head, walked into the house, turned on the lights, and pulled down the shades. Then she checked the bedrooms and the closets and under the beds and in the shower. Satisfied she was safe, she locked the doors, built a fire in the old wood-burning stove, and put on a pot of water for her tea.

Sarah hadn't intended to fail her man. She'd given everything she had to save him, including herself—the price of the pathologist's testimony. She retched at the memory of the skinny, hairless talking corpse with the penciled mustache. When he'd emptied, he'd patted her on her naked butt and told her she could get dressed, as if he'd been the examining gynecologist.

She worried about Ringo in that foster home. The Cynthia Foley woman seemed kind enough. But a son needed his mother. It was as if she were a doe and her fawn was safe in the zoo, but the fawn needed its mother, not the apathetic tending of some zookeeper, even if the zookeeper were kind.

She'd thought of kidnapping Ringo in the night, and by morning they'd be many miles away.

Kidnapping her own child?

Yes.

She could steal a car in Laramie, another in Rawlins, a different one yet in Rock Springs. But she had no money for gas or food. Of course, she had her ways. Still, the police would find her and take Ringo, and she'd be in prison, and she'd never see her son again. She must be patient, she kept telling herself. Surely Christopher Hampton would bring her child home again.

She knew she'd have to rear Ringo without a father. What happened to her on the kitchen table had ended her marriage to Ben Eckersly. Even if he were acquitted, the Jaycox ghost would lie in bed with them and stare at them at breakfast. Suddenly, she jumped up and grabbed the meat hammer from the drawer and began beating at her precious antique table.

She beat it!

And beat it!

And beat it until she could no longer lift the meat hammer!

If the table hadn't been there, she could have fought him, like any woman would fight. But Jaycox had grabbed her and kissed her, and she'd fallen back against the table, and he'd followed her down as she fell against it, and he'd ripped at her dress, and then he was on her, and she'd gotten lost in the struggle, and when she came out the other side, Ringo was there with the shotgun, the man on top of her, her legs spread.

She struck at the table again.

But the old wood didn't crack. It invited the hammer.

She'd lost her man, this man she loved. Yes, she loved him. And she'd killed him. He'd die in the penitentiary. He wasn't the kind who'd take abuse from guards or inmates. He'd be killed, and if he weren't killed, her husband, who'd lived as free as the golden eagle, would curl up and die like the eagle with its flight feathers severed. She shouldn't have made him go back for Jaycox.

The evil irony of it—that by saving her husband from being a murderer, he'd be convicted as one.

She poured the tea and stared into the cup, the leaves settling to the bottom. She felt the abrasions she'd left on the old wood of her precious table and hated herself for the damage. The table was innocent. And she'd left Ringo fatherless, as well as the Jaycox children. *She* was a murderer. She wielded some evil power she didn't understand, like a deadly virus she'd breathed on them, and they'd all begun to wither and die.

When she finished her tea, she took off her black dress and laid it carefully on the bed. Naked, she stood looking at herself in the closet door's mirror. Her body was like roses in the third day of blooming. She felt stiff. She turned her back to the mirror. Every woman had a butt. She ran her hands across hers. Her hands felt rough against the softness of her skin.

She hung her black dress next to her blue Sunday dress with the blue cloth flowers at the shoulder. Her white wedding dress, done up in plastic to preserve it, claimed its place there, as well. The shotgun still leaned against the back wall, behind the dresses. She took pains not to touch it.

Then she put on her bib overalls, her flat-heeled work shoes, and pushed her hair up inside one of those small-billed black woolen feeder's caps that ranchers wore in the winter. She put on her wool-lined denim jacket and walked to the barn in the dark. Old Hard Head whinnied for his hay, and after that, she put a gallon of crushed corn into the feed box, opened the barn door, and Old Boss lumbered in. Sarah dropped the stanchion blocks behind the cow's head.

Old Boss's hide against her cheek felt warm and welcome. The cow's milk squirting in straight streams into the empty pail made tinny music, and the rhythms were from the cadence of her squeezing fingers, small but strong. The sound of the cow chewing the corn, the smell of the cow's body heat, the perfume of fresh hay in the manger were good. Darkness filled the barn except for the single bulb that hung from the ceiling, casting its long, weary shadows.

The foam began to rise from the streams of milk that beat into the pail, and as the pail began to fill, the sounds softened, and she saw that she and the old milk cow were the same. The power was in what was taken. At last, the cow's udder emptied. Sarah lingered on the milk stool, the pail still between her legs. She heard the mice scurrying in the loose boards of the roof. She thought that had she been Mother Mary, she would have chosen to give birth to the Christ Child in that barn with its animal warmth and its animal honesty. If someone had told her that one day she'd be sitting alone in a barn out on the prairie on a cold night milking a cow, she would have thought them daft. She released the stanchion. Old Boss backed out and waited at the barn door for Sarah to open it.

CHAPTER 56

Laramie, Courthouse, 1941

THE PLUMBER, A tolerant man devoted to the disposal of human refuse, was elected foreman of the jury. The older housewife thanked the schoolteacher for nominating her as foreperson, but she said she thought that Mr. Hammersly, the plumber, could do a better job. And there being no further discussion and with appropriate modesty, he took over.

The jurors had been arguing for over two hours about whether it was a crime to dump a dying man on the prairies. The secretary, whose hairdo was like two black wasps' nests set one on top of the other, argued he might have lived. "Only thing we know is Jaycox died. And we know that Eckersly intended to let him die. He admitted it."

"Yeah, that may be so," said the squinty-eyed rancher, who sat on her right. He'd been out on the prairie and looking into the sun for a lot of years. "But we don't know if he woulda died anyway. We can't guess the man into the pen." With one hand, he rolled a cigarette out of a Bull Durham bag, licked it, stuck it in his mouth, and lit it with a farmer's match that he put to fire with a long, fast swipe across the leg of his Levi's. He took a drag off his cigarette. "I'll tell you one thing: I come home an' I find some bastard doin' my wife on the kitchen table, I'm gonna kill him."

"I didn't believe the Eckersly woman," the secretary said. "I think she and her husband made up that rape story and got the kid to testify to it, too. Eckersly had a beef with Jaycox. I feel sorry for Mrs. Jaycox and her kids. I don't know how they're going to make it. He probably didn't have any life insurance."

"Whether Mrs. Jaycox can or can't make it has nothin' to do with the facts of this case," the rancher with the sunburned nose said.

"Eckersly admitted he had a beef with Jaycox," the squinty-eyed rancher said. "He didn't have to. I think the man was tellin' the truth. One thing bothers me, though. Even if his kid shot the deputy, I don't think a father shoulda let the jury know about that. A man has to protect his kid. I think the father shoulda took the blame."

"I suppose you wanted him to lie," the secretary said. "I suppose you think some lies are okay and some aren't. You men are like that. And you don't need to tell me that the Eckersly woman was being raped on the kitchen table. That's the silliest thing I ever heard of."

"Well, that's what makes me think it's true," the professor of Latin Studies said. "As the old saying goes, 'Truth is stranger than fiction.' If she was making it up, she'd have claimed the man threw her on the floor or something like that."

"I never thought of that," the housewife said.

"I didn't like that Lucas," the rancher with the sunburned nose said. "If he talked to me like he talked to Eckersly, I'd a punched the son of a bitch out."

"We can't let things like that govern us," the secretary said. "We're charged with finding the truth here. We took an oath." She turned to the squinty-eyed rancher. "Would you mind not blowing that smoke in my face?"

He squashed his cigarette against the calluses of his left hand, rubbed the dead butt between his thumb and forefinger until it disintegrated, and dropped it to the floor. He shot the woman a testy smile.

"Thank you," she said.

The housewife flipped through the pages of the judge's instructions and started reading at a place near the bottom of the pile. "The judge says here that 'the defendant had no duty to save the life of the deceased person, and his failure to do so is not a crime.'"

"Yes," the secretary said, "but I remember the judge reading us something about Eckersly taking possession of Jaycox, and something about if that caused his death, then we could find him guilty. Something like that."

"Well, that Dr. Lowry said Jaycox woulda died in fifteen minutes if it hadn't been for the tourniquet," the housewife said. "I'm confused. He woulda died without the tourniquet. Then somebody put one on him. Then Eckersly took him out, dropped him on the ground, and left him there. Then Eckersly went back and picked him up to save him. Then Jaycox dies going to the hospital, but exactly when, we have no idea. And exactly how long it took them to drive to town, we don't know. I can't figure this out."

"I think it is terrible the way Eckersly treated Chief Deputy Jaycox," the secretary said. "Even if you believe that little boy's parents didn't put him up to his lies, Jaycox getting his foot shot off was punishment enough, even if he raped her. That man didn't have to be killed and leave that family without a breadwinner." She took out her compact, opened it, and touched up her lips. "If my husband did what that Eckersly did, I wouldn't lift a finger to defend him."

The squinty-eyed rancher tossed a raw sneer at the secretary. "If your old man caught you on the kitchen table with some guy, he'd probably apologize for the interruption." No one dared laugh. The room was silent for a long time.

Finally, Sunburned Nose said, "The bailiff told me that Jaycox was quite a ladies' man. Had quite a swagger to him."

"That is totally improper," the secretary said. "I should report you to the judge."

"You just do that, sister," Sunburned Nose said. "And I'll tell you somethin': The reason you want to put the guy away is because you didn't like his wife. Pretty little thing, wasn't she?"

"How dare you!" the secretary said. "I don't have to sit here and take this."

She got up and started for the door.

"Where you goin'?" Sunburned Nose asked. "You wanna go cryin' to the judge, I'll have a thing or two to tell him myself."

The secretary stopped at the door. "And what would that be?"

"About how you're tryin' to convict this man because you feel sorry for Mrs. Jaycox and her kids. You oughta think about that, sister, before you go shootin' off your crybaby mouth."

The plumber, Hammersly, exercising his power as foreman, tapped his empty water glass against the tabletop. "Now folks, it is one thing to say how you feel about this case. It's another to get personal. You know we're all on the same side here." He glanced from juror to juror to make sure everyone was listening. "Now folks, we may not agree, but one thing we can agree on: We're here to do justice, whatever that might be. So let's hold it down a little and show a little respect for each other." He blushed, embarrassed at the use of such raw power.

The secretary began anew. "I agree with Mr. Lucas. I think it was very cowardly for a father to blame his child for what the father did."

"You got this all wrong, lady," Squinty-Eyed said. "Eckersly coulda just said he got lost, or he blacked out. He coulda made up a whole shitpot full a stories, but he never did. He said he intended to kill him. And lady, if I'd of come home and found that deputy hooked to my wife like a dog stuck to a bitch, I woulda finished him off right then and there. So for my money, the guy was tellin' the truth, and all I gotta say, *again*, is the deputy had it comin'."

"You're prejudiced," the secretary said. "You ranchers all stick together." She glared at Squinty-Eyed.

"Well, now, ain't that a cute argument," Squinty-Eyed said, leaning his chair back and putting both feet up on the table. "I'll tell you somethin', lady, that you don't know. Eckersly runs sheep. I run cattle. If I got any prejudice, it's against sheep men who turn their livestock loose on the public range and eat everythin' that grows right down to the goddamn roots." He slammed his chair back to emphasize his point. "And let me ask you somethin'. If you had a real man for a husband and he comes home and finds some guy rapin' you, what would you want him to do 'bout it?"

"Whatever he did, he wouldn't blame it on his son," the secretary said. "Not if he was a real man. But let me ask you something: Between that boy and that Eckersly, which was the more likely to use a gun on the deputy—the man or the boy?"

"Who the hell knows?" Squinty-Eyed said. "Kids on ranches use guns. Every one of my kids, my two girls included, can nail a grasshopper at a hundred yards."

"Little kids don't go around shooting grown men when they find them in a compromising position with their mother," the secretary said.

"Would you be talkin' from experience?" Squinty-Eyed asked.

"How dare you!"

"I'm gonna have me a cigarette." He got up.

"We're gonna take us a ten-minute break," foreperson Hammersly said. "Then we'll come back and deliberate until suppertime and get us a free meal on the county."

CHAPTER 57

JUDGE EMERY FOSTER called the lawyers into the courtroom. The judge said Ringo's case had been pending before him long enough, and while he had the testimony fresh in mind, he thought it an efficient use of time to take up the boy's case while they awaited the jury's verdict.

Before Eckersly's murder trial began, Hampton asked Judge Foster to step down from the boy's case and assign it to another judge. "After all, Your Honor will come to your own opinion in Eckersly's trial, and you'll carry that opinion over to the boy's case."

Judge Foster replied, "Yes, that's true. I have an opinion in the murder case, which leaves me in a better position to decide the boy's case without a lot of unnecessary fuss in the juvenile court."

Now he ordered that Mrs. Eckersly, Cynthia Foley, his foster parent, and Ringo be in court by nine in the morning.

SARAH ECKERSLY DROVE the long road to court alone. Mrs. Foley was present with Ringo. Christopher Hampton and prosecutor Lucas sat at their respective tables. The clerk handed Ringo's file up to the judge. Deputy Darwin Hullberry stood at the courtroom door to assure that the juvenile court proceedings were private, as required by law.

"Do either of you have anything more you wish to offer before I make my ruling?" The judge stared down at Sarah. His position above her lent a sense of his absolute authority, a deity, his lips pursed to rearrange the universe.

"My boy needs to come home," Sarah pleaded. "He's without his father, and he's been without a mother for too long. Mrs. Foley says he cries at night. This is too hard on a small child. I'm a good woman, and I'm best qualified to take care of my child. I'm a responsible citizen. I was born here. You know my father. He speaks highly of you. I beg of you to let me have my child."

The judge offered no hint of his thoughts. The law required that the interests of the child remain paramount. He would not be moved by the entreaties of the mother.

"Thank you, Mrs. Eckersly," the judge said. "I'll give your concerns due weight. My only interest in this case must be the best interests of the child."

"Yes," she replied. Then she heard herself laugh. She was startled such a sound should escape her lips. Her mirthless laugh must have torn loose to hide her pain.

The judge, surprised, peered down at her. Then he turned to Christopher Hampton. "Do you have anything else, Mr. Hampton?"

Hampton nodded toward Mrs. Foley. Matronly and smiling, she rose, clasping her hands in front of her. "Ringo is a nice boy. He doesn't cause any trouble whatsoever. But I do think he misses his family." She patted the boy on the shoulder and sat down.

Ringo stared straight ahead. The words he heard held no meaning for him. His collar was too tight. "You want to make a good impression on the judge, don't you?" Mrs. Foley had asked. Then she'd tied the tie his mother brought, one that belonged to his father, and the part that hung down too far, Mrs. Foley tucked under his pants. These days, *Fear* followed Ringo wherever he went. *Fear* was a bully he couldn't run from.

The judge turned to Christopher Hampton. "Do you wish to say anything on behalf of your client before I make my ruling?"

"Yes, Your Honor," Hampton said, rising to address the court. He knew this was all an empty formality. The court record would reflect that the judge had listened to the mother, to him, and to the prosecutor. Everyone was granted an opportunity to speak. No appellate court would reverse the judge's decision. Hampton knew the judge had made up his mind. Why play the judge's game? He could as effectively speak to a lamppost on Front Street. But if he said nothing, Sarah would always believe that what he'd failed to say could have made a difference. Still, Hampton himself was a member of the species that by reason of its brief and desperate journey on Earth had learned to hope in the face of hopelessness. "If man were immortal, hope would be useless," he often said.

Hampton looked up at the judge. He wasn't a judge for the people. He was a judge for himself first, and for the law. But the law does not feel. It does not love. The law is quite dead.

"I agree with Your Honor," Hampton began. "The only consideration here must be what's best for this child." He put his hand on Ringo's shoulder. "If there is hell on this Earth, this family has endured it. This child has walked through its fires, and has endured it. Please look at this child, Your Honor. Actually *look* at him."

Hampton waited.

The judge, impenetrable as a stone Buddha, glanced at the boy.

"This is one of the bravest humans I've ever encountered," Hampton said. "He took action to save his mother. He's lived in the house of a stranger all of these months, and if he cried, he cried only alone at night. He stood up before this court and, different from the sycophants who bow and grovel before you, he had the courage to speak his mind. He has never been the source of trouble either in school or to his family. I wish for such a son." The judge looked down, a tired patience stamped on his face. Hampton stopped to gather his fraying forces.

Then he pushed on. "This boy's separation from his father,

whom he adores, is in the hands of the jury as we speak. How long must this child be estranged from his mother? It is time for his hell to end." Hampton sat down.

"Thank you, Mr. Hampton," the judge said. He turned to Ronald Lucas.

Lucas stood at his table. His voice was so low, the judge leaned forward to hear him. "I have no quarrel with this child," Lucas said. "I have but one thing to say: If this jury should acquit his father, I'm convinced we'd be sending this boy home to a murderer. If this jury should convict his father, it seems to me that it would be quite merciless to send this boy to the public schools, where other children would taunt him as the child of a convicted killer. We all know the cruelty of children. I ask the court to take these thoughts into account when the court makes its decision." Lucas sat down.

Hampton was on his feet. "That was an improper argument! The child should not be punished for whatever crime his father may or may not have committed."

Lucas spoke without rising from the table. "I speak only for the benefit of this child."

Judge Emery Foster cleared his throat. "Are you ready to receive my decision?"

CHAPTER 58

"I'VE GIVEN THIS case much thought." Judge Foster's voice was as dry as old sticks. He cleared his throat and peered at the invisible crowd in the empty courtroom.

"This child has been presented here as an innocent boy of eleven. Yet he has no respect for the authority. But that's not his fault. We don't know what the verdict will be in his father's case. I'm told the jury is still deliberating. I know how I would have decided the case. The defendant, Eckersly, found his wife in the arms of another man and decided to murder him. If this jury acquits Mr. Eckersly, I quite agree with Mr. Lucas: I'd be sending the boy into a home in which the head of the house is a murderer, from whom the child would have learned that he can take the law into his own hands and get away with it."

Refreshed by his notes, he began anew. "I have no doubt that an attitude of lawlessness exists in this household, as was reflected in the conduct of this child. He didn't hesitate to lie for his father. Most children would not possess the ability to do so and still withstand the expert cross-examination of Mr. Lucas."

Avoiding any visual connection with Sarah Eckersly, the judge continued. "This boy must learn right from wrong. I refuse to send him home to his mother, since I believe the full story of what transpired between her and Chief Deputy Jaycox has not been candidly presented. In short, I did not believe her testimony. Not the first word."

Momentarily, the judge turned to Christopher Hampton. "How could I possibly send a boy into a household where its members so readily use their child as an excuse for their conduct and lie so easily as the occasion suits their needs? To return him to such a family could hardly be in the best interest of any child."

When he saw Sarah Eckersly staring at him as if seized in a catatonic state, he quickly turned from her. "I have observed Mrs. Eckersly during these proceedings. Her demeanor does not comport to that of an innocent woman. I noted that she laughed while she was addressing me. From what tarnished soul does such an inappropriate response escape?"

To prosecutor Lucas, he said, "I admire the composure the prosecution has shown in this boy's case and, indeed, the prosecutor's compassion. We all share empathy for this child, but it must be distilled into sound judgment. Mr. Lucas will draft an order requiring the sheriff of Albany County to deliver custody of this child to the superintendent of the Boys' School at Worland, to there remain for an indefinite term and until further order of this court."

"My God!" Sarah Eckersly cried. "No! No! Oh my God, no! Dear God, please, Judge, no! He's innocent. *Innocent*." She staggered toward the judge and fell to the floor, gasping. Then she struggled to her feet.

As if he were deaf to her entreaties, the judge turned to Christopher Hampton. "Mr. Hampton, you may advise this boy that if he behaves himself, he can be out in short order, not to be returned to his mother, but to, say, Mrs. Foley. Perhaps at the boy's reformatory, which is under the superintendence of Mr. Ralph Delaney, who operates a stellar institution, one that promotes the moral, mental, emotional, and physical well-being of errant boys—perhaps under his tutelage this child will become appreciative of his duty to the law and to society. When evidence is presented to me that he has made sufficient progress, I will reconsider my ruling."

As if it was an afterthought, the judge spoke to Sarah Eckersly. "I do not intend any cruelty to you, madam." His eyes were focused above her hairline. "You understand I cannot consider your feelings in this matter, but only the welfare of your son. My door is always open to you, as it is to all parents, for whatever report you may wish to make from time to time concerning your progress. Our goal is for both the advancement of the child and the child's parents. I wish you well in your endeavor to hone your skills as a parent in such a way that you can provide a suitable environment for the return of your son."

Judge Emery Foster slammed his gavel three times, rose from the bench, and retreated to his chambers, the tail of his black robe following after him like an evil shroud.

Deputy Hullberry lumbered forward in determined steps to lead Ringo away. He grabbed the boy's wrist, but Sarah was holding on to Ringo, both sobbing and shouting at the empty bench, "How could you take my child, you heartless, evil son of a bitch?" Then she screamed at the judge's shut door. "You are an agent of the devil!"

Ringo clung to his mother.

"Let loose of the kid." Hullberry was trying to pull Sarah away from Ringo.

"Take it easy," Hampton said in a quiet voice. "Give her a minute." The deputy stood back. Sarah, sobbing uncontrollably, held on to Ringo with both arms around him.

"All right, lady, this has gone far enough," Hullberry said after a few seconds. He grabbed Sarah's bun, jerked her head back, and stepped in between the mother and the child. He took Ringo by the collar of his coat, as if lifting a pup by the nape of its neck, and walked toward the door of the courtroom, Ringo's feet fanning at the floor. Sarah came running behind them, screaming, "Please don't take my child! Please! I beg you, please."

Hampton stepped in front of her and put his arms around her. "We can't stop this, not right now," he said.

She held on to Hampton, her body heaving in uncontrolled spasms. "My baby! Oh, my baby!"

The boy looked back at his mother. "Don't worry, Mom. I'll get out." Then flailing at Deputy Hullberry with both fists, he shouted at the deputy, "And when I get out, I'm gonna kill you." Forthwith, Hullberry dragged Ringo to an empty cell, his arms thrashing in the high, thin air.

THAT SAME AFTERNOON, Eckersly recognized the sounds of familiar footsteps. He looked up as Christopher Hampton and the old jailer stopped at his cell. Eckersly examined the face of his lawyer for a clue. Hampton's face was a blank tablet. Old Plowman's head was turned down. He opened the jail door and let Hampton enter the cell. Then abruptly, he left in silence. Hampton sat down on the cot by Eckersly, reached over, and patted him on the thigh. Bad news usually comes coated in imposed kindness.

"The judge sent Ringo to the boy's reformatory," Hampton said in a soft, fatherly way.

"What?" Eckersly asked, dismayed. "*What* did you say?" He jumped to his feet.

Hampton slowly shook his head in confirmation.

At last, Eckersly was able to ask, "How's Sarah taking this?"

"Not good," Hampton said. "She went back to the ranch alone. I didn't have anyone to send with her."

After minutes, Eckersly finally spoke. "I kept her penned up there too long—kept her for myself." His face was pushed up against the steel bars. They left their marks against his sallow skin. "Never knew what it was like for her until they put me in here. She had no friends except me and Ringo, and we weren't her friends. We were her responsibilities."

Hampton watched Eckersly drowning in agony.

"I've tried not to get riled up with my emotions, to think things through and do right. Then I got trapped in my emotions." He stopped and turned slowly to face Hampton. The skin under Eckersly's eyes was swollen like blisters. His hair, beginning to gray, hung over his ears. "How's Ringo?"

"Ringo's feisty. Good sign. Said he was going to kill the deputy."

"It's in our genes, I guess," Eckersly said. "When I get out of here, I'll get Ringo out, too, if I have to kill a dozen of the sons of bitches."

"Better think about what you're saying," Hampton said.

"I am going to get out of here, aren't I?"

"The jury's still arguing," Hampton said. "Let's hope they never stop."

CHAPTER 59

THAT AFTERNOON, SARAH Eckersly drove the highway from Laramie through the long prairies and onto the single-track trail that led to their house. Her mind was frozen and she could hear nothing but the sounds of gravel against the old truck's tires and the rattle of its loose fenders.

She and her child were trapped, but in separate traps. She couldn't escape the ranch, any more than Ringo could escape the reformatory. She felt a sinking sense of helplessness. She felt old, and so exhausted that she might lose the strength to hold on to the wheel. She should let go, let the old pickup die there on the prairie, let the snow blow up around it, and around her.

She drove on.

In the deep shadows she saw a faceless phantom reach up and spread her legs on the kitchen table for Jaycox. What power the demon within—to concoct its black, snarling schemes below the surface of her mind! She had not planned it, none of it. She would swear to that looking into the eyes of Jesus. The phantom had captured her and was moaning and panting when Ringo walked in with the gun. Suddenly, her anger rose up like a stepped-on snake. She was glad Jaycox was dead. She wished she'd killed him.

She drove on.

If she'd ensnared her husband into evil by convincing him to drive Jaycox to the emergency room, she'd not known of the phantom's plan. If her testimony had destroyed her husband's defense by her telling the truth, she'd not been a party to such wickedness. If Lucas's cross-examination had made her appear as a liar, it was that same malignant ghoul that had spread her legs on the table.

She drove on.

If she housed such an accomplice of the devil, it should be exterminated. She remembered as a child when her father had burned down the chicken house to rid it of a disease the veterinarian claimed was buried in the boards and caused the hens to stop laying. She thought of the shotgun in the closet. The blast would end her pain and free her. Suddenly, she felt a sense of serenity, something light blue in color, like warm, distant summer skies.

THAT NIGHT, RINGO couldn't sleep. The drunk in the cell next to him was vomiting and making noises as if he were choking. In the shadows of his cell Ringo saw the face of his mother. Her eyes were bursting in terror, her face like the inside of the dried sheep pelt hanging over the fence, the rawhide yellowed, the red veins running through it. In her terror, his mother was not beautiful. The judge had hurt her—the judge and that lawyer, Lucas. Then Ringo pulled the blanket up over his shoulders. The wool scratched at his throat.

Fear crept into his cell. He saw the fiends at the reform school with their black whips, the ones Billy had told him about. He saw them forcing the boys to eat shit for supper. *Fear* crawled under the blankets and began to gnaw at his belly. They'd have to whip him like Ham's old man whipped him, until his back was bleeding and he couldn't stand up, and still he'd never eat shit.

In the morning, Deputy Hullberry led Ringo to his squad car in cuffs, pushed him into the backseat, and started off on their trip to the Boys' School at Worland. "That kid is dangerous,"

Diggs had warned. "Keep him cuffed, or he'll try to pull some-thin'."

Hullberry didn't speak during the daylong trip, the radio blar-ing country music. Once, the deputy stopped to piss and let Ringo out, uncuffed him, and held his gun on him. "You try somethin', kid, and I'll shoot you on the spot. Now go ahead and piss."

They stopped at a drive-in at Casper for a hamburger and a Coke. Hullberry cuffed the boy's hands in front of him so he could eat. "Better enjoy this, kid. It'll be the last decent meal you're gonna get for a while."

When Hullberry pulled the patrol car up along the side door of the main reformatory building, he said, "Maybe you'll learn somethin' here. I doubt it." He jerked the boy out from the back-seat. "I'll say one thing for you. You're a tough little son of a bitch. You never cried once."

He led Ringo up to the main door. "And when you get outta here, if you come sneakin' around me, I'll shoot you six times through your fuckin' head."

The doormat in front of the main door of the reformatory read WELCOME.

CHAPTER 60

SEVEN DAYS AFTER the jurors began their deliberations, Judge Foster ordered Lucas and Hampton to appear before him forthwith. The townsfolk had heard the rumors, and the courtroom was packed. A conviction, finally. Only a few of the odd ones, those who saw the sun shining from behind the clouds, held out for an acquittal. The low humming voices of the spectators sounded like bees at the hive. The room smelled of people's bodies, a thick, repugnant smell not of the earth.

The clerk of court was poised at her desk, looking solemn. The clerk nodded to the bailiff, who nodded to the jurors, who'd been lined up in the hall behind the courtroom. Eckersly watched them trudge in. He wanted to remember the twelve faces of his own species when they announced their decision that would end his life. None of the jurors even glanced in his direction. Bad sign, Hampton had once told him. "If they won't look at you, it means they've done it to you." Then Judge Emery Foster took the bench like an ascending Solomon.

Sarah Eckersly sat in the first row of pews, next to the rail that separated the audience from the court officials, the attorneys, and her husband. Judge Foster took the bench. Sarah's mind had dried up. She had trouble breathing. She tried to see her husband.

Eckersly was ready for it. If the law wanted him, they could have him. Nothing worth a damn was left of him. Those who stood for the law had destroyed his life. The law had been their weapon. That less than an animal Jaycox had destroyed the Sarah he knew. The law had taken Ringo. The jury would find him guilty. What more could the law seize?

Hampton tried to read the jurors' faces—faces of people who'd forgotten how to love. Perhaps they'd never been loved. Hampton put his hand on Eckersly's. His hand was cold. Most of the jurors had lived law-abiding lives and hugged the law like infants on the tit. If the jurors wanted the sheriff to keep them safe, they had to believe the sheriff. Otherwise, the sheriff and his deputies would throw up their hands and say, "What the fuck's the use? The damn juries turn 'em loose every time." After that, nobody would be safe.

What about "proof beyond a reasonable doubt" and "the presumption of innocence"? That was so much bullshit that lying lawyers argued. Why would the prosecutor charge an innocent man? And for Christ's sake, why was a plumber who worked every day cleaning out somebody else's shit allowed to run the jury? Hampton saw the familiar look he'd seen on jurors' faces before. He squeezed Eckersly's hand again, perhaps if only to hold on to somebody.

The judge reached for his gavel, slammed it hard three times, and sat down. He cleared his throat. "One of the sterling attributes of the law is that it is patient. I've given this jury seven days to decide this case. The jury has not been able to agree. I've monitored their deliberations, being careful not to intervene in any way.

"I do not believe a judge should impose his entreaties upon a jury to come to its decision. Once the case is in their hands, the matter is totally within their domain."

With unbridled disgust, he surveyed the jurors from one end of the jury box to the other. "To me, the decision was clear. But I am told this jury has been hopelessly deadlocked from the first day, and, therefore, I have no choice but to declare a mistrial."

The judge gathered his papers, stuffed them into his file, and marched out.

Hammersly, the foreman, walked over to their table and smiled at Eckersly as if he were an old friend. "I done you the best I could. One of the women wanted to put you away for life." He shook his head. "Jesus, she was a mean bitch. Wouldn't give an inch. Rest of us, all eleven of us, wanted to turn you lose."

"Yeah," Hampton said, "I know the one. I thought she smiled at me too much."

PROSECUTOR LUCAS LET Eckersly rot in the Albany County jail for two more months, and every day of those months Christopher Hampton could be found perched in Lucas's office, beseeching him, arguing with him, begging him to drop the charges and not to try the case again.

"Only one of the jurors wanted to convict Eckersly, and she was breaded in hate and fried in misery," Hampton argued. "We both gave it our best shot, Ron. I thought you had me beat. You made the most convincing argument I've ever heard in a courtroom. You'll never do better if you try it a hundred times more." Then one day, as if it were his idea, Lucas dropped the charges and Eckersly went home.

Christopher Hampton had said it more than once. "No man can survive a murder charge, even if he's innocent and acquitted. You can't live through that fire of fear without something in you burning up and leaving scars."

Sarah wept in joy, and Eckersly fought his own tears. He and Sarah held on to each other, their elation spread across the surface like thin frosting on a cake, each trying to fulfill the expectations of the other. Eckersly was not the same, and Sarah was that stranger in the house.

They had long conversations about trivia, any trivia, and they told each other the same stories they'd told each other countless times before. But they avoided any mention of the rape or the hellish whatever it was that had occurred in the very room where they ate three meals a day, and took the sustenance of their lives from on top of that damnable table.

He spent longer hours with the men and the sheep. He said he owed it to Longley and Hansen for the support they'd given during the trial. He said he thought Sarah had "done marvels." No other woman could have run the ranch as she had. But there were details a woman wouldn't see. The tractor needed over-hauling, the corrals were piling up with dung, and the chain on the manure spreader needed new links. There was a lot of fence down—no fault of hers—and the flume across the creek was leaking.

They pretended they were secure lounging before a well-stoked fire with all the doors locked. They tried to deny ugly memories, not to ask questions, to accept each other and to go on, because there was no other place to go.

Eckersly never asked Sarah why Judge Foster had released Ringo from the reform school so soon. She only said she'd met with the judge, and after that he'd ordered the boy released, even against the stern admonition of the superintendent, who warned that the boy was inherently violent.

Ringo had come home and finished his time at Bear Creek School under the tutelage of Mrs. Sheehan, and he'd gone to high school in Laramie and roomed with Mrs. Foley. When he left home to go to high school in Laramie, he stayed with Mrs. Foley. In exchange for his board and room, he helped her with the children. He knew the pain of frightened children. He couldn't erase their fear. But he cared. And caring is contagious.

Ringo passed from grade to grade—no honors. He wasn't an athlete—just another student passing through. There'd been no violence. He seemed hidden from his classmates in a self-imposed anonymity. He had no friends and came home on the weekends. Arturo was his only companion.

The family pretended things were the same. Ringo joined them in their denial of the past. He couldn't change history. He could only try to forget the unforgettable, to let time bleach the memory like blood is bleached from the cloth, but the stain remains.

Then one night after supper, and after Ringo had gone to bed, Eckersly was drinking his coffee, and, as usual, he said it was the best damn coffee a man could drink, and he gave Sarah that same soft smile. They talked about how Ringo seemed to be coming out of it. "He even laughed when Arturo told him some joke in Spanish that Ringo seemed to understand," Eckersly said.

When there was nothing more to say, Eckersly got up from the table. They'd begin docking in the morning, and he wanted a full night's sleep. Unexpectedly, and void of thought, the words came bursting like a terrible ghoul born of an evil egg. "How did it feel?" He was stunned by his words.

Horror grabbed Sarah's face. "What are you talking about?"

"I didn't mean anything by it."

"You meant something by it. You've never tried to understand, have you." It was not a question.

He stood staring at her. He felt unsteady, and momentarily, as if searching for support, he reached out for the table.

"Ben," she cried, "the table!"

Rage, blind rage connected only to itself, exploded.

Eckersly grabbed the meat hammer from where Sarah had left it on the counter, and began beating the table.

He beat it.

And beat it.

And beat it.

Choked in horror, Sarah lurched backward to the kitchen wall. He saw blood on the table.

At last, the force of his blows splintered the table's plank-thick top.

Gasping for breath, he stopped and stared at the pieces, which stared back at him like the dead demanding retribution. He dropped the meat hammer and grabbed an unbroken table leg, and with both hands he beat it across the old potbellied stove until the leg cracked and fell in two.

He stood panting, surveying the aftermath. He felt no shame. No remorse. He felt a sense of victory.

At last, he saw Sarah. Yes, it was Sarah standing there. Her eyes were alive in a way he'd never seen. She pushed herself up to him. Her breath was hot, and she kissed him with an open mouth. As she released him, she said in a soft, seductive voice, "Take me to bed."

And he followed her into the bedroom.

CHAPTER 61

Bear Creek Ranch, 1947

RINGO STOPPED HIS pickup at the gate where the two-tracked trail met the highway. He dragged the gate open and drove in. Once, he'd been afraid to leave the ranch. Now he was afraid to return. He wasn't brave. He bit at his lower lip, squeezed the wheel, and rattled down the two-track trail toward the ranch.

The ranch was waiting.

Always waiting.

The truck's exhaust emitted a long trail of lazy blue fog. The prairie dogs at the brink of their holes scolded at the charging monster and at the last moment disappeared into their holes, and the horned larks with their yellow heads and black sideburns cried their warnings, scattered, and settled again.

Ringo locked his focus on the trail. The settlers who'd given birth to it ruts had suffered their desolate lives there, died there, and the wooden markers of their graves and the scars of their burials had long ago been digested by the earth.

His father would say nothing about his having dropped out of school, but his silence would condemn. And his mother would run to him and hold him and and fight against tears. He held on to the wheel with both hands, his hands soft, washed, but not cleansed.

His memory of his days at the reformatory had become clouded as the mind scabs over and tries to heal. He remembered how as a boy of eleven and on his first day there he'd attacked the guard with his fists, and he'd been locked away to cool and to cure in a padded cell that was as dark as his parents' closet. For ten days, he saw only the guard when he came with the bread and water. The guard did not speak to him.

Then one day, he was suddenly released—something about the judge's having ordered it. As he followed the deputy out, the other boys jeered at him. One hollered that his mother must have fucked the judge. He would have tried to kill him, but the guard dragged him to the deputy's car.

The deputy drove him to the ranch, and when Ringo saw his mother, for a moment he didn't know her. She'd aged, and her hair, uncurled, hung down out of the short-billed black feeder's cap she was wearing. Her face was gaunt and tight. But when she saw him, she suddenly came alive. Her eyes brightened and her face lit up, and he knew that this was his mother, that she was very beautiful, and that he loved her. She ran to him, and as if he would disappear were she to release him, she held him with her strong arms for a long time.

"Where's Daddy?" he was finally able to ask.

"He'll be home soon." But her voice had no bottom. She offered him fresh lamb chops for supper, but she fed him fried eggs and pancakes with butter and syrup because he said he couldn't wait until breakfast for them.

That first night home from the reformatory, Ringo had awakened to the wailing of the coyotes. Again *Fear* crept under the covers and clawed at him. He cried out and Sarah came rushing into the bedroom and turned on the light. When he realized he wasn't locked in the padded cell, he told his mother he was all right, and after she kissed him dearly on the cheek and tucked him in, he tried to sleep, but he did not sleep for a long time.

THE MORNING FOLLOWING his return from the university, he went with his mother to the docking chute and took his place beside the men. He was ashamed of his failure as a student. But he felt a certain freedom from the demands of the professors. He was glad to be home. He felt safe. And he'd learned one thing for certain: He could never be a lawyer.

CHAPTER 62

ALTHOUGH RINGO'S CALLUSES were soon reborn from pitchforks and posthole diggers, he'd often set up his easel behind the barn. In spare moments, usually on a Sunday, he'd paint on the burlap of old wool sacks, on Masonite that he'd gessoed white, or on worn canvas that had once blocked an irrigation ditch in the hay fields. He painted portraits of his soul. He painted his memories of Meg, which took on the forms of both ravens and robins, and of blue tumbling numbers flying through space. He stacked the paintings in the granary. No one saw them, not even his mother.

The canvases bore great blotches of black where his anger had exploded, and small, tender strokes of loneliness in yellow, and when he painted the light blue, the color of forget-me-nots that, as a boy, he'd found blooming in the shadows by the creek, he felt joy. Sometimes he painted until exhausted. Then he'd lie down on the barren ground, the sun beating on him, the heat burning and searing the pain.

He saw her face.

He hadn't bothered to withdraw from the university, and another fall had come around like a greyhound in its endless chasing of the mechanical rabbit.

Of late, his mother was complaining of her back and neck. "Some people suffer arthritis at a younger age than others," the doctor told her, "but we all get it." Her back had been laid to every task from hoeing in her small garden to lifting the ninety-four-pound cement sacks from the pickup for the concrete she mixed by hand to repair the headgate.

Ringo saw his mother's hands, the veins beginning to show like meandering blue tubing. And even in the years following his father's return to the ranch, she often joined him in his work to take the place of another man who would cost Longley and Hansen, for, as had become the liturgy of their lives, they owed their bosses. Otherwise, Eckersly might still be in prison.

They never spoke of Chief Deputy Jaycox, nor of Eckersly's trial, nor of Ringo's time at the reformatory. And Eckersly never asked her how she'd convinced Judge Foster to release Ringo early. The family was satisfied to bury the past like one buries something diseased and contagious. A certain comity existed between them—a respect for tender places that, if touched, might bring on a sudden onset of pain.

One thing Ringo had come to realize: Pain and death were certain, and so the family, together once more, took small pleasures in the company of one another—his delight in the chocolate cake Sarah baked on some Sundays, or her joy over a poem he'd written about a rattlesnake he'd encountered. He'd refused to kill it, and a week later perhaps the same snake appeared at the door of the barn.

> I've come to adore you,
> You heard my rattling cry for mercy
> And you did not impale me
> With the hungry steel of your shovel.
> I have come to display
> My most charming slithers
> Like a belly dancer at your table.

"What does the snake stand for?" Sarah asked. He was sitting across from his father at the kitchen table, a steel table with chrome legs and a red Formica top they'd ordered from the Sears, Roebuck catalog. His mother was pouring their after-supper coffee.

"It doesn't have to stand for anything," Ringo said. Then he read on.

> *Do not kill me, not now,*
> *Not after we've loved*
> *In this strange way.*
> *I do not come to harm*
> *Where harm composes*
> *The menu of the day,*
> *Where old ewes weep*
> *And small lambs bleat*
> *Into the deafened ear*
> *Of eternity.*

"I don't understand, Ringo," his mother said. "But I like the way you read it."

> *I've come to lay my slippery tongue*
> *Upon your muted lips*
> *And by my kiss, to break down*
> *The walls of purgatory.*

As Sarah listened, she absently ran her fingers along the cold metal edge of the tabletop.

"I should call the poem the 'Kiss of the Snake,'" Ringo said. "Like in Adam and Eve."

"I guess so," his mother said. Then she cleared the table and put the dishes in the sink.

"I have to go milk," his father said.

"I'll go," Ringo said.

CHAPTER 63

Ringo often revered the day when Mrs. Foreman had told him she loved him.

He was a child when she'd said that. His mother was loving. But she never said those words. Why, he didn't know. And he'd loved Mrs. Foreman. Her killer had never been identified. Ham had confessed to killing her to escape his father, but Ham was innocent. Sheriff Diggs seemed to lack interest in solving the case. That was because Diggs had murdered Mrs. Foreman.

Diggs met Mrs. Foreman at a rally when he was running for his second term, and she'd campaigned for him—gave him sound advice—and one morning they ended up in the same bed. That proved to be more than satisfactory for Diggs. The woman was good at listening, and she was able to predict his every need in and out of bed, and yes, she was hot, and their connection deepened naturally from there.

Then came a time when Mrs. Foreman wanted all of Diggs. He couldn't, he said. She should understand that. The election was coming up, and being the shining star of law enforcement in the county and married and all—well, she should understand.

But what about her? she asked. Much anguishing and arguing replaced the high, heated hilarity of the prenuptial bed. She said their relationship shoud be "open, honest, and real," and if what he'd been saying to her was true, he had to tell his wife, and if he didn't have the courage, she'd tell his wife. That proved to be a fatal mistake.

A fatal mistake?

Yes.

Fatal.

If their affair were discovered, it would cause a hell of a lot of problems for Sheriff Diggs in the coming election, not to mention at home. If he didn't have the sheriff's job, he'd have to go back to selling used cars. She had to go. Shame she had to go, he thought. In ways, she reminded him of his mother.

He asked himself what was more important, his career, which had kept the people safe and the fucking deadbeats and pukes in line, or the life of this teacher? Yeah, she was getting a little old, and she'd been "pretty spicy." But things just didn't work out.

One night a couple of weeks before the election, and staggering drunk, Diggs gathered up the nerve to finish it with Mrs. Foreman. He stabbed her. She gasped, kicked around on the floor, shuddered like one suffering chills, and died. She didn't even cry out. He ran from the scene, but he forgot his knife. And he was afraid to go back for it.

The sheriff never figured out what happened to his knife, the one that Ringo pulled out of Mrs. Foreman's chest and that Swanker, believing it belonged to Ham, stole from the scene and thereafter disposed of. Somehow, Lady Luck always seemed to smile on the sheriff. Luck has its favorites, even the ugly and the evil.

Term after term thereafter, Sheriff Diggs was reelected. Finally, no one contested him in his bids for reelection. He'd become a revered institution. If he got drunk, he was forgiven. His occasional wayward forays simply proved he was human. Diggs kept the pukes in the county to a minimum, and didn't fuck around with a lot of expensive trials and bullshit. If the sheriff was on your ass, you'd better plead guilty and get it over with. The citizens of Albany County, Wyoming, liked that about their sheriff. As one citizen observed, "Jesus Christ would have made a piss-poor sheriff."

Once, Deputy Hullberry thought about asking Diggs what had happened to his knife. "There are three kinds of questions," Hullberry opined. "There's the question you should ask, there's the question you better not ask, and there's the question you did ask." Hullberry never asked the sheriff what had happened to his knife.

Ham, who was as innocent as the lambs in the docking pen, served his time at the reformatory. Years later, he brought a declaratory judgment action against Diggs and the state of Wyoming to clear his name. No one, including Diggs, contested it. Silence has its reasons.

Thereafter, Ham was admitted to study archaeology at Princeton. How that happened, nobody would have predicted, except that Princeton had a penchant to select the cream of the crop, beginning with James Madison and Woodrow Wilson, not to mention John F. Kennedy. Ham had finally found his home in academics.

"What goes around comes around," as the old saying goes. Ham's father, the bestial bastard, was serving ten to twenty for dealing in drugs—a drug dealer who hid his business behind the white board fence surrounding his mansion out there on the prairie. Feds got him. Ham's father gave Ham a general power of attorney, and Ham came back to take care of the horses.

Finally, confronting the obvious, that he wasn't born to nurture horses or to tend to the demands of ranching, he sold everything and returned to the university, where, in due course, he was awarded a doctorate degree. In the academic world, he began to bud and to bloom. Soon he joined the faculty of Princeton and became widely acclaimed as the first and last word on the endemic influence of the New World on the culture of its European exploiters.

CHAPTER **64**

Bear Creek Ranch, 1948

THAT MORNING, MEG saw that Ringo's chair was empty, as usual. For weeks, she'd kept hoping the door would open and in would walk that strange, dear, deep man in his turned-over boots. But on that day when Professor Johns finally found his way into the classroom and closed the door, she'd at last surrendered: Ringo would never return. And all that remained were the ashes of an old love.

She pushed on. The train of life is like that. Take the ride or let the train go by, and all you'll get is the sound of its whistle. She'd passed econ and her other courses as well, and she thought she got better grades than she deserved. She tried to make friends with some of the students, but their heads were as empty as the beer cans they threw in the street.

She would finish school, but she got a new job and a new apartment, one that didn't have Ringo's ghost.

She'd been packing her clothes from the closet when she came upon the painting. With trembling hands, she set it up on the couch. She stepped back to view it and stared at it for a long time. Then she grabbed the painting, ran down the steps to her old car, and slid the painting into the backseat.

When she drove into the ranch yard, the dust from the corrals was so thick that she could see only the dim silhouettes of the men working the sheep. In high-pitched voices, they yipped and hollered and heyed as they sorted the herd, the noise like the pleading masses at the gates of hell. It was weaning time. They were separating the lambs from their mothers.

As she drew closer, she was able to recognize Ringo. She heard Ringo's voice hollering at the ewes. Looking over at an adjoining corral, she saw a man who must be his father, a man as tall as his son, with a deeper voice that carried an authoritative ring. "Arturo," he hollered, "hold up a minute. We got this pen of wethers full."

"Lot of good eatin' for rich men in L.A." Arturo laughed.

"Those lambs pay our wages, Arturo," Eckersly hollered back.

Meg stood at the corral, watching the men work. She licked the dust away from her lips and squinted into the bedlam. Then she saw Sarah carrying a milk bucket of hot lamb stew in one hand and in the other a basket with bowls and spoons. Ringo looked up when his mother called. Then he saw the woman standing at the corral. Curiosity nudged him toward her. He was only a few feet away when through the dust he could see her face, her teeth biting at her lower lip to stop its trembling.

He froze.

He could never escape her. How easily she'd broken down the gates of hell.

Pain came flooding through.

"I brought your painting back," she said. She could think of nothing more to say.

Sarah was at the corral. "Why Ringo, I didn't know you had a lady friend at school."

It was then that his father hollered, "Stop that bitch, Ringo!" A stubborn ewe was scrambling over the sidebars of the cutting shoot to get to her lamb. Ringo turned into the noisy melee, threw his arms around the ewe, and turned her back.

"We met in class and became good friends," Meg said to Sarah.

"You must know what a wonderfully talented son you have. He did a painting once, but he never had a chance to finish it. I was coming out this way, and I thought I'd drop it by."

"How thoughtful," Sarah said. "I'm embarrassed at how I look." She smoothed the wrinkles of her shirt. "But, as you can see, we're a working family."

"I know what it's like to work," Meg said. "I work as a waitress at the Paris Café—Chinese place—and I'm attending the university. When I get my teaching certificate, I'm going to teach grade school kids in Laramie."

"You must be very happy about that," Sarah said. She thought the young woman seemed happy.

"I am happy. Some of my best friends call me 'Happy,'" she said, and laughed.

"Well, we all know how to work here on this ranch," Sarah said. "And that's for sure."

"I feel like I already know you," Meg said. "Ringo has spoken of you so often. He's such a genius with a paintbrush, and I love him to death."

As timely as noontime chimes from the village clock, the men at the corrals stopped their work and headed for the barn, where Sarah's steaming fresh lamb stew was waiting.

"You must be ready for some lunch, dear," Sarah said to Meg. "It's a long way out here. I'm not a fancy cook, but the men say my lamb stew is the best in the West. Come with me." Sarah took Meg by the arm and led her to where the men were sitting on grain sacks at the door of the barn, the air rich with the sounds of workingmen, their laughter and chatter in Spanish. Ringo took a seat next to his father. Meg watched Ringo stirring the stew.

Stirring the stew.

Stirring the stew.

Meg kept hoping Ringo would look up, and when he did, she tried to smile at him, but he quickly looked away. His eyes had grown soft like the lambs' before docking and his lips confessed a faded grief. He took a bite of the stew and tried to chew.

Sarah filled a bowl and offered it to Meg. "I'll leave you now so you can visit with your friend Ringo." She turned to go.

"I'll come with you," Meg said, carrying her bowl. "We had a small misunderstanding at school, and I don't think we're ready to talk about it." The two women walked toward the house. "It must be wonderful living out here on this ranch, no one to bother you—just you and your family together, all peaceful and quiet."

Sarah liked the way Meg talked, her openness.

"Well, a woman gets lonely for a woman to talk to," Sarah said. "Woman talk is different. And it's hard for a married woman on a ranch to have a life of her own." She didn't know why she was carrying on like this. She hadn't known the young woman but a few minutes. "I'm glad you'll have a life of your own. Teaching children will be very fulfilling."

Sarah filled the sink with fresh hot water, poured in the soap, and dropped a kettle into the suds. "I could dance when I was younger," she said. "I wanted to go to New York. It sounds so silly now."

Meg watched as Sarah scrubbed at the kettle. "Here," she said, handing Meg the rag. "Maybe you could clean the table. It's a mess. I didn't have time to do the breakfast dishes."

Meg gathered up the dirty dishes and hauled them to the sink. Then she quickly scrubbed at the table.

"My mother was the wise one," Sarah said. "She convinced me not to go east. She said that trying to get to the top, I could end up being nothing but 'a common whore'; that's how she put it." Sarah seemed embarrassed at her words. "You know what I mean. And some girls might, I suppose. I wouldn't have." Her voice was flat. "But you're too young to know much about that."

From the kitchen window, Sarah could see the men at the corrals working again, and she saw the straight, slender figure of

Ringo in the dust. Her son was home and safe. She would have given her life to save him. She had given far less. She felt a sudden sense of having won. Staring out the window, she said, "He's quite beautiful, isn't he?"

"Yes, he is beautiful," Meg said, standing behind her with a waiting dish towel.

"I wouldn't have tripped around from bed to bed in New York to climb the ladder," Sarah said again. "I wouldn't do that."

"Some do," Meg said. "I read once about a poor Mexican mother who slept with the railroad men in vacant boxcars down on the tracks to make enough to feed her kids. I'd do that if I had to."

"It's not what a woman gives; it's why," Sarah said. "But I don't know why we're talking about this."

"If you give it for love," Meg said, "it's okay, I guess. I get confused sometimes."

"I suppose one of those women could love somebody," Sarah said.

"I suppose so," Meg replied. The last of the dishes done, Meg smiled at Sarah. "I have to go." Then Meg embraced her.

The woman smelled clean to Sarah, sweet-clean, like a child. Sarah followed her to the car. Meg pulled the painting from the backseat, walked to the barn with it, and leaned it up against the wall. Then she called, perhaps too cheerfully, "Good-bye, Ringo."

"Ringo, aren't you going to say good-bye to your friend?" Sarah asked.

"You'll come back again soon, I know," she said to Meg with downy eyes.

Ringo ambled slowly to the gate. "Good to see you again, Isabelle," he said. His voice was deeper.

"Isabelle?" his mother asked.

"That's her name," Ringo said.

Then Meg turned from him, got into her car, and drove off.

At once, the old heap became locked in the two tracks of the trail ahead of her. She felt caught in the merciless ruts of history. She felt dry inside. She wept without tears.

Sarah and Ringo stood watching the car disappear into the distance. Then Sarah said to Ringo, "She's a nice girl, and so happy. I hope you find a nice girl like her sometime."

Ringo turned the painting face out and, with trepidation, stepped back to view it.

"I don't understand that painting," his mother said. "It looks so—so tangled and all."

Ringo carefully laid the painting on the passenger seat of his pickup. He ran to the barn and returned with his paint box and easel, and tossed them into the back of the truck. At the house, he stuffed his things into his old black tin suitcase and tied it shut with a worn piece of lariat. Then he mounted his truck.

"Where are you going, Ringo?" Sarah asked.

"I have to finish a painting," he said. Something different in his voice, something that sounded like a man speaking to the new moon. He didn't say good-bye. Truth appears when words take to hiding like ghosts out of favor.

Sarah watched as his old truck disappeared over the far horizon; she watched as mothers do when their sons leave home forever.